GOLF CURSE

a novel of slasher horror
by CAMERON ROUBIQUE

ISBN: 9781092673976

This book is for my Indian Tree Family.
There are way too many of you to name here,
but I have to mention
my best friend Kyle Doran,
who got me the job,
and Scott Gibson,
the best boss a goofy, purple-haired,
140lb. kid could ask for.

Author's Note:

I have the utmost respect for
Native American people, their culture,
and their beliefs. There are no real
tribes or people mentioned in this book,
and it was not my intention to write
any political or social commentary.
This is simply a work of fiction,
meant to be read for fun
on a dark and stormy night.

– Cameron Roubique

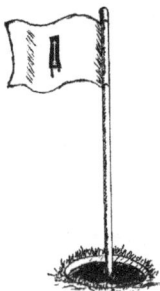

Monday, May 18ᵗʰ, 1981

Long before the golf course was built, the high slope on the western edge of town—now known as Hackberry Hill—had been called Indian Hill, and terrible things happened there. Like most people who lived there, Ronnie Wilford knew nothing about its dark history. As far as he knew, Indian Hill was just a plain old public golf course, there were hundreds just like it all over America. If asked, he would've assumed that the Indian Hill name was something someone made up to appeal to all the old-timers that golfed there everyday.

Ronnie had never even heard of the Indian Hill Golf Course until last year when his old friend Mark Rowe told him he could get him a summer job there on the maintenance crew. At the time, summer break between his freshman and sophomore years of college had been coming up, and he needed to do something to replenish his dwindling savings account. He dreaded the thought of having to go back to bagging groceries as he had done back in high school. Mark's offer seemed tempting but there was only one problem.

"But I don't golf," Ronnie had explained. "Well, maybe putt-putt, but I've never played, like, y'know, *real* golf."

"So what? You don't have to know how to golf," Mark said with a wave of his hand. "You'd be working with me on the maintenance crew."

Ronnie was even more doubtful about that. Hard physical labor and handyman stuff was maybe okay for a guy like Mark who was strong and athletic. He was kind of short and stocky, but he lifted weights and had played on baseball teams his whole life. Ronnie was only five foot nine though, and skinny as a scarecrow. At the time, he only weighed one hundred and twenty pounds.

"I don't know. I don't really know how to fix anything," Ronnie said.

Mark laughed. "It's not *that* kind of maintenance. You sit on a mower most of the day. It's super easy." Ronnie shrugged. He couldn't really picture himself fitting in at a job like that, but Mark was persistent. "Trust me, you'll love it. Look, honestly the hardest part about the job is waking up at the crack of dawn and getting there by 6:00 AM everyday. Other than that it's a breeze."

Now, over a year later, on a warm Monday morning in mid-May, Ronnie's alarm clock blared at 5:00 AM sharp. He rolled over and shut it off, groaning as he pulled his scrawny legs out from under the covers and sat up. It was still completely dark in his room at this hour so he clicked on the lamp. He squinted at the harsh white light and rubbed sleep out of his eyes, then reached for his thick, black, horn-rimmed glasses lying on the night table. His eyesight was terrible, and the glasses, combined with his skinny, pale build, gave him a stereotypically nerdy appearance. But so what? He had a good sense of humor about it. He had learned early on in life that it was always hard for people to make fun of a guy with a good sense of humor. The world came into focus behind those lenses and he sat there staring at the poster of Olivia Newton-John hanging on the wall across the room, trying to force himself to wake up a bit.

Mark had been right: these early mornings were definitely the worst part of the job. He had quickly discovered though, that once you were up, you were up. Also, getting off work early at 2:30 in the afternoon was great. He had every afternoon and evening to himself, plus every weekend off. For a twenty-year-old guy working a summer job in between semesters in college, he really couldn't ask for better hours.

"Okay, enough's enough," he muttered after glancing at the clock and seeing that twelve minutes had somehow already passed. He threw on a pair of blue jeans, an old white T-shirt, and a fading Indian Hill trucker hat over his mop of black hair. He strapped his Walkman onto the waistband of his jeans and slung his big tan Koss headphones around his neck, letting the curly cord dangle down unplugged. He gave Olivia Newton-John one more appreciative glance before shuffling downstairs to practically sleepwalk through the rest of his morning rituals. Every workday was the same: he ate a bowl of cereal, threw some snacks in a paper bag for lunch, brushed his teeth, and snuck off to work before the rest of his family woke up.

A half hour later he was on the road in his rusting beige 1964 Mercury Montclair. Driving west through town, he saw the sun rising in his rearview mirror, and flipped on the radio. It was tuned to a

3

country station and he heard John Denver's "Take Me Home, Country Roads" just beginning. Smiling, he turned the volume up a bit. Ever since he started working on the maintenance crew at Indian Hill, he had developed a taste for country music. Sure, some of that really shit-kicking stuff was a bit too much, but he liked the songs about driving down the road and the wilderness and camping, stuff like that. This song was a perfect soothing, early morning song, and it really felt right as the suburban neighborhoods began to give way to the rural farmland on the west side of town.

He turned left, heading south on Old Wentworth Road. The rising sun silhouetted the cornfield and the old barn on his left, and painted the irrigation ditch and tall trees on his right with golden light. Straight ahead of him, rising high into the air, was Hackberry Hill. The tall slope was so steep that they had diverted Old Wentworth Road around it rather than building it up and over. It was covered in patchy scrub grasses and loomed over the town. One tall, knobby old Hackberry tree stood right at the peak.

Coming up on the right side of the road, the entrance sign to the Indian Hill Golf Course came into view. It stood in between two driveways that curved in and out of the golf course parking lot. If he'd had a bird's eye view, the two driveways would have looked like two parentheses facing the wrong way. Mounted on the sign were the words *INDIAN HILL Golf Course* in tree-branch letters. It stood in the middle of a flowerbed filled with bright orange lilies and was flanked by two colorful totem poles.

Ronnie turned in and drove down into the nearly empty parking lot. The big, fancy clubhouse and the squat U-shaped maintenance shop sat on opposite ends of the parking lot. He pulled the old Mercury into his usual spot at the back end near the maintenance shop,

4

surrounded by the other maintenance guys' cars and trucks. Ronnie and Mark were two of the four young guys on the crew, the rest were retired guys who only worked so they could enjoy free golf. They usually arrived at work much earlier than any of the younger guys.

Zeke, Ronnie's favorite old-timer, stood back behind his car smoking a cigarette and watching the sunrise stoically. He did this every morning and their boss, Bill, never called on him to get to work like he did with everyone else. Zeke was a soft-spoken lanky guy in his seventies with a shock of white hair, a deep tan—that Ronnie assumed came from decades of never wearing sunscreen—and a crooked smile. Mark had told Ronnie that the old guy had been working at the golf course forever, since it had opened sometime back in the late forties. Zeke never really spoke much during normal conversations with the other guys, but sometimes he would tell Mark and Ronnie long stories about the old days that were mildly interesting. To Ronnie, he had a way of saying things that really made a person think.

"Mornin', Zeke," Ronnie called to him.

"Mahnin, kid," Zeke answered with a grin. Ronnie left him to his cigarette and his morning thoughts, whatever they were.

He was about to walk across the curving driveway when Mark's shabby old Chevy van appeared. Ronnie waited on the median that separated the parking lot from the driveway and held out his thumb as if he were hitchhiking. Mark drove past grinning with his middle finger up and Ronnie burst out laughing.

Ronnie had two older sisters that had both moved out of the house, but, in many ways, Mark had always felt like an older brother. They were the same age and had grown up together on the same street, but had different groups of friends in high school. Mark was more of a popular jock guy, whereas Ronnie was sort of a geek. Mark stood up for Ronnie though, and didn't act as if his popularity were in jeopardy if he spoke to him in the halls of DeAngelo High. Even after they both graduated two years ago, and Mark moved into an apartment with a couple of his friends, they still kept in touch. They had been closer than ever since last spring, when he had gotten Ronnie the job.

Mark pulled in right next to Ronnie's Mercury and got out. He was wearing faded jeans and an old gray Atlanta Braves T-shirt with blue sleeves.

"Hey, look who it is. It's the Urban Cowboy," Ronnie teased.

"Oh fuck off," Mark retorted. He had been going to a country roadhouse every Sunday night to try to pick up girls with his roommates. He always invited Ronnie to come, but Ronnie always declined. "I keep tellin' ya, man. You gotta come down one of these nights. The chicks there are *unbelievably* hot."

"I'm sure they are," Ronnie agreed. "But I keep tellin' *you*, I am not going to a country bar and line dancing and all that shit. I like country music okay, but not *that* much."

"Your loss," Mark shrugged. As they walked toward the maintenance shop, Mark launched into the story of what happened at the country bar last night, and Ronnie listened politely.

The maintenance yard was fenced in and fully paved with concrete, surrounded on three sides by the high walls of the cart barn, mower barn, and maintenance shop. As they walked in, a line of golf carts drove out from the open garage door of the cart barn on the left. First thing every morning, the golf carts had to be driven up to the clubhouse building and parked in rows outside the pro shop. Then a separate cart crew came in the evening, drove the carts back down to the maintenance

6

yard, washed them in the spillway near the big gas tanks, and parked them back in the cart barn. Ronnie and Mark waved to Butch, Pete, and the other old-timers in the golf carts as they drove past. Mark had taught him early on that everybody waves to everybody out on the golf course.

They walked in through the open maintenance shop garage door on the right. This was where Brian, the mechanic, had all his tools, his bulky orange automatic mower blade sharpening machines, and his hydraulic lift. Ronnie and Mark walked into the small office just to the right of the garage door where they punched in at the time-clock and grabbed a couple of handheld Walkie-Talkie radios.

Ronnie let Mark clock in first, remembering the first time he came into this office for his job interview last spring.

Bill Carlson, the superintendent and Ronnie's future boss, was a stocky bald guy in his early fifties. Ronnie had smiled politely during the interview and tried to sound enthusiastic and confident, but he could tell Bill was eyeing him suspiciously. Under that doubtful gaze, Ronnie felt a little like he was being scrutinized by the father of a girl he was picking up for a date. Thankfully, Mark had been standing behind him for moral support.

"You think you can make it through the summer here?" Bill had asked, thinking that this little pencil-neck wouldn't last a week.

"Yeah, definitely," Ronnie said with an enthusiasm that he didn't really feel.

"Of course he will," Mark stepped in. "I've known this guy most of my life. He's a great worker. Trust me."

"Yeah right," Bill said sarcastically. "You two dipshits'll probably be screwing around all summer."

Ronnie looked wide-eyed at Mark, he hadn't

been expecting profanity, especially in a job interview of all places. Bill Carlson, as he would come to find out, was a blunt easy-going guy. Mark just laughed.

"Oh come on, Bill. No we won't," Mark argued. He dropped into a terrible fake thick New Jersey accent and held up two pinched fingers in a mafia-like gesture. "We'll be the best fuckin' workers you've evah seen in yo entiah life."

"Shit," Bill laughed. "You better be. And no screwing around."

"Minimal screwing around," Mark corrected. Bill and Ronnie shook hands and the job was his. At the time, Bill thought he definitely wouldn't last all summer, but Ronnie had proven him wrong.

While Mark put their lunches in the small refrigerator, Ronnie pulled his time-card out of the slot and stuck it into the battered time-clock. The numbers 5:58 were stamped in red ink with a loud *chunk* and Ronnie returned his time-card to the slot.

Outside the office, he stopped and looked up at the chalkboard hanging just outside the door. Every person on the crew's name was listed, and the jobs they were scheduled to do were written out every day by Bill. Ronnie's usual Monday schedule was up there:

RONNIE - CUPS B / TEES / REFACE BUNKERS / TRIM

A *B* or an *F* next to a job name stood for either the back nine or front nine holes.

Mark joined Ronnie at the board.

"Ugh, cups.   I fuckin' hate cups," Mark grumbled.

"Yeah," Ronnie agreed. "It's still better than bagging groceries for a bunch of cranky assholes though." Mark shrugged. He had never known the

8

torture of working at a grocery store as Ronnie did.

Ronnie and Mark turned around and went toward the back of the maintenance shop building. Past all the mechanic's stuff was a crowd of parked golf carts and mowers. They squeezed past the carts and through a tight little aisle between two mowers and the wall, making their way into another little storage room in the corner. This was the tool room, a cool, dingy, windowless room lit by a few fluorescent lights. Just about everything in the tool room was coated with dust. Shovels, rakes, and other long handled tools stood upright in a wooden rack. Up in the rafters, dozens of spare flag sticks were stored out of the way, their flags hanging down a few feet overhead.

In the far left corner of the room sat all of the tools for changing out the cups. Ronnie and Mark each grabbed three spare flags and a tool bucket in one hand, a round metal cup cutter in the other. The cup cutters' curved blades scraped loudly against the concrete floor as they picked them up. With their tools in hand, they headed back out to the work carts.

Joe and Jeff, the other two young guys on the crew, were walking up from the office and the chalkboard. Both of them looked hungover and half asleep with dark circles under their eyes. They were a few years older than Ronnie and Mark. Most of the time they pretty much kept to themselves, though they loved playing pranks on Ronnie and Mark, as well as antagonizing the old guys whenever they got the chance. They dressed the same and had the same long Rod Stewart-ish spiky-shag hair. Jeff was older though and had dark hair and a thin beard, while Joe had blonde hair and only the scraggliest hint of a goatee. Mark liked to call them JoeJeff, all one word.

Ronnie hopped in the nearest work cart, and Mark jumped in the one next to it. They dumped their

9

tools in the back bed and settled the extra flag sticks in the notch between the two seat-backs. Joe and Jeff each stood blocking their carts and looking off aimlessly. Jeff stretched and Joe ran his hands through his hair. Ronnie and Mark pulled the gearshift levers that were down near their calves, putting the carts into reverse and setting off a loud high-pitched warning tone. Joe and Jeff still stayed where they were, their eyes wandering around the room, trying to look innocent. Ronnie and Mark looked at each other and rolled their eyes, this was another one of their dumb pranks.

"Ay JoeJeff. Move your ass," Mark demanded angrily over his shoulder.

"Did you hear somethin?'" Joe asked Jeff. Jeff only shrugged.

Ronnie shook his head and rolled his eyes. These guys played this joke on them about once a week. Mark tapped the horn button twice with his foot, the whiny high-pitched beep exploded in the early morning quiet of the maintenance garage.

"Get the fuck outta the way! We got shit to do," Mark shouted. Joe and Jeff began to laugh. Mark got up to confront them and they finally moved, hopping onto a couple of greens mowers.

"Enjoy your cups," Joe said smugly. Jeff snickered to himself too. Changing the cups was a much harder job than mowing the greens. Mowing only required you to sit on the mower and occasionally get off to dump the excess grass out of the buckets.

"Heh heh--fuck you," Mark said, which only made them laugh even harder. Ronnie ignored them and backed up out of the garage after Mark.

He was about to drive off to the back nine greens to get started on his cups when Mark waved at him to stop.

"Hey, I'll race ya," Mark challenged.

Ronnie only laughed and shook his head. "Dude, you always beat me."

"So what? There's always that chance. One of these days you'll beat me." Ronnie rolled his eyes. "Look, I'll even give you a head start. Five minutes. Plus I'm doing the front nine, so there'll probably be golfers out there already. They'll slow me down."

Ronnie sighed resignedly. "Okay, you're on."

"All right! Better get goin.' Five minutes starts...now."

Without another moment's hesitation, Ronnie hit the gas and tore off into the parking lot. He took a few quick glances back over his shoulder to make sure Mark was actually waiting for him, and, sure enough, he stayed true to his word. Ronnie knew he was probably going to lose yet another cups race, but he didn't really care. When you lost to a good friend like Mark, it didn't really feel like losing.

Ronnie put his big headphones on over his ears and hit play on his Walkman. With a mix-tape of country and rock blasting in his ears, he went to work.

The sun was rising in the clear blue sky, promising a beautiful late spring day. A light breeze sent some bright pink blossoms off the crabapple trees fluttering down over Ronnie's cart as it passed. He crossed the parking lot, curved around the pro shop, glancing up at the old, grim-faced, wooden cigar-store Indian statue that stood outside the door to the pro shop. It was kind of a creepy old thing, but it fit in nicely with the clubhouse's rustic western motif.

He drove past the tenth hole tee boxes and ventured out onto the back nine. He stayed on the cart path as it ran alongside the wide lake and went over the bridge toward the curving fairway and the tenth green. There weren't any golfers out on the back nine yet, and he practically had the whole south half of the course to himself. Just breathing the fresh cool air and knowing he wouldn't be cooped up inside classrooms all day made Ronnie feel great. He reached the green and parked on the fringe, then grabbed his tools and walked toward the hole.

On Ronnie's first day last year, Mark had taught him how to change the cups, it was the first thing he had ever done at the golf course. You went out to each green with a bucket of sand, a cup cutter, and a spare flag.

"You gotta do this about every other day, or else the hole just gets beat to shit," Mark had explained while setting the cup cutter down on a fresh spot on the green. It was a T-shaped metal device about three feet long with a handle at the top and two semicircular blades at the bottom exactly the size of a golf hole. First they knelt down and hammered both blades into the ground as far as they would go with a battered rubber mallet. Next they pulled the white plastic cup out of the old beat-up hole and filled it with their freshly cut round dirt plug. Then finally they filled the new hole with the white plastic golf cup and the flag.

"And that's about it. Easy, right?" Mark had said, placing the new flag back in the new hole.

For Ronnie, it hadn't been easy at all, at least not at first. The first time Ronnie tried to cut a new hole, it took him about thirty awkward hits with the rubber mallet before just one blade was all the way in the ground, and he'd been panting and sweating. It only took Mark about seven hits on each side of the cup cutter, and his breathing hadn't increased at all. By the time Ronnie finished his first cup, his whole arm was sore and he felt exhausted. Mark had said, "Okay, only seventeen more to go." Ronnie had given him a look like he was about to pass out. After a summer of hard work though, he had gotten the hang of it. His boss, Bill, had told him what a great job he did, and had even taken Joe and Jeff off of cups and put Ronnie and Mark on it all the time. It wasn't that he wanted to give Joe and Jeff special treatment, they were just too sloppy and lazy when they changed the cups.

Now as Ronnie pounded his way through the cups on the back nine greens, he hummed along with the music and felt a light sweat break out over his forehead. At the twelfth hole, he looked up and saw a huge bird circling overhead. He took his headphones off, heard its loud cry echoing, and wondered if it was a hawk or an eagle. It disappeared behind the leaves of a big cottonwood tree over near the next hole and Ronnie continued his work.

As he worked his fingertips became caked with dirt. He hurried, but saved as much energy as he could without slowing down. He didn't want to wear himself out before he even got started on the rest of the day's tasks. After finishing the thirteenth green on the southwestern corner of the golf course, he hopped in his cart and sped off toward the east. He drove through the rough along the southern border of the course, weaving around the pine trees. Driving the golf cart full sped over several grassy berms, he felt like he was on the last few hills of a roller coaster. The ground began a slow uphill climb as he drove toward the southeastern corner of the course. The seventeenth hole sat in that corner, and it was highest point on the golf course, not far from the peak of Hackberry Hill.

He pulled up next to the fourteenth green. It wasn't quite as high as hole seventeen, but from this vantage point, he could see most of the back nine, the pro shop, and even a few of the front nine fairways. He looked for Mark on either six green or nine green, but couldn't spot him.

"Where are ya, you bastard?" he muttered. He gave up the search and pounded out the new cup on fourteen as fast as he could. Mark frequently beat him by three or four greens whenever he challenged Ronnie to a cups race. Luckily for him, Mark was still nowhere in sight.

Maybe today I really will beat him, he thought. *Though if I do, he'll probably just say, 'Well, that's because I gave you a head start.'*

As he walked back to his cart, he looked down at the ninth green and saw one of the dark green maintenance carts pull up alongside it. Mark jumped out before the cart even came to a complete stop, slammed his own cup-cutter down, and began hammering.

"Shit!" Ronnie said aloud. "How the fuck does he do it so fast?"

Ronnie threw the bucket and the cup-cutter into his cart and stepped on the gas. He was determined to get at least the seventeenth hole done before Mark made it up here and declared himself the winner.

The fourteenth and seventeenth greens were very close together, divided by a couple of sets of tee boxes and a little wooden rain shelter. Ronnie drove onto the cart path, speeding around the retaining wall that held up the championship tee boxes. He took the hard left curve too fast and his tires screeched on the concrete. For a second he imagined that he was one of "them Duke boys" in *The Dukes of Hazzard*. He had to duck under the low hanging limbs of a big pine tree that stood near the cart path.

He spun the wheel hard to the right as he came around in front of the wooden shelter and around the retaining wall for the other championship tee box. The seventeenth green was just past there. The image of Mark hopping into his cart with his fists raised triumphantly in the air made him grit his teeth with determination.

"Come on, come on," he urged his cart faster.

A weeping willow stood close to the cart path on this side, and Ronnie held up his hand to shield his face from several of the low hanging fronds. They slapped his arm and brushed the top of his trucker hat. He instinctively squinted his eyes shut even though his glasses protected them. He was about to look back for Mark, but did a double take as he noticed something big in the cart path directly ahead of him.

A dead man lay face down across the cart path less than five yards away.

Ronnie jammed on the brakes and his heart leaped up into his throat. His jaws clenched and he yanked the wheel as hard as he could to the left. The cart skidded off the path, leaving burnt black rubber skid marks. His tires screeched in protest. The front left tire came within and inch of the dead man's dirty, worn-out sneaker. The skid marks became muddy green smears as he slid down the incline towards the seventeenth green. Now clear of the dead man, he yanked the wheel back to the right again to avoid tearing up the delicate bent grass on the green. If he tore up any of that thin, short grass, Bill would have a cow. Finally the cart came to a reluctant stop. Ronnie's forward momentum tried to throw him over the steering wheel, then he slammed back against the seat.

Ronnie sat there for a second panting in stunned silence. His glasses had almost flown off his head, the bridge dangling crookedly off the tip of his nose. He pushed them back up and turned around to look at the dead guy. That carefree all-is-right-with-the-world-feeling he'd had only a few minutes ago had evaporated.

The man lay face down in the grass with his legs splayed diagonally across the cart path. Ronnie got out of his cart and walked quickly back up the incline to get a closer look at him, stopping at a safe distance of five feet away. The guy's face was turned away to the left and was covered by his long, greasy graying hair, not that Ronnie even wanted to see his face. He looked like he had just keeled over sometime either last night or early this morning. He wore old faded jeans and a matching denim jacket, both looked damp with morning dew.

"Oh my God," Ronnie whispered to himself. "Holy shit." He had never seen a dead man before, and the thought that this was the first dead body he'd ever seen made his stomach feel queasy. He looked down at his tire tracks and saw just how close he'd come to running over this guy's legs. "Jesus!"

A high whiny horn beeped behind Ronnie. He whirled around to see Mark driving towards him with his fists up in the air, cheering like Rocky Balboa at the end of a fight. Mark's grin melted as he came closer and saw the pale, terrified expression on Ronnie's face and the lump that lay on the ground near Ronnie's feet.

Mark pulled up close and walked over to Ronnie and the body.

"What the fuck is that, dude?" Mark asked breathlessly. He now looked just as pale and nervous as Ronnie. They stood near the dead man's feet and peered over his shoulder, not wanting to look directly at his face. Ronnie felt his panic rising and looked over at Mark, but the look on Mark's face didn't lend him any comfort either.

"You...you think he's really dead?" Mark whispered, as if talking out loud would somehow disturb the body. Ronnie only shrugged. Mark tapped the sole of the guy's ratty, old tennis shoe with his own clean Adidas sneaker. The guy didn't move.

"Oh God, he really *is* dead," Ronnie whispered. Mark tapped the dirty old guy harder up near his knee. He still didn't move. "Sh-should we go get Bill?" Mark ignored his question and stepped forward. He nudged the guy near his rib cage with the toe of his shoe.

Suddenly the guy woke up with a loud gasp and a jerk. Both Mark and Ronnie let out short startled screams and jumped back. Their hearts raced as they watched the guy writhe around on the grass, groaning and making unintelligible noises.

"Hey, man. You okay?" Mark asked. "You scared the shit out of us."

"Yeah, we thought you were dead," Ronnie added.

The guy spun around on his back, his red bloodshot eyes darting back and forth between the two of them. Now that he was facing them, they could see the Grateful Dead T-shirt he wore under the denim jacket, it was cratered with tiny battery acid holes. Also his jeans were fraying in the knees. To Ronnie, he looked like an old hippie that had his mind fried by way too many drugs back in the psychedelic sixties.

After a moment of warily looking back and forth at Ronnie and Mark, he seemed to decide that they didn't mean him any immediate harm and allowed himself to look around. Recognition dawned on his face and he craned his neck back over his shoulder. Ronnie followed the man's line of sight up the hill past the high tee box for hole seventeen, and saw the gnarled old hackberry tree at the top of Hackberry Hill.

The man's head snapped back around and he looked directly at Ronnie. For a second, he squinted his eyes, peering at him intensely. Ronnie immediately felt uncomfortable and took a step back away from him.

"I know you, man," he said in a slurred dazed voice. Mark looked over at Ronnie in surprise.

"What?" Ronnie asked.

"Yeah. Ih'ss you. I saw you in a vision...man." He added the *man* at the end of the sentence almost as an afterthought. He struggled to get up onto his feet and

17

slurred more words that neither one of them quite caught. "This izza year, man. I saw it comin.' Th'blood...year'a blood. Sheephs...sheephs comin'...comin' back..."

"Look, do you want us to call a cab for you or something?" Mark asked him, interrupting his mumbling. The man ignored Mark, barely giving him a glance as he staggered to his feet. Suddenly one of his dirty hands shot out and grabbed Ronnie by the shoulder. Ronnie jerked back instinctively. Mark jumped between them, shoving the guy backwards with his forearm. The strange old hippie's eyes never left Ronnie.

"You better ge'outta here while ya still can, man," he warned, crooking his index finger at Ronnie.

"Hey whoa. Easy, dude. Just take it easy." Mark held his fist back ready to swing if the guy tried anything. Ronnie stood speechless, his eyes refusing to look away from the hippie.

"Better not be here after th'sun goes down. This place is cursed."

"Hey, why don't you get outta here, okay?" Mark said forcefully. "Don't make us have to call the cops on you."

The man finally looked at Mark, turned back to Ronnie, then took one last glance around, as if considering Mark's suggestion.

"Yeah yeah, good idea, man. Let's get outta here. Place's gotta curse on it, man." He turned around, still mumbling to himself and began to walk northeast down the hill, back in the direction of town. He held his left arm out and began to press down invisible frets while his right arm began to strum an air-guitar, jamming out to some old song that only he could hear.

As soon as he was out of earshot, walking through the small sand trap next to the sixteenth green, Mark finally spoke up again.

"What a freak."

"Yeah, you're telling me," Ronnie said dusting off his shoulder where the guy had grabbed him. "For once I'm actually glad you finished cups before me."

"Ohhh yeah," Mark laughed, he had completely forgotten about their cup race. He looked back at the old hippie. "Do you know that guy or something?"

Ronnie shrugged and shook his head. "I don't think so. Never seen him before in my life."

"What was up with that *'I saw you in a vision'* shit?"

"How the fuck would I know? Guy's probably high on LSD or something. Probably smoked one too many *dooooobies, man*," Ronnie's voice fell into an imitation of the burnt out old hippie and they both cracked up. They looked back just as the air-guitar man awkwardly climbed over the split rail fence on the eastern edge of the course.

"Come on, I'll change out sixteen for ya," Mark offered, and they went back to work finishing the cups. Every few seconds they glanced back toward the air-guitar man until he disappeared into the trees.

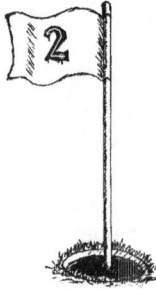

Other than the weird encounter with the air-guitar-playing homeless guy, the rest of the morning turned out to be pretty good.

After they finished changing the last of the cups, they went back down to the maintenance shop. Bill was standing inside near the big hydraulic lift talking to Brian the mechanic as he replaced a fuel filter on one of the golf carts. Brian was a big beefy guy in his early thirties with long auburn hair and a handlebar mustache. He didn't talk much and always seemed to be spitting out chewing tobacco. To Ronnie, he looked a bit like a time-traveling bartender from the wild west. Ronnie and Mark grabbed their spare flag sticks and cup cutting tools from their carts, then walked over and told Bill and Brian what had happened with the air-guitar man.

"A vision, huh?" Bill shook his head. "Guy must've been hopped up on something. I'm just glad he didn't freak out and try to hurt you boys."

"Yeah, you can say that again," Mark agreed.

"I wonder what the hell he was doin' out here. I mean, we're pretty isolated out past all the farms. It would be a long walk from town."

"My guess is that he was probably drawn here by his hard-on for this guy," Mark joked. He poked at Ronnie's ribs with the blunt ends of the flag sticks in his hands.

"Ah!" Ronnie flinched away from him. "Get away from me, you creep."

"Come on, *maaaan*," Mark teased in slurred voice. He was trying to imitate the air-guitar man's voice but he sounded more like Tommy Chong. "I saw you in a vision, *maaaan*." Both Bill and Brian broke up laughing as Mark chased him around the shop relentlessly poking him with the flags. Ronnie screamed a high, girly *Nooooo!* that he knew would make them laugh even harder.

Finally, Bill stepped in and broke up the horseplay. "All right, dipshits. *Get to work!*" he said still laughing.

"Okay," they both said sulkily.

They put their cup cutters, flags, and buckets back in the storage room where they belonged, then went straight for two of the three small orange tee mowers parked along the back wall. Bill called out to them before they started up the mowers.

"Hey, if you guys see that crazy homeless guy again, you call me up on your radios, okay? We can't have homeless guys out there messing around with the golfers or getting hit in the head with golf balls or anything."

"No sweat, boss," Mark said with a big thumbs up.

"And just take your time out there," Bill continued. "We've got the *Laaadies* out there on the

21

front nine right now. So try to stay out of their way." He said the word Ladies in a nasally voice dripping with sarcasm.

"*Laaadies*, ugh," Ronnie repeated in that same nasally, disgusting voice. The Ladies were a group of about twenty-five old women who golfed two to three times a week. They were a constant thorn in the sides of everyone on the maintenance crew because they loved to complain about any little thing the maintenance crew did. Every bad shot they made they blamed on the maintenance guys, the condition of the golf course, or the weather.

"Oh, good one, Gladys," Mark said in a cracked old lady voice.

"You too, Martha," Ronnie replied in the same voice.

Bill shook his head smiling. *"Get to work!"* he yelled again, then turned back to continue his conversation with Brian.

The old tee mowers reluctantly started up. Their engines roared, echoing off the concrete and cinder block walls of the maintenance shop. Ronnie and Mark both settled their big Koss headphones over their ears to block out most of the noise. They throttled up once they were out of the garage bay door, their exhaust pipes coughing out thin clouds of smoke. The mowers could only reach a speed of about fifteen miles per hour at their fastest, so they slowly made their way across the parking lot and up past the circular drop-off lane. The lot was already half full now, and they passed several golfers pulling their clubs out of their trunks. Clusters of elderly men and women in golf attire stood around chit-chatting, and practice putting on the two large practice greens in front of the pro shop as they waited for their turn to tee off on hole number one. Ronnie and Mark slowed down and wove between them, waving politely to anyone who made eye contact with them.

They drove around the clubhouse to the backside, parked their mowers next to the five foot rock retaining wall that elevated the tee box for hole number seven, and killed their engines. They pulled their big headphones off and let them hang around their necks. Part of the daily ritual of mowing tees was stopping inside the clubhouse restaurant for a couple of drinks before they headed off onto the course. As they walked toward the clubhouse, Mark said *Hi* to someone that Ronnie didn't know. Mark seemed to know everyone here and they all knew him. It was like they all were one big extended family. Ronnie hoped that after he spent enough time here, he would also gain that sense of familiarity with everyone.

From the outside, the clubhouse was designed to look like two giant tepees built onto the side of a mountain lodge. The parts of the building with the rounded tepee roofs were the restaurant and the pro shop. The lodge part of the building contained large, spacious banquet rooms that people could rent out for parties. Inside, the whole clubhouse had even more of a rustic mountain lodge motif. There were brown Native American patterns and symbols painted on the orange walls, and various western decorations hung up here and there. Ronnie and Mark walked in through the back doors and went down a long hallway that stretched all the way to the front of the building. This long hallway separated the banquet rooms from the restaurant and pro shop.

The place was immaculately clean. Mr. Hamilton, the head professional, was in charge of the golf course, and he was very particular about keeping the clubhouse spotless. Ronnie glanced into the large trophy case built into the wall on his right. It was filled with golf tournament trophies and plaques with the names of golfers he'd never heard of. He saw Mr. Hamilton's black and white picture in there underneath an old 1800s musket with a bayonet. He was a tall thin man with stern, pinched features and tight curly hair. Neither Ronnie or Mark liked him very much, he seemed like too much of a stickler. Every time Ronnie saw his picture, he had the sudden urge to draw a mustache and devil horns on the glass. The idea left his mind as soon as he turned left and followed Mark into the dimly lit restaurant.

It was a small crowded bar that opened up into a wide dining area under the high tepee-shaped ceiling. The dining area was completely empty at the moment, but there were a few groups of golfers sitting at the tall tables near the bar, eating eggs and bacon for breakfast. A big screen TV surrounded by fake plants sat against one wall near the bar, blaring out the morning news. A weatherman was talking about a big rain and hailstorm that was supposedly heading their way that night.

Ronnie and Mark stepped up to the bar and looked down at Judy, the lady who ran the early morning shift at the restaurant. She was in her mid-fifties, very short, and always seemed to be stressed to her breaking point.

"Guten morgen," Mark greeted her in German and grinned. Ronnie suppressed a laugh.

Judy let out an exasperated sigh. "What do you guys want now?" She spoke to them in a complaining voice as if they had been in there all morning bugging her for various things while she was trying to serve a hundred customers. In fact, this was their first trip in all day, and most of the golfers were outside.

"Can I get a Cherry Pepsi please?" Mark asked.

"We don't have Cherry Pepsi," she snapped back.

"Sure you do," Mark insisted amiably. "Just

pour me a Pepsi and then put a little grenadine in it."

"A little what?"

"Grenadine. See that bottle back there with the red liquid?" he pointed to the bottle of grenadine on the shelf crowded with various liquor bottles behind the bar. "My one true love Tanya made me one of those last week." Tanya was the older of the two sisters that worked at the restaurant and on the beverage cart in the afternoons and evenings. Judy glanced back at the bottle, then frowned and turned back to Ronnie and Mark.

"I suppose you want one too?" she asked Ronnie.

"No, too early for me. I'll just have water."

"Grenadine, grenadine," she muttered to herself as she turned back to get the bottle. It was too high for her to reach and she had to go grab a stool from back in the kitchen.

Sitting on the bar next to where Mark stood, was a circular wire rack filled with large individually wrapped chocolate chip cookies. As soon as Judy's back was turned, Mark reached over and plucked out two cookies without even turning his head. He sneakily handed one to Ronnie under the bar, and they both made them disappear into their pockets. Stealing cookies was also one of their daily rituals, and they knew well enough to leave them in their pockets until they got far out on the course so the prying eyes in the pro shop wouldn't see them eating.

A soft hand fell on Mark's shoulder and he turned to see Wendy, the younger of the two sisters.

"I saw that," Wendy whispered to Mark. He silently held up his index finger to his lips, pleading with her to keep quiet. She grinned at them. "Hi Ronnie."

"Hey, Wendy." Wendy was a year older than them. She was more timid and quiet than her older sister,

25

Tanya, who everyone thought was drop dead gorgeous. Wendy seemed to constantly be living in Tanya's shadow, but Ronnie liked her better than Tanya. She had a pretty face dotted with a few freckles. Her dark, shoulder-length hair was pulled back into a loose ponytail, with her bangs spilling over her forehead. As she walked back into the kitchen, Mark called out to her.

"How's your sister doing? Can you tell her something for me?" he asked, waggling his eyebrows.

"No," Wendy said rolling her eyes. She disappeared into the kitchen.

"Tell her she completes me," Mark called out.

Ronnie suppressed a grin as Judy returned to the bar holding the bottle of grenadine. With an irritated look on her face, she poured their drinks into large paper cups.

"One water and one Cherry Pepsi," she said, pushing them across the bar toward Ronnie and Mark.

"Thank you," they said simultaneously and turned to walk back out to their mowers. Ronnie looked back just before they left the restaurant, hoping he could catch one more glimpse of Wendy. No such luck.

Once they were out of the clubhouse again, Ronnie turned to Mark. "Why does she hate you so much?"

"I have no idea, man," Mark shrugged. "But if you thought *that* was hate, you should see her with JoeJeff. She *really* hates them. Have you ever--" Mark suddenly glanced all around him and lowered his voice. "Have you ever noticed how just about every old person hates young people?"

Ronnie laughed and shrugged. Mark wanted to press the issue further but took another look around and saw that he was surrounded by elderly golfers. He decided to keep his mouth shut and got onto his mower. They put their cups in the side-mounted cup-holders, and started up their Walkmans and mowers again. Mark listened to a tape of Glen Campbell's greatest hits, while Ronnie had the new Journey album *Escape*. "Stone in Love" began to blast in his eardrums. They had both gotten addicted to Journey after watching *Caddyshack* at the movie theater last year.

Ronnie loved mowing tees. It was an easy job that managed to eat up about three hours of their long mornings. Sure, he had to get off the mower and move the tee markers, but most of the time he was just sitting, mowing lines back and forth, listening to music, and enjoying the warm days and sunlight.

Luckily for them, there were no golfers teeing off yet on hole number one, so they were able to jump right onto the tee box and get to work without waiting. The first hole had only one big tee box right behind the practice green and the door to the pro shop. The fairway for hole one was relatively long and straight, lined with large bunkers up to the green.

Mark started mowing diagonal lines in one corner of the tee box, pressing the foot pedal to drop the blades as soon as they crossed over from the rough to the short tee box grass. Fresh cut grass flew out in front of the spinning blades, looking like a misty green cloud from a distance. While Mark mowed, Ronnie got off his mower and pulled off all four sets of oversized golf ball-shaped tee markers, getting them out of Mark's way.

They worked as a team, with Ronnie pulling tee markers before Mark's mower hit them, and putting them back after Mark had passed by. All the other holes had multiple separate tee boxes, and they would both be mowing and pulling markers, but since there was only one tee box on this first hole, they split the duties. Finally, Mark finished all the diagonal lines and mowed a cleanup circle around the outside of the tee box, leaving a nice round edge, and Ronnie put the black championship tee markers into place near the back. They finished up at roughly the same time and drove off before any golfers approached.

As they drove up the fairway toward the tee boxes on hole two, Ronnie glanced over at Mark and saw him passed out while still driving his mower. His arms bounced limply at his sides, his head slumped back, and his mouth hung wide open as if he were in a deep sleep. Ronnie lost it and cackled laughter, Mark began to grin.

They couldn't really talk over the roar of the mower engines and the blasting music in their headphones, so Mark held up a finger as if saying: *Wait, watch this*. He glanced over his shoulder and made sure there were no golfers trying to tee off yet. Satisfied that they still had the fairway to themselves, he yanked his steering wheel hard to the right and then pretended to fall back into his open-mouthed deep sleep. His mower spun around in a circle as he "slept." Ronnie threw his head back and laughed even harder. The image was so ridiculous that he couldn't help it. Mark "woke up" and sped back towards Ronnie.

Now Ronnie slumped over his steering wheel and gave his own take on the sleeping mower joke. Mark caught up and Ronnie opened an eye to see him laughing hysterically too. Ronnie was about to pull the circle stunt when Mark glanced back and saw a group of old ladies doing stretches on the number one tee box and pulling their drivers out. Mark cocked a thumb back at them and mouthed the word *Golfers*. Ronnie immediately perked back up, and they both pulled off into the rough on the left side of the fairway to get out of the golfers' way.

They pulled their stolen cookies out of their pockets and ate them as they drove the rest of the way to hole two. Every few seconds they glanced over their shoulders to make sure no golf balls were heading directly for them. Ronnie had learned quickly when he started working here to keep an eye out for golf balls flying at him while he was out driving around on the course. It became second nature after a while, and so far, he had never been hit.

Twenty minutes later, Ronnie and Mark sat off to the side of the the high hilltop tee boxes for hole number three with their mowers throttled down. They had to wait for a group of ladies to finish teeing off before they could mow again. A song faded out on his headphones, and Ronnie faintly heard a voice squawking out of the radio on his hip. He pulled his headphones down around his neck and listened closely to the radio.

"Mark and Ronnie. Bill to Mark and Ronnie," Bill said.

Ronnie picked up his radio and held it out to Mark. "Hey, Bill's calling us."

Mark pulled off his headphones and gave Ronnie a confused look. "Why you giving it to me? Just answer him."

Ronnie shrugged. Mark usually did all the talking for them on the radios because Ronnie always felt awkward and uncomfortable talking on them. He held down the talk button.

"Uhh hey, Bill. This is Ronnie. Come on back," he finished in a southern accent, the way he imagined a trucker on a CB radio would sound. Mark often answered Bill like that.

Bill responded sounding irritated. "Are you two clowns fuckin' around out there?"

"Ummm, no," Ronnie said hesitantly. He honestly didn't know what Bill was talking about. At the moment they were just sitting there quietly. "We're just out at number three waiting to mow."

"I just got a call from the pro shop saying that you guys were on number one screwing around, driving

29

in circles, and acting like a couple of idiots," Bill snapped.

Ronnie suddenly remembered their fake sleeping. "Uhh, oh yeah. Sorry about that."

"You guys better quit fuckin' around out there, or you're gonna be finding another job, got it?"

"Okay. Sorry, Bill," Ronnie replied sheepishly. Bill did not respond. Ronnie turned to Mark and gave him a clenched nervous jaw and hissed in breath.

"What did he say? I couldn't hear over the mowers," Mark said.

"He was super pissed. He must've heard about the sleeping thing. You know, on number one?"

"Oh shit," Mark said guiltily and gave him his own tense, tight-jawed look. Ronnie told him exactly what Bill had said over the radio. Mark sighed and shook his head. "Those fucking tattle-tail assholes in the pro shop. I bet it was that fuckin' kid Chip. He probably saw us through the window and went and told Mr. Hamilton, then he bitched out Bill."

"Shit, I hope Bill isn't too mad," Ronnie said. Rarely had he been yelled at by a boss at work like that.

"Naw, don't worry about it. He'll get over it, he's a mellow guy. Hey, we're up." Mark pointed at the empty tee box. The ladies were driving off, heading down the fairway toward the green. They both sped off and continued mowing.

The tee boxes on holes four and six were close together so Mark took six, while Ronnie took four. Old George Withers sat in a golf cart parked on the cart path alongside the tee boxes for hole four. Old George was in his late eighties and was a regular at the golf course. On Mondays, when the Ladies had one of their bi-weekly tournaments, Old George would drive out to the fourth tee with Thermoses full of coffee. He would flirt with them and serve them coffee in little paper cups as they played. Like the ladies, he also gave the maintenance crew a hard time.

Ronnie hopped off his mower and began pulling off the red Ladies' tee markers. Right on cue, Old George came hobbling over, yelling and mumbling at him. Ronnie politely pulled a headphone off one ear.

"Ya can't do it! Ya can't do it! They're havin' a tournament," Old George yelled.

"I'm sorry, man, but I have to," Ronnie said and continued what he was doing, wishing he had taken hole six and Mark had taken hole four instead.

"But ya can't do it! Ya gotta put 'em back!"

"Look, I'll put them right back in the exact same spot when I'm done, all right?"

"But ya *can't!*"

"Look, I already told you, I have to. Sorry." He almost turned away, then on impulse added one more thing. "If you have a problem with it, then talk to my boss, Bill Carlson." Ronnie put his headphone back on and ignored Old George as he continued to yell from the side of the tee box. As Ronnie began to mow he could see the old geezer glaring at him from the seat of his golf cart. Ronnie was glad when he was finally able to finish and get away from the annoying guy. As he drove off to the hole five tee boxes, he shook his head.

Boy, am I gonna get it for that one. Bill's gonna chew my ass out for sure. Thankfully, Bill never mentioned Old George.

The rest of the tee mowing went a lot smoother. They got ahead of the Ladies somewhere around hole number eight, and were able to continue without having to wait for anyone or get in anyone else's way. Some of the older guys on the maintenance crew were mowing fairways with the big tall mowers on the back nine. Ronnie and Mark felt more comfortable around their fellow coworkers. Between several of the holes they ran into herds of geese and chased them with their mowers. The mowers were too slow to catch the geese, and they seemed to know it. They never flew away, they only spread their wings and ran just fast enough to stay ahead of the mowers.

Around hole seventeen, Ronnie was reminded of the strange air-guitar man. He kept a watchful eye out for him as he mowed, but the guy was long gone. Ronnie's mind wandered back to the incident that morning as he mowed diagonal lines on the big figure-eight-shaped tee box. *I saw you in a vision. This place is cursed.*

There's no curse. And he probably had no "vision" about me either, Ronnie thought. *If anything, this place has been more of a blessing to me than a curse. Where else could I find a summer job this good?*

Ten-thirty was approaching when they finished the last tee box, hole sixteen near the parking lot exit, and drove back into the maintenance shop to wash their mowers. There was a wash bay in one corner of the maintenance yard just past the cart barn and the gas tanks. They usually had to pull out the long hose and spray gun that were attached to a pressure washer that sat permanently inside the cart barn, but today they ran into Merv, one of the old guys on the crew who was washing his big fairway mower.

Mark went into the building to use the bathroom and allowed Ronnie to wash his mower first. Merv handed Ronnie the pressure washer hose when he finished.

"She's all yours, Mark," he said to Ronnie.

"I'm not Mark. I'm Ronnie."

"Uh, well, whatever your name is. I can't keep track of all you youngsters anymore." This wasn't the first time Merv had gotten Ronnie's name wrong, but Ronnie didn't take it personally that he never seemed to be able to remember his name. He just laughed as the old guy drove forward to gas up his fairway mower, and began washing the clumps of wet grass off the bottom of his tee mower with the thin, powerful jet of water from the pressure washer.

"At least you didn't call me Joe or Jeff," Ronnie mumbled to himself.

*   *   *

Each spring, all four of the young guys on the crew had to go out to all thirty-six bunkers on the course and cut a fresh new edge around them with a flat, sharp sod-shovel. They would haul off the old overgrown sandy edges and dump them in a big storage area near the fourth green on the north end of the course. Bill called it refacing bunkers. It was a hot, hard job that they usually only did in the mornings because the heat of the afternoons made it just too unbearable. The process usually took about six weeks, and between Ronnie, Mark, Joe, and Jeff, they only had a few bunkers left to do.

Joe and Jeff were riding around with their smoked Aviator sunglasses on and their sleeves rolled up over their shoulders to avoid getting farmer's tan. They were also trying to avoid work. An hour ago they had refaced one of the smallest bunkers near the sixteenth green, but now they were just driving around the lake on the north side of the driving range, trying to make it look like they were working.

"What time is it, dude?" Jeff asked.

Joe looked down at his wrist watch. "Uh, ten forty-seven."

Jeff tipped his head back in agony. "Fuck, this day is fucking dragging."

"Maybe we should go do another bunker. Get

'em done so we can stop worrying about 'em, know what I mean?" Joe was usually the voice of reason and had a mildly stronger work ethic than Jeff.

"Ooh, y'know, I really want to but I'm really busy at the moment," Jeff said sarcastically.

Joe laughed. "Bill's gonna be pissed if he catches us."

"I don't give a f-- *Goose!"*

Jeff spotted a goose standing by the lake near the tall grass, hissing at them like mad with its pink tongue hanging out. It even advanced toward their cart a few steps. Around this time of year, the geese were always aggressively protecting their newly hatched fuzzy yellow chicks, and Jeff loved to antagonize them.

He took up the goose's challenge and slowed the cart down.

"Come on, little asshole. Whatcha gonna do, huh?"

Joe laughed at how seriously Jeff seemed to take the challenge. Jeff hit the gas pedal and surged a few feet closer to the goose, trying to intimidate it and get it to run away into the tall grass. The goose held its ground and hissed harder, it even advanced a few steps closer.

"Okay, so it's like that, huh? Come on. You want some of this?" Jeff threatened. Joe continued to giggle in the passenger seat. Jeff turned the cart, putting Joe on the side near the goose. He tapped the gas and surged forward again, stopping within five feet of the goose.

Instead of running away, as both Joe and Jeff suspected it would, the goose suddenly started charging toward their cart, hissing madly and going straight for Joe's legs with a look of pure animal hatred in its beady black eyes.

"Shit, dude! GO GO GO!" Joe screamed. He protectively pulled his legs up away from the goose. Jeff

yanked the wheel to the left and stomped down on the gas.

"Oh shit," he muttered under his breath. The cart sped off and the goose chased them for a few yards. Joe and Jeff looked back over their shoulders and saw the goose out in the middle of the fourth fairway, hissing and warning them not to come back near its little ones again.

Joe continued to laugh. "What the fuck? I never thought I'd be chased by a goose before. Look at it. You pissed it off to the max."

They faced forward again and caught sight of the younger kids, Ronnie and Mark, refacing one of the big bunkers near the fourth green.

"You thinkin' what I'm thinkin'?" Jeff asked.

"Yep."

They sped off towards the bunker.

*   *   *

There was no shade around the bunker and the sun reflecting off the hot sand made the comfortable eighty-five degree temperature feel twenty degrees hotter. Ronnie dumped a heavy shovel full of sod into the back of their work cart and pushed his glasses back up on his sweaty nose. Mark mopped sweat off his forehead with the back of his forearm, and saw Joe and Jeff driving toward them down the fairway.

"Hey, look who it is," Mark said. "It's Lenny and Squiggy." Ronnie looked up and saw the older guys driving up too. "About fuckin' time they showed up and helped us do some real work around here."

Joe and Jeff pulled up next to the bunker near Ronnie. As they slowed down, Ronnie started to say, "Well, well, well, look what the cat--"

Then Joe immediately tossed a cup full of icy cold water at Ronnie, completely soaking his T-shirt and

35

the front of his jeans. Ronnie gasped in shock and stood up straight as the ice water shocked his senses. Joe, Jeff, and Mark all immediately began to howl with laughter and the two older boys sped off. Mark dropped his shovel in the sand and doubled over from laughing so hard.

"I'm-I'm sorry, dude. I'm sorry, but that was fuckin' incredible!" Ronnie tried to give him a furious glare but he couldn't help the smirk that was spreading across his face and the laughter bubbling up from his guts. In the sweltering heat, he actually felt re-energized from the cold water.

"You know somethin'? That actually felt amazing," he said truthfully. He held his arms out and sighed with relief as Mark continued to laugh.

*   *   *

Mornings lasted from 6:00 AM until noon when they broke for lunch. With only two hours left in the day, the short afternoons were usually kept open for busy work like trimming around trees where the bulky rough mowers couldn't reach, or picking up trash and stray limbs. This upcoming Saturday, the course was hosting what Mr. Hamilton liked to call "the biggest tournament of the year." According to him, the course had to be in perfect shape for the tournament, so Ronnie and Mark were sent off to trim around trees with two string trimmers.

They were back on the north side of the driving range near the lake and the bunker they had re-edged a little while ago. If asked, they would say they were searching for trees to trim around, but they weren't searching very hard. They were busy driving around quoting their favorite lines from *Caddyshack*.

Suddenly, in mid-quote, Mark slammed on the

brakes and Ronnie flew forward for the second time that day. His glasses threatened to fly off the bridge of his nose again but his hand flew up to catch them. He half expected another person to be lying face down in the grass, just like the air-guitar guy had been this morning. There was no one in front of them, in fact, Ronnie could see no reason at all why they stopped.

"Jesus, man! What the hell?" he asked.

"Do you see that girl over there? Ay chihuahua!" Mark said.

Ronnie squinted through his glasses, searching for the rumored "hot girl." The only female Ronnie saw was golfing with an older man down the middle of the fifth fairway more than a hundred yards away.

"Who? Her?" Ronnie asked. Mark only nodded, still staring at the woman. "Look dude, I hate to break it to ya, but she's probably a grandma."

"What? No way. She's young man, probably in her twenties. That's gotta be her dad out there with her."

"Since when do you ever see hot younger girls —besides Tanya—out on this golf course in the middle of the day? It's always old people out here."

"No way, José. I can tell. We're going over there."

"Oh God, no. Don't go over to her," Ronnie protested. "I'm tellin' you, she's a grandma. I'll bet you five bucks she's a grandma."

"You're on."

Mark immediately stomped on the gas pedal and raced forward. He straightened his Indian Hill trucker hat, trying to feel if it was perfect. Ronnie continued to protest as Mark took a roundabout route over toward the man and the alleged "hottie" or "grandma." He drove up on the hill near the fence that curved around the northern border of the golf course, and casually stole a few glances at the woman as they approached. Ronnie caught sight of her long long salt and pepper hair and the deep crow's feet around her eyes. She couldn't have been any younger than fifty-five. Not wanting to seem like a creep, Ronnie intentionally turned and looked at Mark. He gave him an *I Told You So* look. Before Mark could respond though, the older woman looked over at them.

"Mark? Mark Rowe, is that you?" she asked.

"Oh hi, Mrs. Landry," Mark said. "I, uh, thought I recognized you so...I wanted to come say hi."

"Oh that was so nice of you. How's your father doing?" she asked.

"He's good." After making small talk for the next few minutes, Mark hurriedly ended the conversation. "Gee, well, we'd better get back to work. I'll let you get back to your game."

"All right. Nice talking to you, honey."

Mark drove off toward the bunkers near the fourth green and he and Ronnie sat in silence for a minute until they were out of earshot.

"Boy, that was one hot girl. Let me tell you," Ronnie said sarcastically. "I'm surprised you didn't ask for her number. She seemed like she was into you the way she called you *Honey* and everything."

"All right, wise ass," Mark cut him off. "She and my dad work together, okay?"

"Wow, I guess you're really going for the older ladies, huh?"

"Shut up," Mark said. He slowed the cart down, dug in his pockets, and handed Ronnie a crumpled five dollar bill. "Here ya go, you bastid," he said in a nasally mafia accent.

"Mark and Ronnie, come in," Bill's voice suddenly squawked out of their radios. Mark picked up the radio sitting in the little cubby-hole of their cart.

"Oh great, what'd we do now?" he asked Ronnie. He clicked the talk button and answered Bill.

"This is Mark. What's up boss?"

"I just got a call from one of the marshals that there's some kind of dead bird, maybe a hawk or an eagle over near thirteen green. I need you guys to grab some shovels and go clean it up."

"Copy that," he said and clicked off the radio. "You catch that? Another dead animal, ugh. Apparently an eagle this time."

"An eagle? Really?" Ronnie asked curiously. "Whoa, that's a new one." Occasionally, Ronnie and Mark had to clean up dead geese or dead cats that wandered out onto the golf course and were ripped to shreds by coyotes. Dead animal disposal was one of the most unpleasant aspects about the job, but luckily it didn't happen very often. They had never had to pick up a dead eagle before.

"Yeah," Mark agreed. "I wonder if it's the same one I see flying around over the back nine sometimes." Ronnie was reminded of the eagle's high-pitched cry he would sometimes hear echoing over the quiet golf course whenever it was on the hunt.

"Oh yeah, I've seen him flying around too. Come to think of it, I saw him flying around this morning when we were doing cups. That's sad," Ronnie said mournfully. Mark agreed and drove them back to the maintenance shop to go pick up some shovels, gloves, and a trash bag.

A few minutes later they were back out on the course, heading toward the thirteenth green.

"I think I see where it is," Mark said. He pointed to a spot up ahead between the curve on the twelfth fairway and the thirteenth green. A tall, hundred-year-old cottonwood tree with a massive, deeply cracked trunk stood there. Ronnie saw a golf cart parked near the cottonwood, and two men kneeling on the ground looking down at something. "What the fuck are those guys doing? Do you see that?"

"Yeah I see them. I have no idea."

As Ronnie continued to watch the two men, he saw that one of them seemed to be bowing down to the slumped shape in the grass in front of him, while the other knelt with his head hanging solemnly. Mark slowed down and stopped the cart about fifteen yards from the two men. Thinking that this was some kind of prank, he snorted out a little laugh.

"The hell is this?" he said in a louder voice than he intended.

Both men slowly looked over their shoulders and glared at Mark. They could see that both guys were big and muscular. Ronnie guessed that with their long black hair, deep tan skin, and similar likenesses, they were brothers and of Native American descent.

Ronnie shot Mark a look and a small scolding whisper, *"Dude."*

Mark finally wrapped his mind around what was going on. They had interrupted something sacred, a Native American ritual of some kind, and guilt hit Mark like a ton of bricks.

The closer of the two men had stood up now and was approaching the cart.

"Oh shit," Mark muttered to himself without even looking at Ronnie. Both Mark and Ronnie sat still in the cart. They could see that both men wore black button-up, short-sleeved shirts tucked into acid washed jeans, and despite the fact that they were playing golf they wore cowboy boots. From the mean, tough expressions on their faces, Ronnie and Mark felt like they were about to get their asses kicked.

Mark spoke first, trying to diffuse the situation and act innocently. "Uh, hi, how ya doin,' sir?"

The man glared at him for a second before he finally spoke. "What's so funny?"

"Funny?" Mark asked, and shook his head as if he didn't know what the man was talking about.

"What are you laughing at?"

"Laughing? I wasn't..." Mark began, then he decided to come clean. "Okay, look, I'm sorry. I really didn't mean anything by it. I honestly thought this was some kind of joke."

"This is no joke. This land has lost a great protector."

"Umm, are you talking about the dead bird? We were sent to come clean up a dead--"

"The great eagle. *Respect*."

Mark fell silent. Both men looked at Mark with stern gazes and waited a moment, letting him squirm in his uncertainty. The closer of the two looked back at the other, then turned back to Mark with the faintest trace of a satisfied smirk on his face. They had intimidated Mark and they knew it. Mark almost broke the awkward silence when the man finally spoke again, the confrontational tone in his voice softer.

"Do not mind us. We will be finished here shortly. You must know that the eagle is a great protector, he is the symbol of freedom and strength. He watches over us and frightens away evil spirits. He is a messenger to the Creator. We are making sure he has a proper burial."

"Oh. Uh, okay," Mark said lamely. "I'm sorry. I, uh, I didn't know."

"We will be finished shortly," the man said. Without a pause he returned to the dead eagle and knelt back down.

Both Mark and Ronnie shared a relieved look. They tried to look away, but stole casual curious glances at the ritual. Neither one of them had ever seen anything like it before. From this distance they could hear a muffled chant in a language that neither one of them recognized.

After another few minutes, the two men stood up, silently walked back to their golf cart, and drove off down the fourteenth fairway. Their long black hair blew back in the wind as they drove off.

"Shit, that was a close one," Mark sighed as soon as the brothers were out of earshot.

"What the hell is wrong with you, man?" Ronnie said.

"I wasn't trying to disrespect those guys or anything. Honest. I seriously thought they were pulling some prank on us."

"One of these days you and your big mouth are gonna land us in some deep shit, you know that?"

"Yeah, well, it could've been a lot worse. At least I didn't raise up my hand and say *How.*"

Ronnie grimaced at yet another ill-timed joke. "You're an idiot."

Mark drove up to the dead eagle, parked the golf cart, and picked up the shovel out of the back. They both looked down over its still body. Its brownish black feathers looked a little ruffled and out of place, as if the great bird were very old. Its eyes were squinted shut and its powerful beak hung open slightly. Just the sight of such a majestic animal laid to rest like this made Ronnie sad.

"Man, look at how big it is," Mark said. Its body was easily the size of a small dog, and though its wings were folded, they looked like they would spread out at least six feet. Its scaly yellow feet and black hooked talons looked incredibly sharp. "Well, I suppose..."

Mark walked around in front of the eagle and slid his shovel under its head, trying to work the blade toward the center of its body. Ronnie put on the latex gloves he had brought and whipped the black trash bag up and down to open it. Still holding the shovel handle, Mark walked around to the side of the eagle so its head would be free to slide into the open mouth of the trash bag. Ronnie held the open ends of the bag out as far away from his body as possible, not wanting to touch the dead bird.

"Ready?" Mark asked and Ronnie nodded his head. Mark gave a short countdown to three, then lifted the eagle up off the ground and dumped it headfirst into the trash bag.

"Wow. I didn't think it was gonna be that light, y'know, considering how big he is," Ronnie said, testing the trash bag's weight. Mark nodded in agreement. Ronnie laid the bag delicately into the back of the cart and they took off for the maintenance shop.

Once they made it back down, they stopped at the large blue dumpster that sat just outside the fence and the main gate.

"I wish there was some better way to get rid of them, the dead animals I mean," Ronnie said. "I hate just throwing them in the dumpster. It feels....I don't know...wrong I guess."

"Yeah, I know exactly what you mean," Mark agreed. "Oh well, it's not like we killed it or anything. We're just the poor schmucks that had to clean it up. It's just nature, man. The circle of life, y'know?" Ronnie only shrugged. He took the trash bag out of the back of the cart and laid it down gently on top of other piles of trash and dead limbs.

"Sorry, buddy," he said to the bag and walked back to the cart.

A half hour later, Ronnie and Mark both punched out for the day. Ronnie saw dark clouds gathering in the west, heading straight for them.

"Damn, look at that. Stahm's blowin' in," Mark said, finishing in a downeast accent.

43

"Yeah they said on the news that it's supposed to rain like hell tonight."

"Hopefully it rains tomorrow too so we get the day off from work."

"Wouldn't that be nice?" Ronnie agreed, although, he really didn't mind coming to work. Rainy days were nice to have off, but they meant that his paycheck would be smaller. "Well, I'll see ya tomorrow.... Maybe." Mark said the same and they both aired out their hot cars before getting in. Ronnie cranked down the windows, turned his engine on, and pulled out of the parking lot. He drove back up the driveway and turned left out onto Old Wentworth Road again. In his rearview mirror, he could see that knobby, old hackberry tree standing tall and proud at the top of the hill in the background. It was the last time he ever saw it.

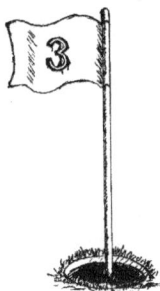

Lightning ripped across the dark, cloudy sky and was followed immediately by a crack of thunder so loud that even Mack Rosenberg heard it over the country music blaring from the speakers in his friend, Travis Burnham's truck.

"Can we turn this shit off?" Mack asked, yelling over the music. Travis heard vague words coming from Mack's mouth.

"What?" he yelled.

"I said: Can we turn this shit off? I fuckin' hate country." Mack reached forward and yanked the volume knob down. Travis reached over and turned it right back up again so he could hear Eddie Rabbitt singing about how much he loved a rainy night at full blast.

"My truck, my rules," Travis said with a grin.

"You fuckin' cracker," Mack laughed.

"That's me, y'all. HOOOOOEE!" Travis let out his best southern sounding scream before taking a long swig out of his can of Schlitz beer. Mack thought he sounded as shrill as Granny from The Beverly Hillbillies.

Mack rolled down the window and stuck his head out, letting the wind blow his long dark brown hair back. He looked up at the sky for a moment, waiting to see another flash of lightning, but it remained dark and brooding.

Two more of their friends sat scrunched up in the center-facing jump seats of Travis's extended cab, and they fired off a couple of good-natured insults of their own. One of them was a preppy looking kid in a polo shirt named Jimmy Bloom who had braces on his teeth, and the other was a chubby guy named Bernard Martel, they all called him Heff (short for Hefty or Heffer).

Travis finished his beer, crumpled the can, tossed it on the floor, and reached back over his shoulder. "Gimme another one o' them beers!" Heff handed him another from the brown paper bag at his feet.

They tore past several empty cornfields as the sky continued to rumble and flash farther west. The storm hadn't quite reached the outskirts of town yet, so they still had time to fuck around outside. They roared onto Old Wentworth Road, the tires on Travis's truck bouncing and screeching in protest. The back end of the truck wanted to fishtail off the road, but the tires gained traction at the last minute and the old Ford lurched forward.

"Jesus, man! Slow the fuck down!" Jimmy shouted from the back.

Mack and Travis only laughed loudly. "What'sa matter, Jimmy? You pussy!" Mack taunted.

"Check this out!" Travis hit a switch on the console. The headlights went out and the old country road disappeared, complete darkness fell over the speeding truck. Travis let out a fake squawky scream in the green glow of the dash lights. He swerved back and forth across the road, tugging on the steering wheel like a little kid would. Mack and Heff continued to laugh.

"Hey, watch it, man! You're gonna miss the entrance," Jimmy protested.

Travis flicked on his headlights again and the Indian Hill Golf Course sign with its two totem poles was immediately illuminated on their right. The truck was going fifty miles an hour, way too fast to make the turn for the entrance. In a flash, Travis slammed on his brakes and yanked the wheel hard to the right, turning into the exit instead.

"Here we are, boys," Travis shouted over the music. "Indian Hill!" Mack stuck his head and shoulders out the window as they drove down the exit driveway. He let out a loud Indian war cry, patting one hand over his mouth. As soon as the other boys got their hysterical laughter under control, they all copied him.

The Ford peeled into the empty parking lot and Travis spun the truck around in tight circles, laying down black donut skid marks on the clean pavement.

"Old man Hamilton's gonna shit a brick when he sees those skid marks in the morning," Jimmy laughed. He had a part-time job on the cart crew at Indian Hill in the evenings, washing the golf carts and parking them in the cart barn for the night.

"Will you two quit fuckin' around and get to it already?" Heff asked from the backseat.

"Yeah, really," Jimmy agreed. "You're makin' me sick back here."

Travis let the truck skid to a stop and looked back over his shoulder at Jimmy. "You puke in my truck and you're a dead man." He faced forward again and looked up at the peak of Hackberry Hill dead ahead of them. Lightning flashed inside one of the clouds, momentarily silhouetting the old hackberry tree that

47

stood at the top of the hill.

"There it is, man," Travis said to Mack. "Are you still gonna do it?"

"Fuck yeah, I'm gonna do it," Mack replied arrogantly. "Never said I wouldn't do it."

"He won't do it. He'll fuckin' chicken out just like he did at that Rollerville place the other night," Heff said from the back.

On Saturday, two nights earlier, they had been celebrating the end of another school year at DeAngelo High, and had taken a similar drunken joy ride over to the abandoned Rollerville Disco Skating Rink. After throwing a bunch of rocks at the building, Mack had told them he was going to go inside, but he turned back as soon as he stuck his head inside the broken front doors. He thought he heard someone moving around and laughing in there. So he herded them back into his own car and sped back to the Westview Mall parking lot. Travis and the others had been giving him a hard time over it for the last two days straight.

"Shut up, fat boy," Mack shot back. "I'll kick your ass."

"Ooooh, I'm really scared of you, Ghost Boy," Heff said sarcastically.

"Yeah, better hope you don't see any g-g-ghosts up there on the hill. Oooooh," Travis added in a quavering, fearful voice while shaking his knees.

Mack shrugged his shoulders confidently, trying to act like he didn't care about their comments. "Arright, fuckers. You gonna keep talkin' or are you gonna get me a goddamn golf cart? I'll drive up there right now and I'll cut that big ol' tree right the fuck down."

"Yes, sir. Get the man a golf cart," Travis said promptly.

"Pull up to the maintenance yard. It's that fenced-in area back there," Jimmy pointed it out. "I left it dummy-locked so we can get in."

Travis pulled up to the maintenance yard, slamming on his brakes dangerously close to the chain-link gate.

"Jesus, man! Will you cool it? I--" Jimmy began, but it was too late. Travis tapped on the gas pedal and the truck lurched forward into the gate. The chain holding the two sections of fence together held for only a second before it snapped. The two sections of fence flew backward, slamming against the wooden fence on the right, and a parked Cushman work cart on the left. Mack, Travis, and Heff roared with laughter. Jimmy felt a stab of fear for his job when he saw that the middle support poles on the chain-link gate were dented in the outline of Travis's front grill.

"DUDE! Are you out of your fucking mind?!" Jimmy shouted.

"Oops!" Travis laughed.

"I just told you I left it unlocked, man! All you had to do was wait for five fuckin' seconds."

"So what?"

"So I'm fucking dead if anyone finds out I was here with you guys."

"Who's gonna tell 'em?" Travis said. "Now quit cryin' and get him a cart, will ya?"

"You fuckin' asshole."

Mack got out of the truck and pulled the lever under his seat, tilting it forward so Jimmy could squeeze his way out from the back of the extended cab. He walked around to the back of the truck and reached over the side of the bed to grab the chainsaw that Travis had swiped from his dad's garage before they headed out on their little mission. Holding the chainsaw in one hand and his can of beer in the other, Mack jogged over to the cart barn to catch up with Jimmy who was looking around nervously.

"You better hope to God no one else shows up here," Jimmy told Mack.

"Don't worry. The only ones out here besides us are the ghosts," Mack joked. Jimmy only gave him one snort of a laugh. He was the only one of Mack's friends who actually believed his story about hearing the ghosts at the roller disco, not that he would have admitted it to any of them.

He rolled up the garage door. The shuttle cart sat right in front in the darkness, ready to help the maintenance crew pull the carts up to the pro shop the next morning. Jimmy didn't have the key to the shuttle cart, it was locked safely away in the pro shop. He wasn't high enough on the totem pole to have access to that building. Below the seat, the gearshift lever was set to forward, Jimmy pulled it halfway over, putting the shuttle cart in neutral. He and Mack pushed it out of the barn with Jimmy steering it over toward the gas tanks.

Travis and Heff had gotten out of the truck and were still screwing around over by the gate. Mack and Jimmy watched as Heff climbed up on one of the two parked tractors and pretended to drive it. Travis wasn't in sight, which made Jimmy worry even more.

"What the fuck's he doing now?" Jimmy muttered to himself.

Once the shuttle cart was out of the way, Jimmy searched through his keys again and found the tiny silver universal golf cart key on his key chain. He almost gave Mack his whole key chain, but something told him that giving Mack all of his keys was probably a bad idea. He worked it off the key chain and held it out to Mack.

"Here you go," he said. "Try to bring it back in one piece, okay? I'm probably gonna be in enough trouble as it is."

"No sweat," Mack replied. "Be back in ten."

Mack snatched the key out of Jimmy's hand and

handed him his can of Schlitz. He sat down in the cart that had been parked right next to the shuttle cart, and put Jimmy's key in the ignition. One foot stomped down on the gas, and the cart pulled forward at full speed.

"Watch the--" Jimmy yelled, but Mack swerved in time to avoid the garage door track.

Mack drove off past Travis's truck and saw him standing at the dumpster outside the maintenance yard's gate. He was spray-painting the words *GOLF SUCKS* in big white, drippy letters.

"TIMMBERRR!" Travis called out to him as he drove by. Mack laughed. He cut across the parking lot and drove onto the course past the L-shaped tee box for the sixteenth hole. He was glad to be rid of the three of them.

Travis finished his graffiti and threw the can of spray paint in the back of his truck. He and Heff walked up to Jimmy who was still standing near the cart barn checking his watch.

"Gimme a key, I wanna go up there and see this," Travis said.

Jimmy held out his empty hands. "That's it, that's the only key I had."

"What?" Travis and Heff asked at the same time. "Aww. Drag, dude."

"Quick honk your horn, so he'll come back and get us," Heff suggested.

Travis considered it. "Nah, I don't want anyone to hear it. Come on, let's go park the truck where we can see it fall."

*   *   *

Mack left the comforting glow of the streetlights in the parking lot and was swallowed up in the darkness out on the course. As he drove up the sixteenth fairway,

51

he looked around nervously at the black shapes of the trees. Even though they were technically still in town, those black pine tree shapes made him feel like he was miles and miles from civilization. A nervous tension crept into his shoulders so gradually that he didn't even notice it. This was starting to feel just like the other night when he stuck his head into that haunted Rollerville building.

I don't care what those dumbfucks say. I heard someone laughing in there.

"Just stop. Don't think about that shit," he said to himself. "Just get this over with. Whoa!" The small sand trap that sat just outside the sixteenth green seemed to appear out of nowhere, and he had to swerve to avoid it. *Jeez, didn't even see that, it's so damn dark out here. Gotta pay closer attention.*

The golf cart struggled as he drove uphill past the seventeenth tee box and worked his way toward the top of Hackberry Hill. A few yards past the tee box, at the southeast corner of the course, there was a split rail fence blocking his path. Jimmy had warned him beforehand that the course didn't go all the way to the tree. This must have be the spot where he would have to get out and walk. He stepped out from under the golf cart's roof and felt the first raindrops tapping against his arms and shoulders.

"Fuck," he whispered to himself. He considered turning around and telling the guys that it was starting to rain and maybe they should come back another night. Looking back over his shoulder, he saw Travis's truck back in the parking lot. His tailgate was down and Mack could see the tiny shapes of all three of them sitting there watching him and drinking more of the cans of Schlitz that Heff had stolen. He imagined their reactions to him driving back to them without cutting the tree down. *Oh there you go again, you pussy. What a fuckin' chickenshit. Big Bad Mack afraid of the dark.*

It's just a little rain. Who cares? Better get moving, he thought.

With the chainsaw in his right hand, Mack climbed over the fence and began walking through the tall, patchy grass toward the old hackberry tree. The dry grass tickled his calves and seemed to whisper in the wind. Overhead, the dark purple storm clouds flickered with lightning. The hill grew steeper and steeper until it suddenly leveled off. Mack found himself standing at the top of the hill in a flat little clearing with the old hackberry tree dead ahead of him. This place had a lived-in, used feeling that he didn't like. He didn't feel like he was out in the woods anymore, he felt like he was trespassing in a stranger's backyard.

No, it's not like a stranger's backyard, he corrected himself. *It's like I'm in an old church where I'm not welcome.* As he walked toward the big old Hackberry tree, he imagined it as the big wooden cross that sat behind the pulpit. Wide flat rocks were placed sporadically around him in the grass, they were the empty pews. He felt like he was being watched on all sides.

Mack finally stopped in front of the hackberry tree and looked up at it in awe. It stood forty feet high, silhouetted against the wide view of streetlights and porch-lights all over town. He wondered if anyone down there would look up and hear the chainsaw running. Would anyone see him?

Don't be ridiculous. It's pitch black dark, who's gonna see anything up here?

The tree itself was an ugly old thing, with knobby limbs and a thick, cracked trunk. The sandstone at its base had eroded away, leaving exposed roots that looked like old bony fingers clutching the ground. There were a few leaf buds sprouting out from the tangled

53

branches, but even this late into the spring most of the limbs looked like they were still in the dead of winter.

"Here goes nuthin.' Sorry tree, this ain't personal. It's just...y'know...."

He began yanking on the chainsaw's pull cord. Pull after pull, the engine refused to turn. Mack began to work up a sweat and his fingers gripping the narrow little plastic end of the pull cord began to ache.

"Fuck. Start, goddamn you!" He gave it three quick pulls in a row and the small engine began to choke and turn over on its own. Encouraged, Mack tried it again, giving the throttle a couple of squeezes. Finally the engine roared to life. Mack hit the throttle sporadically with his finger, letting the engine warm up and cough out gray smoke. *Rrr Rrr RRRRRR!*

Down at the parking lot, Travis and the others faintly heard the chainsaw start up.

"Oh shit, you hear that? There he goes," Travis said. Heff and Jimmy nodded and began to laugh. Travis held out his hand and felt the rain starting to come down harder now. "He better hurry before he gets soaked."

Mack brought the whirling chainsaw blade around to the side of the trunk that faced town and angled it down. His father had taught him how to properly cut down a tree when they were up at their family's cabin. He had explained that the trick was to cut a wedge out of the side where you wanted it to fall, then on the other side, you cut the first half of another wedge and let its weight take it down.

The rain began to fall a little harder as he started sawing through the old trunk. The blade bounced against the cracked old bark at first, and Mack had to put all his arm-strength into holding it steady against the trunk. Finally the blade gained some traction, cutting a deep channel through the bark. He worked the blade back and forth, helping it descend into the old wood. The smell of sawdust began to rise and mix with the stink of gasoline and exhaust spewing from the chainsaw. A thick spray of sawdust shot out from underneath the blade, dusting the hill and Mack's pants.

The blade caught on some hardwood deep within the tree. It slowed and ground to a stop, and the engine died.

"Ahh *fuck!*" He tried yanking on the blade, wiggling it back and forth, but the wood held it tight. "Come on, you little fucker. Get the hell outta there."

Mack stopped to catch his breath and something scratched against the tree inches away from his head. At first he thought there was some kind of animal climbing down from a high limb, maybe a squirrel or a mouse or something. He jumped back instinctively, not wanting some diseased creature to crawl onto his shoulders or in his long, feathered hair. There were no animals around though, not on the tree trunk, or on the ground scampering away.

Scritch scratch scratch scraaaaaatch....

There it was again, only now he realized the scratching wasn't coming from the outside of the tree, it was coming from within. Something was scratching under the bark.

"What the fuck?!" He stepped back away from the tree. All of a sudden his heart was hammering in his chest. He felt the exact same panic he had when he heard that low chuckling inside Rollerville, but somehow this was even worse.

The scratching fell silent. Everything around him seemed to fall silent. The wind, the dry grass swaying, and the rumbling thunder in the sky all took a pause, as if bracing themselves for something. He started to notice a faint electric smell, kind of like the ozone odor of slot cars or the electric train set that went around the Christmas tree. The air itself even began to feel tense and charged, and the hair on his arms and the back of his neck stood up. Mack realized a second too late what was about to happen.

Lightning tore out of the sky only a few feet in front of Mack, striking the tree. It looked as if the world in front of him ripped open, and white light brighter than the sun shot out of the gash in reality. The clap of thunder that came with the lightning was so loud that it temporarily deafened him. It blew him backwards, he landed on the ground fifteen feet away from the tree.

Down at Travis's truck, all three boys jumped and flinched away from the lightning. They all let out equal screams of surprise and watched as the thick white bolt crashed out of the sky. It struck the tall old hackberry tree in the dead center of the trunk less than five feet off the ground. They watched as the tree split open down the middle and exploded into fiery splinters. It fell backwards with a loud series of groaning, ripping sounds, and thudded against the downside of the hill, the side that faced town. Even on the tailgate of Travis's truck they felt the vibrations of the tree when it hit the ground.

They sat in wide-eyed silent shock for a second, their own hearts hammering before they started yelling at each other, arguing over whether they should go up after Mack or not.

Mack squinted and shook his head in a daze. His ears were ringing loudly and everything under the ringing sounded dull, as if he had just gotten out of a loud rock concert. His eyes were struggling to readjust to the darkness again. All around him were little shards and splinters from the hackberry tree that were all either blackened and smoldering, or still on fire. Now that the lightning had struck, the rain returned with a vengeance, quickly turning into a downpour.

He panted in a deep panic, trying to force himself to believe that he was still alive. The cold rain brought him out of his shock a little and he frantically felt his own chest and legs with his hands. Aside from the ringing in his head and the flash of the lightning that had burned onto his retinas like a giant camera flash, he was physically all right. He scrambled to his feet.

The big tree that had stood in front of him was gone. A splintery, jagged stump sat where it had been only a few seconds earlier. Now he could see all of the town without it blocking his view.

Instinctively, Mack turned to run back to the cart, even took a few steps toward it, then he remembered the chainsaw. It was still stuck in the tree. If he didn't get it back to Travis's father, all four of them would have some serious explaining to do. Travis's father wasn't the nicest guy in town, in fact, he was probably one of the biggest, meanest drunks Mack had ever met. He wasn't the only problem either. What if the police saw the chainsaw sitting there? Surely they would come up here sometime within the next half hour or so, if not sooner. His fingerprints were all over that chainsaw. He had to pull it out of the tree and get the fuck out of here. There was no other way, no other options.

He ran back to the fallen tree and looked for the chainsaw. His eyes searched desperately through the grass. *Please God, don't let it be crushed under the tree. Dear God, please.* There was the yellow engine cover lying flat in the grass, about ten feet down the slope of the hill right next to the splintered, sagging remains of the trunk. The weight of the tree had pushed it against the ground, but it wasn't crushed. He dared to hope that it might have even been loosened with the impact from the lightning strike and the fall.

Mack climbed down the hill, his feet sliding in the wet grass. He bent down, wrapped his fingers around the handle, and pulled hard. It wiggled the slightest bit, but still felt like it was stuck just as tight as it had been before. The rain pounded even harder, the cold droplets pelting him as they began to harden and solidify. Mack couldn't believe it, but the rain was turning to hail. Little icy kernels of hail smacked down against his head and shoulders. The wind began to howl.

"Fuck fuck fuck! Hurry up, goddammit!" He bent down low, his face close to the splintery fragments of the tree, and screamed with the strain of trying to pull it out. *"Come on! Fuck! Come out of there goddamn you!"*

The splintery fragments within the blackened part of the tree trunk shifted. Mack looked over, wondering if his eyes and ears were playing tricks on him. It felt like something had moved from within the tree, but it was hard to tell with the hail bouncing down off the trunk and the wind blowing like it was.

Mack turned back to the chainsaw and the woodchips within the tree moved again. He let go of the chainsaw and jumped back, staring down at the shredded trunk. He remembered the scratching sound that had come from inside the tree just before the lightning hit. Whatever was moving around now must be the same thing that had been scratching against the inside of the tree.

But nothing could've survived a lightning strike like that, his mind protested. *Surely whatever was inside the tree had to be dead.*

Something rolled and shifted again. Mack watched it this time squinting through the hail. Several shredded fragments of the tree almost looked like shoulders rolling and fingers flicking open and shut. Mack could hear them crack and pop. They didn't look very much like pieces of the tree anymore, they looked more like old bones.

Just get the damn chainsaw and get the fuck out of here, his mind yammered.

He reached for the chainsaw and tugged on it, ignoring the moving thing within the tree. Everything fell still and Mack looked back up again.

A bony skeleton hand shot forward seizing him by his windpipe. He yelped as the sharp bones dug in, crushing his larynx and cutting into the skin of his neck. His bladder let go as a dirty skeleton head rolled up to face him. The last thing Mack Rosenberg saw were black empty eye sockets, wisps of long grayish-black hair, and its gnashing, clicking teeth.

*   *   *

A siren sounded in the distance. Down in the parking lot, Travis, Heff, and Jimmy all turned in its direction.

"Fuck! It's the cops!" Travis shouted. He immediately slammed his truck tailgate shut and ran for the driver's side door.

"You think they're coming here?" Jimmy asked.

"No shit, they're coming here!" he shouted. "Come on, let's get the fuck outta Dodge."

"What about Mack?" Heff screamed. "We can't just leave him!"

"And what about the cart? My boss--"

"Fuck your boss. And your cart. We've all been drinkin.' We smashed that gate. This is some heavy shit, and I'm not gonna get caught."

"But the--"

"Get in or stay! I'm leaving right now." He started up the truck and both Heff and Jimmy jumped in, crowding him in the wide front seat. The truck's tires peeled out, spraying rainwater and hail behind as he floored it. He drove the Ford out through the exit and took off down Old Wentworth Road at an insane fifty miles per hour. He didn't slow down until they were far away from the Indian Hill Golf Course.

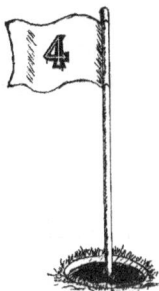

Tuesday, May 19th, 1981

Ronnie knew he was standing out on the golf course because one of the greens was right in front of him, but everything out here was all wrong. For starters, the light was wrong, it was almost totally dark. He was never out on the course at night, only during the day. The darkness made him feel lost, even more than he'd been on those early days after he first started working there and hadn't yet memorized the twisting layout of all eighteen holes. He spun around in a circle, trying to spot any familiar landmarks, but it was all grass and trees.

The wind was blowing hard and there was some kind of ripping, thundering noise. At first he thought it was a chainsaw, but that couldn't be right either because this noise was all around him. It almost sounded like a really hard rain pouring down, but the course was completely dry. Only the wind whipped his black hair wildly around, and that noise continued to thunder in his ears.

Lightning flashed nearby, and he saw the silhouette of the old hackberry tree farther up the hill.

Seventeen, that's what hole I'm on. The closest hole to that old tree, he thought. He turned around again and now recognized the green. The flag whipped in the wind. *Seventeen, yeah. How did I not realize that in the first place? I'm right near where--*

(He's comin' back)

--we saw that weird homeless guy this morning. Oh God.

He did not want to be here. That homeless guy had been creepy enough this morning in the daylight. Now being back here at night in that same spot made him more nervous than ever.

(Chief's comin.' Chief's comin' back.)

Chief. Was that what he had been trying to say? This morning it had sounded like he said something more like *sheep*, or *sheaf*, or maybe even *she's*. But Chief, that hadn't occurred to him this morning. Now it made sense. *Chief. Like an Indian chief. Maybe the same chief who's in charge of those two strange guys that did the burial ceremony for the dead eagle.*

Lightning flashed again, drawing his attention back to the green. Thunder followed quickly, cracking so loud he clapped his hands over his ears and instinctively ducked his head. The ground seemed to shudder and vibrate with it, and somewhere below the freshly manicured golf course grass there was a deep rumbling. He could feel the tremors in the ground through his bare feet.

Something was moving under the seventeenth green. Ronnie watched as the white cup slowly rose up, wiggling its way out of the hole he had pounded out this morning, as if someone were pushing it up from beneath the grass. More lightning flashed as the cup rose all the way up and tipped over, spilling the flag stick out onto the green behind it and rolling away.

Then the ground itself was rising, like a great big bubble made out of the fine, short Bent Grass. Through the circular hole where the cup had been, Ronnie could see some black, rotten thing squirming around under the grass.

He began to back away, his heart pounding. His feet moved slowly like he was walking through water, and he began to pant and wheeze for breath. Somehow he knew he wouldn't be fast enough to get away from whatever was crawling up from under the green.

Jagged eggshell cracks ran down the sides of the grass bubble, and the sod began to peel back and fall away. Two dirt clotted bony hands shot up from between those cracks. They slammed down onto the green and dug in, leaving muddy gouges. One of the hands held an ancient tomahawk with dark symbols painted on it.

Ronnie tripped over his feet and fell back onto his butt. He tried to crab-walk away from the dead thing pulling itself up out of the ground.

Chunks of mud fell off a horrible wrinkled skull-thin face, and black liquid poured out of its sunken eye sockets. A set of bony shoulders and a moldering rib cage lifted themselves up out of the ground. Its dirt caked jaw hung open as it rolled its head back and forth, uttering a gravelly, demonically low scream. Black feathers from a full headdress on top of its head fluttered back and forth in the wind. It pulled itself up out of the hole past its tattered rib cage.

Ronnie tried to scream but no sound came out of his mouth. A rush of air tried to force its way down his throat as the wind blew into his mouth.

The dead thing snapped its head in Ronnie's

direction, fixing those wormy black eye sockets on him, and it began to pull its legs out, coming for him....

With a short cry of terror, Ronnie kicked himself awake. The bed sheets were all tangled and bunched up around his legs. That pounding sound and the crack of thunder had somehow followed him out of his nightmare and into the real world. Ronnie looked over to his window and saw sheets of hail rapping harshly against the glass. It was hammering the roof and was deafeningly loud in his upstairs bedroom.

He caught his breath, sitting up in bed and rubbing his bleary eyes. The image of that dead thing crawling up out of the ground was still fresh in his mind. His stubborn brain refused to let it go. He shook his head a few times trying to will it away.

"Shit. What time is it?" he muttered to himself. He picked up the clock and had to squint at the narrow hands to see that it was 1:27 AM. He let out an exhausted sigh and laid back down. The sheets were still tangled so he took the covers in both hands and tossed them back down, letting them settle in a straight position again. He hated crumpled, tangled up sheets.

Still feeling a little tense from the nightmare, he turned on the radio on his alarm clock. The country station kept him company as he fell back asleep. The nightmare was already fading in his mind, but one word kept repeating, a word that he didn't quite understand anymore.

Chief.

*   *   *

He barely remembered the nightmare when his alarm clock blared at five o'clock the next morning. All the details had fogged over in his brain. It had something to do with the golf course and some creepy horror movie thing had been after him, but that was all he could remember. He figured it probably had a lot to do with the strange things that had happened yesterday.

After fifteen minutes of stalling and trying to keep his eyes open, Ronnie finally got out of bed. He put on his thick horned-rimmed glasses and shuffled over to look out the window. The rain and hail had stopped sometime in the night and everything outside had a wet, washed-out look. There were still clouds in the early morning sky but they looked used up and weak, like the last remnants of the storm, soon to give way to yet another sunny day.

Ronnie shrugged. *I guess there'll be work today after all. So much for that rain day*, he thought without much regret.

Forty minutes later, he turned onto Old Wentworth road. It was chilly under the overcast sky, so he wore a thin Windbreaker. Back near his house the hail hadn't caused much damage, but out here the road was covered with broken tree limbs and debris. It looked to Ronnie like the windstorm had been much worse out here.

He glanced up at the hill looming ahead of him and did a double take. The old hackberry tree, the landmark that he saw everyday on his way to work, was gone.

"What the hell?" For a brief second he thought that he must've taken a wrong turn down some unfamiliar farm road. No, this was Old Wentworth Road all right. There was the old abandoned barn and the empty cornfield. Up ahead he could even see the Indian Hill Golf Course entrance sign and the totem poles. Ronnie looked back at the hill, it looked naked and unnatural without that big old tree. "My God. It must've blown over in the night." Suddenly he felt the tires on the right side of the car crunching and bumping along the narrow dirt shoulder. With a jolt of surprise he looked back down at the road, saw that he was inches away from driving into the ditch, and quickly veered back into his lane.

Ronnie kept his eyes focused on the road until he pulled into his usual parking spot at work. He slung his Koss headphones around his neck, grabbed his brown-bag lunch, and got out of the car. Old Zeke stood behind his car a few spots down, smoking a cigarette. Instead of staring at the sunrise as he usually did, he stood staring up at Hackberry Hill. Ronnie walked over to him.

"Mornin,' Zeke," he said.

"Mahnin'," Zeke replied in his downeast accent without taking his eyes of the hill.

"Can you believe that big ol' tree fell down last night?"

"Nope. She stood there watchin' over us longer than you or I've been alive."

Ronnie shook his head. "Man, that must've been some wind."

"Oh, it was more than just wind," Zeke said, and finally turned to face Ronnie. "Had us some visitors last night."

"What? I don't get what you mean."

Zeke cocked a thumb over his shoulder in the direction of the maintenance shop. "Go take a look at what they did to the shop."

"Who? What'd they do?" Ronnie asked, suddenly curious.

"Take a look," Zeke repeated gravely.

Ronnie walked toward the maintenance shop quickly, curious to see what the old man's cryptic words meant. He wondered how Zeke ever got to be so strange.

The first thing that struck him was the police cruiser parked next to Bill's old pickup truck near the maintenance yard fence.

"Uh oh, that's not good," he said to himself. He began to hurry in towards the shop. If the cops were here that meant that something really crazy had to have happened. He looked toward the maintenance building, expecting to see catastrophic damage, but from here everything looked mostly intact.

Something white caught his eye off to his right. The blue dumpster that sat just outside the gate had the words *GOLF SUCKS* spray painted across it in white. The letters looked drippy and faded, as if they were the font on some horror movie poster that couldn't decide whether it wanted to be spooky or bloody. Ronnie guessed the rain must've washed some of the paint away before it had a chance to fully dry.

He continued forward and noticed the big dents in the metal support posts of the chain-link gates. They looked as if they'd been rammed with a car or truck.

"Shit," he whispered to himself, brushing his fingertips over the dents. He scanned the rest of the maintenance yard for more damage. The tractors looked fine, the big gas tanks were okay, and all the garage doors looked the same as they had yesterday afternoon when he left.

Maybe the inside of the shop is ransacked, he thought. He imagined the interior of the maintenance garage in shambles, but as he turned into the open garage door, he saw that everything was still in place. *Maybe the rain scared them off.*

The homeless air-guitar man's words echoed again briefly in his mind. *Better not be here after th'sun goes down. This place is cursed.*

Up on the chalkboard, he saw a big X scratched over everyone's job listings. He took a few steps toward the office to punch in for the day, but the door was closed. Through the narrow little window above the door handle, he could see Bill, Brian, and the head pro, Mr. Hamilton talking to two police officers.

Mark came into the garage in a rush, wearing an old baseball shirt with long green sleeves and the number 8 on the front.

"Holy shit, dude," he said, pointing back over his shoulder with his thumb. "What's goin' on? Why are the cops here?"

"I have no idea, man. Looks like someone rammed the gate," Ronnie said.

Mark almost walked into the closed office door just like Ronnie had a moment ago. The office door was rarely ever closed so it was a force of habit for them to just walk in. He peered through the window and saw the group standing inside talking.

"Whoa, Mr. Hamilton's here?" he said, looking at the immaculately dressed head pro. "That guy never gets here earlier than nine o'clock. You know it's serious when he's here this early."

Bill noticed them looking in through the window and excused himself. He popped his head out the door.

"Don't worry about clocking in," he said quietly. "I'll fix your time cards later."

"Okay, Bill. What's goin' on?" Mark asked.

Bill gave an exasperated sigh. "I'll give you guys the details later. We had some vandalism and a huge hailstorm last night. Just ignore what I had on the board and go pull carts. Then when you get done with that, I want you guys to each take a cart and go on a debris run. The course is a complete fuckin' mess so I want you to pick up all the big limbs that blew down on the fairways, okay? Ronnie, you take the front nine, and Mark, you take the back. You guys got it?"

"Sure thing, chief," Mark said. That gave Ronnie a start. He glanced over at Mark. Something about that word *chief* made him think of that weird nightmare he had last night. There had been something about the word *chief* but he couldn't remember.

"Ronnie? You got it?" Bill asked.

"Yeah. No sweat, boss," Ronnie replied, not wanting to use that word again. They handed Bill their lunches for him to put in the fridge, and he handed them each a freshly charged radio. Then he went back in the office and closed the door.

"Damn, it must've been pretty bad," Mark said to Ronnie as they walked to the cart barn. "Although it doesn't look that bad to me. No broken windows and none of the equipment's fucked up."

"Butch and Pete will probably know more," Ronnie said. "They always give us the straight dope from the horse's mouth."

"Here's your straight dope, Wilburrrr," Mark joked in a horsey Mr. Ed voice. Ronnie cracked up as he sat down into one of the carts and pulled out of the cart barn.

Up near the pro shop, Butch waited for the two young guys to park their carts before taking off across the parking lot to the cart barn again. Sometime while Ronnie and Mark had been talking to Bill down at the office door, Zeke had joined the rest of the crew pulling carts. He sat silently on the rear-facing backseat of the shuttle cart, looking around at the course thoughtfully and smoking another cigarette.

"Hi there, big fella," Mark said loudly to Butch. It was his customary morning greeting to him even though they were both the exact same height.

Butch responded with his usual, "Hi there, ya little shit."

"You and your little sidekick there didn't fuck up them gates last night, did ya?" Pete asked Mark.

"No not me," Mark said. "I was about five

69

beers in, and ol' Ronnie over here was busy beating his schlong to a Playboy magazine he swiped from his dad's underwear drawer."

"Hey, fuck you," Ronnie shot back and punched him on the arm. The old-timers laughed at that.

Every morning Butch and Pete pulled carts before clambering up on the big fairway or rough mowers. Butch always drove the shuttle cart and Pete always sat next to him in the front. The two always carried on their own loud conversation about the weather, or college football, or some television program. They kind of reminded Ronnie of the two old geezer Muppets that sat in the balcony and heckled everything. The only difference was that they always wore jeans, boots, plaid work shirts, and grease-stained trucker hats.

As they drove back to the cart barn, Butch pointed out all the black tire marks looping around the mostly empty parking lot.

"See all them damn skid marks, Pete?" Butch asked. "They musta' been drvin' around in circles, probably raisin' all kinds of hell."

"Yep. Probably honkin' the horn and hootin' and hollerin' and carryin' on," Pete dutifully agreed.

"Yeah what the hell happened here last night? You guys have any idea?" Mark asked, casually breaking into their conversation.

"Goddamn little pissants drove in here, busted up the gate back at the shop, drove around in circles all over the parkin' lot. They dumped beer cans all over too, but we already picked those up."

"They somehow got into the cart barn and stole one of the carts too," Pete added. "Probably took it joyriding all over the course. God knows what we're gonna find out there."

"Wait, what? They stole a cart?" Mark asked. "Whoa, I didn't know about that."

"Yep, probably ain't never gonna see that cart again neither," Butch cut in.

"I come in here at quarter of five this morning, just like always, and I sees Billy and that Hamilton already here waitin' for the cops to show up. And Billy says the cart barn was open this mornin,' the shuttle cart was out, and one of the carts was missin.' How d'ye like that?"

Butch stopped the shuttle cart in front of the cart barn. Pete, Zeke, Ronnie, and Mark all got off and walked into the barn to pull up four more carts. Mark examined the garage door and the track as he walked in.

"The door looks okay," he said. "Doesn't look like they broke in or anything."

"Little shits probably had a key from someone," Pete said. "Either that or the goddamn cart crew kids left the door unlocked. Them kids is gonna have hell to pay, I can guaran-dem-tee ya that."

Pete put his cart key in the ignition and sped off toward the pro shop again, Zeke also sped off silently. Mark looked over at Ronnie and rolled his eyes, then they both hit the gas.

Back up near the pro shop again, they parked their carts and Butch was pointing to the wooden cigar store Indian standing outside the pro shop's main doors.

"You kids see what those little assholes did there?" he asked. Ronnie and Mark looked over. The wooden Indian's carved, stern, war-painted face was missing, it had been completely sawed off. Somehow seeing the faceless wood carving made Ronnie feel sad. Some pranks were funny, like the stupid spray paint on the dumpster, but this was one of those pranks that went too far and showed people's ugly sides more than anything else. None of them knew that the four pranksters hadn't even been near the pro shop last night.

"Jeez," Ronnie exclaimed.

71

"What the fuck did they do that for?" Mark asked.

"Shit, you oughta' know better than I would, kid," Butch said. "You know, Pete, these kids today, they just ain't got an ounce of respect no more, you know it?"

"Nope, they sure as shit don't," Pete dutifully agreed.

"You know, someone oughta' cut them kids' nuts off and feed 'em to the cat."

"Hey, come on now. Not all of us are bad," Mark protested. "Just take ol' Ronnie and me for example. We're the best of the best. We're the future leaders of America." Mark slung his arm around Ronnie's shoulders and puffed out his chest self-importantly. Ronnie imitated him.

"Shit, if you guys are the future leaders of America, then this country's in big trouble," Butch laughed.

Mark continued to toss insults back and forth with them, but Ronnie looked back over his shoulder at the faceless wooden statue in front of the pro shop. Somehow, it just didn't fit the pattern. It looked too neat for ordinary teenage vandals. Also, why just cut off the face? Why not the whole head, or why not just spray-paint it like they had with the dumpster?

He glanced over at Zeke and saw him staring at the Indian statue with a suspicious squint. He wondered if the old man was thinking the same thing he was.

*   *   *

The course was a soggy mess, the ground constantly squelched and sprayed rainwater underneath their golf cart tires. Cottonwood limbs big and small were strewn about everywhere. Some of the poor crabapple trees that had been in a bright pink, colorful

72

bloom yesterday now looked ravaged and haggard from the heavy hailstorm.

Both Ronnie and Mark began to fill up the graffitied dumpster in no time. As ordered, they focused on the biggest limbs first. Bill sent the old guys out on the fairway mowers even though it wasn't originally on the schedule. He sent Joe and Jeff out to mow the greens. All the smaller twigs and debris got chopped up by the mowers and gradually the course got back into shape.

Ronnie was driving back down to the dumpster with his third cartload of limbs, listening to Gordon Lightfoot's "Carefree Highway" through his big headphones. He had stacked the limbs so high that he had to hold them down with one arm behind his back. As he glanced around the course looking for any other last minute limbs he should grab, his eyes fell on the decorative tepee over between the fourth and fifth fairways. He looked away, but that weird feeling came over him again like something was out of place. Taking another look back at the tepee, it finally hit him: the tepee was still standing, and it didn't look out of shape or disheveled at all.

There were limbs all over the place and a few of the weaker trees had even toppled over in the fury of the storm. But why hadn't the tepee fallen over? Surely the wind should have blown hard against the tepee's canvas sides and knocked it down. He had seen it happen before in smaller windstorms, and had even helped Bill put the thing back up again. There it stood though, somehow completely untouched by the storm.

Still driving, he watched the dark hole that opened up into the tepee, and began to get a creepy, prickly feeling on the back of his neck, like someone was watching him from the darkness. Squinting, he tried to see if anyone was hiding in there. Maybe that weird homeless guy had come back.

Then the cart bounced over a low divot in the fairway, and he felt the huge stack of limbs in the back fly up.

"Oh, shit. No ya don't, no ya don't," he gritted his teeth and clamped his arm down tight on the load of limbs. He took it slower the rest of the way back down to the shop, and kept his eyes focused on the ground ahead of him, swerving to avoid any other divots.

Back at the dumpster, he began unloading the limbs. A few minutes later, Mark pulled his cart up beside him with another full load.

"Bill's gonna have to call this dumpster off pretty soon," Mark said. "She's fillin' up fast."

"Yeah, you can say that again," Ronnie agreed. "I see the cop car left." He pointed to the empty parking spot next to Bill's truck.

"Yep," Mark agreed. "I saw Bill and Brian go driving up to seventeen tee a few minutes ago."

"They're probably looking at that big old tree that fell down."

"What tree? The one at the top of Hackberry Hill?"

"Yeah. Didn't you notice that it fell down? You could totally see it from the road driving in."

Mark dropped the bundle of limbs back into his cart and walked towards the parking lot where he could see up the hill. "I'll be damned."

Ronnie laughed. "How the hell did you miss that?"

"Shit, man. You know how it is. I'm really only half awake until about ten o'clock every morning."

Ronnie nodded agreeably. "The wind must've knocked it down last night. It's so weird because it really wasn't all that bad at my house. All the trees in my neighborhood were fine. And something els--" He was about to tell him about the tepee still standing out on the course, but Mark interrupted him.

"Let's take a ride up there," he said.

"Up where? Past seventeen?"

"Yeah, Bill and Brian are up there right now. I see their cart parked up there. I wanna go take a look at that tree."

"You don't think Bill will get mad?"

"Fuck him." Ronnie snorted out laughter knowing that Mark didn't really mean his disrespect towards Bill. "No, he won't get mad. Come on, I wanna take a look at it." Ronnie shrugged.

Once their carts were empty, they drove up the hill toward the seventeenth tee boxes and the fallen hackberry tree. They parked their carts next to Bill's near the corner of the split rail fence. Ronnie followed Mark as he hopped over the fence. They hiked up through the tall grass towards the top of the hill.

At the top, Ronnie looked around in wonder. He had never been on the highest part of the hill before. He was struck by how flat it was up here and what a great view he had of town spreading out to the east. Bill and Brian stood next to the jagged stump near the edge where the hill began to slope down again. Ronnie could tell by the mass of exposed twisted roots that it was the base of what had once been the tall old hackberry tree.

Bill glanced over his shoulder as they approached. "Hey, how's it coming, you guys?"

"Pretty good. Dumpster's almost full though," Mark replied.

"Already? Shit, I'm probably gonna have to call for one of those big roll-offs."

"Damn, lookit that thing," Mark said as they took a long look at the charred, exploded center of the dead tree lying in the tall grass. The exploded fragments and splinters of tree trunk were strewn everywhere on the hillside. "It looks like someone took a stick of dynamite and lit it off in there."

"Yep, it got struck by lightning at about one thirty last night," Bill explained.

"I've never seen a tree that got struck by lightning before," Ronnie said.

"Yeah, well get this," Bill began. "Those kids that fucked up the gate last night, one of them was up here trying to cut the tree down when it got hit."

"What? Are you serious?" both Ronnie and Mark said amazed.

"Look at that cut." Bill pointed to a deep gouge in the underside of the tree trunk that was too perfectly straight to be anything made in nature.

"And look at the sawdust," Brian added pointing at the ground where they stood. The soggy remnants of sawdust squished under their feet.

"Do they know who did it?" Ronnie asked.

"I think it was one of those boys on the cart crew and some of their friends. There's no way they could've gotten into the cart barn and taken a cart like that without having a key. The cops are out questioning him today."

"Ooh, someone's gonna be in trouble," Mark said tauntingly.

Bill let out another sigh and looked back over his shoulder at the golf course.

"I don't know how the hell we're gonna get this place in shape for Saturday," he said.

"What's Saturday?" Mark asked.

"The big invitational tournament. They have it every year on Memorial Day weekend, don't you remember?"

"Oh yeah, I forgot all about that. I forgot this weekend was Memorial Day weekend too."

"Hamilton's all over my ass because he invited

some PGA professional people here and he wants the course to be immaculate."

"Fuck him," Mark said, repeating his joke from a few minutes ago. Both Bill and Brian laughed.

"Oh, if only it was that simple," Bill sighed. "I've been thinking that maybe you guys and some of the other guys could come in Friday evening and work through the night so we can catch up in time for Saturday."

"You mean, like, work all night?" Ronnie asked.

"Yeah. Well, maybe. We'll see how much we get done over the week."

"I'd be okay with comin' in all night," Mark said.

"Yeah, that'd be kinda cool," Ronnie agreed.

"Well, we'll see."

They fell silent as they took one last look at the fallen hackberry tree, the first of many casualties of that long bloody week.

Ronnie and Mark spent the rest of the morning working with Bill, Joe, and Jeff, helping chop up all the downed trees with chainsaws and loppers. They hauled off the branches to an empty spot on the north side of the course near the fourth green where they usually dumped all the overgrown edges of the refaced bunkers. As they worked, the sun burned through the haze and the day became a sunny, beautiful one. All the strange vibes from the morning and last night seemed to be fading away like Ronnie's bad dreams.

Mr. Hamilton asked Bill some kind of question about cleaning up the course for the tournament roughly every twenty minutes, so Bill and Brian left the course for lunch to get away from him. Nearly all of the rest of the guys went up to the clubhouse restaurant for lunch. Ronnie and Mark dumped off their last load of fallen tree branches and went down to the maintenance shop to eat their brown-bag lunches on the picnic table that sat between the two garage bay doors.

When they pulled up, old Zeke was sitting at the picnic table by himself finishing up his own lunch. Mark and Ronnie went into the office to grab their lunches out of the fridge, and saw that Bill had posted a sign-up sheet on the board. *Night crew this Friday night. 9 PM to 5 AM. Time and ½, and Friday off.* Butch, Pete, and Zeke had already signed up.

"Night crew, huh? You wanna do it?" Mark asked.

"For time and a half, why not?" They both signed their names, then went out to the picnic table and sat down across from Zeke.

"Hey, man," Ronnie said.

"Hey there, boys," Zeke replied. "Billy keepin' you out of trouble today?"

"Oh, he can never keep us out of trouble," Mark said. "We bring trouble with us wherever we go. Ain't that right, Ron?"

"Bet your ass," Ronnie agreed in a fake macho voice.

Zeke laughed and shook his head. "Yeah, you college boys ain't nuthin' but trouble." They fell silent for a minute or so, each of them eating their lunches and listening to the radio still on in the shop. For once it was playing something besides country. It was tuned to the rock station, blaring out Journey's "Wheel in the Sky," which ironically seemed to conjure up wild west images in Ronnie's mind.

Mark finally broke the silence. "You guys think the cops'll catch whoever fucked up the gate and tried to cut down that big tree last night?"

"Hahd to say," Zeke said with a fresh cigarette clamped in the corner of this mouth. He popped a match against the dirty old table and lit it up. Somehow his downeast accent sounded thicker whenever he had a

79

cigarette in his mouth like that.

"I'll bet they will catch 'em if it really was one of those cart crew kids," Ronnie said. "They'll probably crack under the pressure. Or they'll say something stupid to the cops and give themselves away. Remember those kids that got caught egging the school a couple years back?"

"Shit, yeah I remember. Man, did that stink," Mark said disgustedly.

"I always heard that the cops found out it was them because one of 'em was bragging about it to some girl. She was the one that told on them. I wouldn't be surprised if something like that happened."

Zeke nodded his agreement. "Where'd you boys go to school?"

"DeAngelo High, home of the DeAngelo Dolphins. I always thought that was a stupid mascot," Mark said. Zeke's eyes went wide.

"You boys weren't at that roller disco thing back on New Year's were you?"

"No," Mark said gravely. Ronnie shook his head. "We both graduated two years ago, class of '79. But there's a guy on my baseball team who's little brother died there."

Zeke shook his head. "That was a hell of a thing. Can't say I was surprised when it happened though. Wish I could. But you know how it is. Every now and then people just go a little crazy. It's always been that way, and I s'pose it always will. You know, when that roller thing happened, I remember thinkin', 'Hell, it sounds just like the Indian Hill Massacre.'"

"Indian Hill Massacre?" Mark asked skeptically.

"You know, the massacre. It happened back in the olden days, maybe a hundred'n'fifty, two hundred years ago. Happened right up where that ol' hackberry tree was." Ronnie and Mark both looked at each other

80

with puzzled expressions. "Ain't you boys ever heard of the Indian Hill Massacre?"

Both boys shrugged and shook their heads.

"Ain't you ever heard of the Tomahawk boys?" Zeke asked.

"No, who were they?" Ronnie asked doubtfully. It sounded like the old man had gone off his rocker.

"*Tomahawk*," Mark joked in a stern Tonto voice. He sat up straight and held up an imaginary tomahawk in one hand as he said it.

"Christ almighty! Don't you boys know your own hometown's history?"

"Guess not," Mark said. Ronnie shrugged again, agreeing with him.

"You know this part of town didn't used to be called Hackberry Hill. No. Them land developers came in and bought up a lot of the farmland around here about, oh, fifteen, twenty years ago. They're the ones that started callin' it Hackberry Hill, because Injun Hill or Redskin Hill—that's what some of us ol' timers still call it—it just don't sound very nice. They wanted to sell more houses to families and young people, attract more people to the area. So they started callin' it Hackberry Hill on accounta' that big hackberry tree up there. The one that got hit by lightnin' and fell down last night."

"Huh," Mark said thoughtfully. "I always thought that Indian Hill thing was just some random name they made up for the golf course. Y'know to make this place sound like it was...I don't know, like, in the wild west or something."

"Yeah, that's what I always thought too," Ronnie agreed.

"Nope. Everyone 'round these parts used to call this whole area Indian Hill. But not anymore. I'll bet in time they'll even change the name of the golf course to somethin' else. And maybe that's the way it should be, I

81

don't know. Hell, you boys get to be my age, and you'll see. You'll look around one day and say, 'Christ I don't hardly recognize this place no more.'" He shook his head in wonder.

"So why'd they call it Indian Hill then? Were there, like, Indians living on it or what?" Mark asked.

"Oh ayuh," Zeke continued. "There was Indians on it alright. Indians by the score. But they didn't live on it, no. It was a sacred place to 'em. 'Twas said to be the place where they buried the Great Father, Chief Eagle Claw. The way I always heard it was that he'd been buried up there with a handful of hackberry seeds, and them seeds grew into that big ol' tree. And it became sort of a landmark for both the Indians and the white settlers.

"They called him the Great Chief or the Great Father, because s'posedly he had three sons, and they formed three big tribes that lived here. Let's see, if I remember it right, there was the Kikawas, the Nawehs, and the Tapachaks. They mostly kept to themselves, but every spring all three tribes would get together up on that hill. They'd come out of the woods, or down from the mountains, or wherever they hunkered down for the winter, and they'd have themselves a huge powwow. A kind of celebration to honor the Great Father and all the other dead chiefs and braves and...all the other dead, I guess."

"So basically it was like the Indian version of Halloween," Mark suggested.

"I s'pose you could call it that," Zeke said, nodding.

Ronnie listened in fascination with one elbow up on the picnic table and his chin resting in his hand. In his head, he imagined the huge powwow up on the hill above the seventeenth green. He could see their tepees set up, and huge bonfires near the hackberry tree, then

82

only a fresh and vibrant young tree. He saw them decked out in war paint and feather headdresses, dancing and chanting around the bonfires, and telling stories in unfamiliar languages.

"It was those three tribes that were the most common at those gatherings. There were others there too sometimes, but it was mostly them three. Far as I know, the Kikawas were the biggest of the three. The Tomahawk boys were part Kikawa too as a matter of fact."

"Who were these Tomahawk guys you keep talking about?" Mark asked.

"The Tomahawk boys were two of the craziest, wildest Indians that ever walked the earth. They was brothers, Chief Tomahawk and Chief Poison Arrow, but everyone just called 'em the Tomahawk boys on accounta' the big brother Chief Tomahawk was the always one in charge. They were cold-blooded killers. All the white settlers and homesteaders was afraid of 'em. It was mostly because of them that the whites stayed out of this area for as long as they did. In their younger days them Tomahawk boys would gather up other angry Indians and ride out on war parties too. They was always killin' and scalpin', and burnin' down farms and trade posts. But every spring they'd come out to Indian Hill to pay respect to the Great Father at them gatherins.' A lot of the other Indians didn't like havin' 'em there, but they let 'em come anyway."

"Why didn't they want them to come?" Ronnie asked. "I thought you said they were chiefs."

"Oh no, they weren't actual chiefs. In fact, they weren't part of no tribe a'tall. They was outcasts," Zeke explained. "They was only half Kikawa, y'see. Their father was a crazy French fur trapper by the name of Foutuer, and their mother was a Kikawa squaw. I can't remember her name. Their father gave 'em white names when they was born. Thomas and Arthur Foutuer, if I'm rememberin' it right. They looked like full blooded Indians though. Later they renounced the white part of their blood and started callin' themselves Chief Tomahawk and Chief Poison Arrow. But the Indians knew they weren't no real chiefs, and they knew they was only half-breeds."

Mark suddenly launched into the chorus of the Cher song "Half Breed" in a husky Cher voice. Neither Ronnie or Zeke laughed at this joke, Ronnie even shook his head. Mark laughed at himself, then quickly shut up and let Zeke continue the story.

"Ayuh, half-breeds, that was part of it," Zeke continued. "But that wasn't the main reason the other Indians didn't want to include them. They didn't want 'em because they didn't *trust* 'em. Them boys was both crazy and they was said to be damned mean. They were born crazy, born with broken minds. That crazy father of theirs was said to be a murderer and a thief, and he passed all his crazy down through the bloodline to them two boys. Especially the older one, Chief Tomahawk.

"When they weren't out on some war party, they lived alone in the woods in a single tepee. They spent their time practicin' all kinds of black magic, tryin' to summon evil spirits, and demons, and Misquamacus, and I don't know what all. They wore headdresses made out of black crow feathers with a dead bat in the middle, because the Indians believed that bats were the guardians of the night. The rumors were that they learned how to do all sorts of nasty, impossible things. They could slip through the shadows without making a sound, and they had an unnatural control over evil animals like the coyote, who the Indians believed was a symbol of the trickster god. I even heard that they could make a man have dark visions, make 'em see dead folks rising up from the ground where they was buried, and other awful things that would drive 'em crazy. They studied all the old Indian legends and learned everything they could to become dark medicine men. But every year they came out to Indian Hill, and they didn't start no trouble. They just paid their respect to the dead, and then went back to whatever blasphemous thing they were doin' out in them woods.

"The older them Tomahawk boys got, the less time they spent ridin' around killin' and scalpin,' and the more time in the woods doin' God knows what. The longer they stayed away, the braver the white settlers became, and year by year they pushed out a little bit farther west towards Indian Hill. Hell, you probably coulda' seen 'em comin' from up there.

"There was a farmer named Wentworth Hamilton who decided to stake his claim this far west first. He was trying to be like his buddy Elias Hart who was the big shot fifteen miles farther East near town, or I should say what little of town there was back then. So this Hamilton--"

"Wait, wait. I'm sorry. Hamilton?" Mark interrupted. "Was he related to our boss Mr. Hamilton?"

"Oh, our Hamilton is part of that line alright," Zeke confirmed. "That old barn you see on Wentworth Road comin' in from the north? That was where the original Hamilton farmhouse stood."

"I see that barn every day when I'm driving to work," Ronnie said.

Zeke nodded. "Well, when this Hamilton staked his claim, the Indian Hill became part of Hamilton Farm's land. He didn't try to grow anything, or build anything on it, but it was his, at least in the eyes of the white man and the U.S. government. And that very next spring, right on schedule, them Indians came back. Must've been close to two hundred of 'em crowded around up on that hill, including them Tomahawk boys.

"So what'd Hamilton do? Well, he rode into town and gathered up ten of the roughest farmers and farm boys, including Elias Hart who was meaner than dogshit and had a special hatred for Indians."

"Ten little Indian killers," Mark joked.

"So him and his cocky little band got on their horses and rode up to the top of that hill. The Indians were in the middle of their ceremonies, dancin' around their big bonfire when them farm boys rode up. They started shootin' in the air and down at the Indian's feet. Most of 'em scattered and ran to their tepees to hide, but old Chief Dry Creek of the Kikawas walked right up to them horses with his hands up and tried to offer them peace. But the Chief didn't know a word of English, and the settlers weren't interested in peace anyway. They was lookin' for a fight and Wentworth Hamilton was tryin' to look tough, tryin' to impress all his men, especially Elias Hart, who was such a big shot in town.

"So Hamilton tossed a rope around the chief's hands just like he was ropin' cattle and he dragged him around in circles behind his horse, tryin' to make a big show and tell them Indians who was boss. The white boys were laughin' and had their guns pointed at the toughest lookin' braves, ready to shoot 'em dead if they made a move to help their chief.

"And all of a sudden, Chief Poison Arrow came slidin' right out of the shadows, and sliced that rope that was tied around Chief Dry Creek. From the other side, Chief Tomahawk ripped Hamilton right off his horse and threw him down onto the ground. Before them white boys even knew what was goin' on, he snatched Hamilton up by the hair and held his tomahawk up, ready to hack Hamilton's scalp off right in front of 'em. But y'see he spoke English unlike the chief. That crazy fur-trappin' father of theirs taught both of 'em how to speak English and French, and they learned a half dozen other

Indian languages from their mother.

"So he turned right to Elias Hart and he said, 'Leave, white man, or I kill him. Then I kill you.' And Hart seen the dead bat and the black feathers and the tomahawk, and recognized who he was.

"He said, 'I know you. You're them Tommyhawk boys. I could kill you, cut off your scalps and get a pretty penny from the U.S. Marshals office for 'em. Probably get a medal of honor too. You're wanted men.'

"And Tomahawk said, 'I know you too, Hart. You kill your own brother, then you run away and hide out here.' That gave him a start, because he *had* killed his brother, except at the time no one knew about it, at least no one in town knew about it. There was no way he could've known that. So naturally, Hart denied it. And Tomahawk said, 'I see all your secrets in great vision.' And he started spillin' the beans on all ten of 'em one by one. He finally turned back to Hart and said, 'You leave now, and maybe we leave you and your wife alone.' Ol' Hart lifted his gun, he was ready to shoot Tomahawk right then and there at the mention of his wife, but Hamilton, tryin' to save his own scalp, begged him not to do it. The other farm boys talked him out of it, and Chief Tomahawk let Hamilton go.

"After Hamilton was safe and back up on his horse, Hart turned back and said 'This is white man's land now, red face. You git off. Next time I see a red face up on this hill, I'm puttin' a bullet in it.' And the ten of 'em rode off with their scalps still on their heads.

"That should've been the end of it, but Hart and Hamilton just couldn't leave it like that. They both had too much pride. Sure enough they came back three days later just as the gatherin' was comin' to an end and they shot a few Indians dead from farther down the hill. The Indians ran off into the woods, and once they were safe

Chief Tomahawk spoke with Chief Dry Creek of the Kikawas. He told him, 'We must not let them stay here. We must kill them now or be killed later. We can call upon the dark spirits to give us strength.' But Dry Creek wouldn't have it, said he didn't want to sour this sacred burial ground of the Great Father with dark spirits. He said he would find a way to reason with the whites, and that war would only lead to death, and that messin' round with that black magic would only lead to madness. Tomahawk respected him, so he said, 'When you are ready to deal with the white men, you come find us.' And he and his brother went back into the woods.

"The next spring they came back, and that first night Hart and Hamilton shot six more of 'em dead while they were doing their dances 'round the bonfire. They scattered into the woods, and the white men rode up the hill and burned their tepees to the ground. The next day, Chief Dry Creek tried to ride into town—without the Tomahawk boys of course—to talk peace, and they beat him and ran him out before he could even say a word. When he made it back to his people in the woods again, the Tomahawk boys came up to him and asked if he was ready to deal with the white men yet. And again, he said no.

"It went on like this for six more years. Hart and Hamilton made it a yearly tradition to kill Indians, called it their yearly redskin hunting party. Between the killin's and the hard winters, the tribes were gettin' smaller and weaker. There was maybe only sixty or seventy of 'em left. And finally on that sixth year, they came back for their gatherin' and Chief Dry Creek himself was shot and killed by Hart and Hamilton.

"So them Tomahawk boys gathered up two of the strongest braves from each of the three tribes and asked 'em, 'Now are you ready to deal with the white men?' By now they was so angry that they would've followed the devil himself. The shootings had gone on long enough. They were too desperate to care whether or not they spoiled the Great Father's burial ground with the Tomahawk boys' black magic.

"The braves and the Tomahawk boys went off to summon strength and protection from the dark spirits. The spirits gave them all a great vision of what they could do to kill the white men, and they planned a major attack on all ten of the farm boys who rode up and attacked them that first night years ago. The spirits showed them exactly where and when to strike.

"They painted up their faces and sharpened up their arrowheads and tomahawks and rode east. They snuck into town in the dead of night, and started setting fire to the farm boys' houses, smoking 'em out. When the whites came runnin' out, the Indians shot them with arrows and scalped 'em. It didn't take long for the screams and the flames to wake up the whole town. The men grabbed their guns, and those that were left alive shot down the wild braves. None of 'em got the Tomahawk boys though. They weren't with the braves.

"They snuck into Elias Hart's house and dragged his pregnant wife out into the street. They scalped her and shot her pregnant belly full of poison arrows. Chief Tomahawk left a Tomahawk in her chest, because he wanted Hart to know exactly who done it. Then he left her to bleed out in the dust. Y'see, they knew from the dark vision that ol' Hart wasn't goin' to be there to protect her. He was staying out at Hamilton's farm on his yearly redskin hunting trip.

"The townies almost caught 'em as they were finishing off Hart's wife, and they started chasin' 'em as they rode off for the hills. Chief Poison Arrow's horse accidentally stepped into a prairie dog hole and flung him off into the dust. The town preacher was the one that caught up to him and he tied him up and took him off to jail. They knew Chief Tomahawk would come back for his brother and that it'd be too dangerous to lock him up in town. So they decided to take him up to the army barracks and let the boys in blue jail him up instead.

"One of the ten farm boys escaped all the madness and chaos in town and rode out to Hamilton's farm to tell him about his wife. When Hart heard the news he went completely insane and rode up Indian Hill by himself to kill as many Indians as he possibly could. Unfortunately for them, a lot of the squaws and kids had snuck out of the woods to watch the carnage in town from up on the hill. Kikawas were always said to be a headstrong and stubborn people, y'understand.

"It started to rain, and Hart rode up almost unnoticed over the sound of the all the thunder and lightnin.' He shot 'em 'til his bullets ran out. Then he tossed his gun down and rode around hacking away at all the women and children with a dirty old scythe he stole from Hamilton's farm. He slaughtered most of the women and children in a wild rage and that hill ran red with blood. That was the Indian Hill massacre.

"After he was done, and all them Indians was lying dead or dyin' at his feet, he just stood there covered in blood, screamin' his wife's name. And that was when Chief Tomahawk showed back up on the hill. He held up Hart's wife's scalp for him to see, and he said, 'I killed your wife. Now I kill you.' And the two of 'em fought the angriest, bloodiest battle ever fought between a white and an Indian. Hart fought for his wife, Tomahawk fought for his brother and his people.

"At the end of it, the Chief got him down on the ground right in front of that old tree, but he wouldn't kill him just by scalping him. No, that would've been too easy. He wanted to make him suffer at the hands of the darkest spirits he could summon. So, as he was calling on them to come claim their prize, he got stabbed in the guts with a bayonet. Hamilton had sneaked up the hill and saved Hart at the last minute.

"Hart wanted to kill him right then and there, but Hamilton made him see reason. He said if they strung him up to that hackberry tree, he'd be a warning sign to any other Indian to stay off Indian Hill unless they wanted the same thing to happen to them. Hart said he was a hell-bound heathen and he deserved to hang upside down, to show everyone what a blasphemous red devil he was.

"For the next couple of days Hart sat there up on that hill watching Chief Tomahawk slowly die. Most people won't tell you the full story, but I heard that Hart and a bunch of other men from town, and even a few women, taunted him by mutilating all the corpses of the squaws and kids he'd killed up on the hill. They cut off their scalps and their ears and their eyes. They cut the breasts off the women, and dismembered 'em right in front of Chief Tomahawk.

"The chief screamed out all kinds of curses while they was doing it. He cursed Hart and Hamilton and their families for generations to come. He cursed all the people in town, and the farmland, and even the Indian Hill itself. Some folks came up from town to join in the massacre and cut them off a scalp or two as a souvenir, but they left in a hurry when they saw what Hart was really up to, and heard the Chief's dark curses. Only Hart and Hamilton stuck around until he was finally dead. Then Hart went home. Hamilton and a few other farmers stacked up all the corpses on wagons and buried them in a mass grave somewhere down the hill. Didn't want the wind carryin' that stink down to his farmhouse."

"Jesus," Mark said. He and Ronnie both had the same disturbed look on their faces. Ronnie wondered just where this mass grave was, maybe it was somewhere out under the golf course.

"Now normally, that'd be the end of the story, right?" Mark and Ronnie nodded their heads.

"Yeah, they all lived happily ever after," Mark joked. He wanted to lighten the mood after that terrible story. "The Indians that survived got jobs acting in those TV commercials crying about the litter on the highway."

Ronnie gave Mark a reproachful look and said, "Ugh. That's terrible, man."

"Okay, I know. I'm sorry. I took that one too far," Mark said, casting his eyes down and grinning sheepishly, still finding some humor in his distasteful jokes.

"Yeah, well there's more accordin' to the way it was told to me. Chief Tomahawk didn't stay dead."

"What?" both Ronnie and Mark asked. Now the old man's story was starting to take a turn for the weird.

"There's an old Indian legend of a creature called a skudakumooch. In English that means, Ghost-Witch. They say that a Ghost-Witch is an Indian who practiced black magic while they were alive, and now refuses to stay dead. During the day, they look like just a regular corpse, but at night they wake up and they feed on the living. If you see one of them at night, or if you hear its cries it'll put a death curse on you, and you'll die in some horrible way.

"I heard that not long after the massacre, Wentworth Hamilton started hearing Chief Tomahawk's corpse screaming out in the night from where he hung. Even from inside his house, he could hear that dead Indian screaming out curses and calling his name all night long. His livestock and all the crops on his farm died within the first year after the massacre. He still tried to make a go of it out here, but eventually he moved back east into town and had to settle for a job working as

92

a farmhand for his old friend Elias Hart. Bad luck and hardships have seemed to plague those families ever since.

"Some decades later, Hamilton's kids tried to make something out of the land they inherited. They built that barn where the old house had collapsed, but they felt the old Indian's curse too and they left that barn to rot.

"Finally in 1947 they donated all that useless land to the town and built this golf course. And here we sit."

"So what happened to his body then?" Mark asked.

"Oh, I imagine it was torn down and eaten by animals," Zeke speculated. "Either that or it fell apart over time. Hell, it could be that the tree even grew over some of the pieces of the body, and if you sifted through what's left of it up there, you'd find ol' Chief Tomahawk's bones."

"Ugh, nasty," Mark said.

"What happened to the other brother?" Ronnie asked. "You know, Poison Arrow."

"Far as I know, he went off to the penitentiary and died rottin' in a jail cell. Lucky for him them army boys did things by the book. The townies would've probably hung him."

"How'd you hear about all this stuff?" Ronnie asked.

Zeke shrugged. "The story's been passed down through time. My father told it to me. He had some Kikawa blood in him, said my ancestors were some of the few survivors of the massacre." Looking at Zeke, it made a lot of sense that he was part Kikawa. He had that deep tan, and stern chief-like facial features.

"Do you believe in the curse?" Ronnie asked, but before Zeke could answer, Bill's voice cut him off.

"Hey get back to work," Bill called out. He and Brian were walking up from the parking lot with Burger King cups in their hands.

"Back to work?" Mark asked. "Doing what? You told us to ignore the board."

"Go trim the edges of the bunkers," Bill said without hesitation.

"Aww fuck. *Nooo*," Mark whined. Ronnie hissed through clenched teeth. Trimming around the bunkers was probably the worst job on the course. It felt like your legs, arms, and face were being pelted with little shards of glass going as fast as bullets.

"Gotta get this course in good shape for the tournament this weekend. Get goin.'"

"Okay," they said.

"Well, thanks for the history lesson there, Zeke," Ronnie said as they got up from the table.

"Yeah, thanks," Mark agreed. "Now I know the curse is real. We gotta go trim around the bunkers."

Zeke laughed. "Anytime, boys. Next time I'll tell you about the Graves murders that happened back in '58."

"Sounds like a fun, lighthearted story. I can't wait," Mark said.

*　　　*　　　*

There were two big bunkers on either side of the eleventh green. Eleven was a short par-three hole, and they found a break in between groups of golfers that allowed them to get to it. Ronnie squinted his eyes shut as bits of sand shot up at his face. He had to wear safety glasses so his regular glasses wouldn't get all scratched under the barrage of sand. He trimmed around the bunker on the south side just as Mark trimmed the one on the north. After they finished, they flicked their trimmers off and met in the middle of the green, wincing and rubbing the tender spots on their faces and arms where the sand and rocks had hit them hard.

"Ugh, God *damn!* I fucking hate that!" Ronnie shouted.

"Yeah, I hear ya, brother! Damn you, Chief Tomahawk. Damn your curse!" Mark shouted, shaking his fist up toward the sky. Ronnie laughed.

"Hey, you think any of that stuff about the massacre and the curse and stuff was actually true?" he asked Mark. "Or you think he's full of shit?"

"Hell if I know," Mark said. "I'll bet some of it is true. Old Zeke's been around here since this place opened. He probably knows all kinds of crazy shit that went down here over the years."

"Yeah, but I wonder how much of it really happened that way. I don't know about the curse and ghost-witch stuff, but I mean, the whole massacre thing with that Hart guy chopping up all those Indians, and then those guys dumping the bodies in a big grave somewhere out here. That I believe."

"You want a massacre? I'll give ya a massacre. Check this out. It's the Indian Hill Trimmer Massacre!" With one pull of the starter cord, Mark started up his string trimmer again. He revved the engine and began to swing the power tool around wildly just like the final shot of *Texas Chainsaw Massacre* where Leatherface spins around swinging his chainsaw in wild fury. Ronnie cracked up and pulled his own starter cord. His trimmer also roared to life. They both swung their trimmers around like maniacs for a few minutes, spinning in random circles.

Finally, Mark became dizzy and stopped spinning. He looked toward the tee box. A group of golfers were standing there impatiently waiting to tee off with their hands on their hips.

"Oh shit! Dude, stop. *Stop!*" Mark called. Ronnie stopped and looked up at the golfers, the grin immediately melted off his face.

"Uh-oh, that's not good."

Mark waved to them and called out, "Sorry!" loudly through his cupped hand. Both he and Ronnie rushed off the green to their parked maintenance cart sitting in the fairway. "Come on, man. We better go say something to them to make sure they don't bitch to the pro shop about us."

"They probably will anyway."

"I hate to say it, but you're probably right." They hopped in, and sped off to go apologize to the golfers.

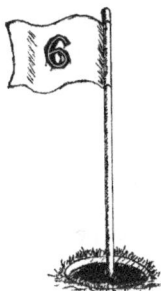

Wednesday, May 20th, 1981

The course had changed. No one noticed the change more than its superintendent Bill Carlson. Sure the big hackberry tree that had stood for maybe two or three hundred years was gone, and half a dozen other trees had fallen down in the windstorm on Monday night too. The loss of a tree always changed the look of the landscape slightly. But that wasn't it. Bill could *feel* a tension in the air, something with a waiting, predatory quality that he didn't like. There even seemed to be fewer golfers around and fewer birds in the trees since yesterday morning. It felt like something bad was about to happen, like another storm was rolling their way. He'd kept his eye on the forecast, praying that they wouldn't have another rainy day and fall even further behind in their work. The forecast showed only sun and a chance for some drizzly rain on Saturday, the day of the big tournament.

On Wednesday morning, Bill showed up at a quarter of six and immediately hopped into his golf cart to drive around checking on the whole course. His predecessor, Fred Davenport, had called it "Looking For Trouble." *Sometimes it's good to just take a ride and go looking for trouble, Billy,* Fred had told him a few months before he retired. That was sixteen years ago now. Bill had stuck by those words in his sixteen years as superintendent, and Fred's preventative approach had saved him a lot of headaches. Although today, because of that odd feeling of wrongness in the air, he didn't particularly want to go looking for trouble. He felt that if he went looking for trouble now he would find it.

He drove down the long fairway on hole number twelve, glancing around left and right. So far everything seemed okay. There were a few dead animals —probably ripped open by a coyote—for the boys to pick up, but nothing major. They had managed to make it through another night without a fresh round of vandalism. He looked off to his right down the long tee boxes on hole eight, a short par-three that sat on the edge of a wide round lake. All four sets of tee markers seemed to be there.

As he faced forward again, his eyes fell on the open door. *Uh-oh, found the trouble,* Fred's voice popped into his mind. The door to one of the old abandoned pumping stations was hanging open, revealing damp darkness inside. Bill pulled over into the rough and parked outside the pumping station.

There were three of these little abandoned pumping stations on the course: one here on the twelfth fairway on the lake's edge, one near the south side of the clubhouse hunkered deep in a shady cluster of sumac trees, and one on the north side of the course between the storage area and the driving range. Back in the 1940's when the course was first built, each of these three pumping stations drew water out of the lakes on the course and used it for the irrigation system. Eight years ago they rebuilt the irrigation system. They had installed the new deep well system and built the pump-house around it on the ridge between the upper lake on the seventh hole, and the lower lake on the tenth hole. These three old pumping stations had been abandoned.

They looked like crumbling little cinder block bunkers buried five feet into the ground with only the top few feet sticking up above the grass. There was an entryway the size of a large basement window well dug into the ground in front of the access door. The old light bulbs inside them were burned out. If you went inside, all you'd see would be a bunch of knee-deep water that had leaked in, cobwebs, and the old rusting pumping machinery.

Bill walked through the tall grass and stopped at the edge of the little entry well, peering into the dark. There was a thin metal latch on the outside of the access door and there should have been a rusty padlock there, but it was gone. He looked down in the entry well for the padlock, but didn't see it anywhere. He couldn't just leave the old pumping station open where curious golfers might go exploring and fall in, and he also had to make sure no one had been screwing around in there during the night.

Wincing against the flares of pain in his knees and lower back, he crouched and hopped down into the entry well.

"Ah," he hissed. "Gettin' too old for this shit." Propping his hands on the door frame, he leaned in. Everything looked okay, there wasn't any graffiti or broken beer bottles. Still he felt the strange sense that someone had been in here.

99

Years ago the water from the lakes had seeped through the crumbling walls and flooded all three of the abandoned pumping stations with stagnant water. Near the back wall of this one, Bill could see a bundle of sticks and branches that had somehow worked their way inside.

"Damn. These walls are in worse shape than I thought if this much crap can get in here," he said aloud. Looking at that pile in the back, he could almost imagine that it was a dead body lying down in the water, it was definitely the right shape and size for it. Bill shook his head at the thought and looked away. *Dead body, give me a break.*

The water came all the way up to the concrete lip at the bottom of the door frame. Even though the water was dark and murky, he saw something metal glinting under the surface not far from where he stood. *The padlock*, he realized.

Bill squatted down, bumping against the back wall of the narrow entrance well. As he set his knees down on the concrete edge, they began to ache almost immediately. Despite the pain, he clenched his teeth and leaned forward to grab the padlock. He stuck his bare hand down into the water and leaned forward reaching for it. He couldn't quite reach the bottom just yet without putting too much strain on his knees. The water felt strangely warm, not the ice cold temperature he'd expected.

"Come on," he urged through clenched teeth. "Come on, dammit."

Suddenly something moved near the back wall. He jerked back, yanking his hand out of the water and letting out a startled cry. The water in the back rippled and Bill looked up to see something slither under the surface near the pile of sticks.

"Fuckin' snakes in here." He held his dripping

arm protectively against his chest, and wondered how close he'd come to touching whatever the hell was down in that water.

He began to feel an overwhelming sense that he wasn't alone. Something was down here in this pump station with him, something other than a harmless snake. It reminded him of the time when he'd caught several drugged-out hippies in one of the bathroom buildings, except this was worse.

"Okay, you know what? Fuck it. I'll just get another padlock later," he rambled aloud, trying to will away the creepy, prickly feeling on the back of his neck. He stood up and turned around, planting his hands on the ground to hoist himself back up out of the entrance well.

Behind him, something shifted and slithered in the water again. Bill stopped cold and looked back over his shoulder. *Would a snake make so much noise?* In his experience, snakes were usually very quiet, not like on TV where they always seemed to be hissing and carrying on.

Then there was a metal *SHINK!* sound like a sharp knife being yanked out of a sheaf and drawn back, ready to stab.

Bill spun around expecting to see some mad hippie standing up in the pump station dripping wet and wielding a rusty cleaver. No one was there. He didn't even see a snake slithering around near his feet.

He heard it again, *SHINK,* but it was too quiet to be right next to him. Then there came a metallic *thud thud thud* sound, and Bill instantly recognized it for what it was. It was only Mark with the metal cup cutter, pounding out a fresh hole over on the tenth green only fifty yards away. He looked over and could even see Mark's head and shoulders as he swung the rubber mallet up and down. The cup cutters made those metal *SHINK* noises whenever anyone picked them up and let the blades fall to the bottom. The sound must have carried over here and echoed off the walls of the entrance well somehow. It was funny how sound played tricks on you when you were in an enclosed space like this.

Bill heaved himself back up out of the hole and when he was back on his feet, he kicked the pump station's door shut with his foot. If there was a snake in there, Bill figured it was best to just leave it alone.

Mark was just putting the white cup into the fresh hole when Bill pulled up in his cart along the edge of the tenth green. Mark saw him, hit STOP on his Walkman, and pulled his big Koss headphones down around his neck.

"Ayyy, Mistah Kott*air*," he joked in a Freddie Boom Boom Washington voice.

"You just scared the shit outta me," Bill said.

"Me? Why? What'd I do?" Mark asked.

"I heard that cup cutter of yours, and I thought it was a knife or something. For some reason, it sounded like it was literally right behind me. I thought there was a crazy guy just about to stab me or something."

Mark laughed and pulled the cup cutter up off the ground suddenly. It made that *SHINK* noise again. "Ohh shit. I get it. That *would* be scary. Sorry about that, man."

"Everything going good?" Bill asked.

"Yeah. Except one thing. How come me and Ronnie have to do all the trimming around here and JoeJeff doesn't have to do any of it?"

"Well, I noticed Joe and Jeff have been slacking on the bunker edging, so I thought I'd give you guys a break and leave the rest up to them."

Mark was pleasantly taken aback. "Oh, I didn't see that on the board."

"I can always put you back on edging bunkers if you'd prefer that."

"No no no," Mark said hastily changing his attitude about trimming. "Trimming is fine. We love trimming."

"That's what I thought," Bill said with a smirk.

As he and Mark talked a little more about the jobs he planned out for them that day and the upcoming tournament on Saturday, the door to the pump station opened up a crack. In the darkness, something watched them and listened.

*   *   *

Over on the front nine, Ronnie was also changing out the cups. He was on hole number two pounding away at the cup cutter with his own battered rubber mallet. Journey's *Departure* album was blaring through his Koss headphones, though he wasn't really listening to it. He had slept badly the previous night, tossing and turning for hours.

He looked up and jumped in surprise. There on the opposite edge of the green stood a ragged looking coyote staring straight at him.

"Whoa, what the hell?" He pulled his headphones down off his ears. He had seen coyotes a few times in the early mornings out here, but they always kept their distance. This one was only twenty feet away though, and stood its ground even when Ronnie stood up to his full height. Its fur was matted all over its body, its thin tail was patchy, and one of its ears had a chunk missing. Despite its ragged appearance, its black eyes seemed to stare at Ronnie intensely, as if it were wondering whether or not it should attack.

"Uh, hey, buddy," Ronnie said to it. "I kinda need to walk back there and grab the flag." He was moving this cup from the very back of the green to the front today. The coyote lifted its upper lip, baring its

103

crooked yellow fangs, and began a low growl.

Oh shit, I hope he's not rabid, Ronnie thought as his heart began to pound. *If he comes at me, I wonder how fast I can get to the cart.* He imagined having to fight off the coyote and clenched his fist around the rubber mallet, preparing himself.

On impulse, Ronnie suddenly did a fake lunge, stomping forward on one foot. That did the trick. The coyote finally flinched and scampered back into the woods through some unseen hole in the golf course perimeter fence. Ronnie listened to its footsteps galloping off into the underbrush and let out a sigh of relief.

He stood tall, feeling brave and confident for scaring the coyote away. "Yeah, that's right. Better run." He smacked the rubber mallet into his bare hand threateningly, then shook his head and laughed at how ridiculous he probably looked and sounded.

Ronnie kept his headphones off and finished changing out the cup on hole number two. He wondered if he should tell Bill over the radio that there was a mangy looking coyote that was prowling around the second green. Then he remembered how stressed out Bill had looked yesterday, and decided not to dump more shit onto his plate. *I'll tell him when I get a chance. The damn coyote probably won't come back anyway. At least not until after dark.*

After Ronnie finished up the cups on holes two, three, and five, he was on his way to the fourth green. He saw the tepee coming up on the left and remembered yesterday when he'd gotten the feeling that there was someone inside it.

Maybe I should run them off like I did with that growling coyote, he thought, still riding high on a wave of confidence. He drove up to the tepee and looked inside. It was a brighter morning than it had been yesterday under all those hazy clouds, and he had enough light to see inside. There was no one in there. Not even any remnants of a person, no leftover belongings or trash. There were only the two wooden benches and a circle of rocks that sat in the middle where a campfire could be lit. These things had always been inside the tepee.

Ronnie shrugged. *Hmm, maybe it was just my imagination yesterday.* He turned and backed out of the tepee, spun around, and almost stepped right on top of a dead cat. Its throat was ripped out, and a look of an agonized struggle was frozen into its dead, furry face. He'd been so focused on what was inside the tepee that he hadn't even noticed it when he first walked up.

"Aww, man," Ronnie said. He immediately felt sad and a little sick at the sight of it. "How many dead animals are we gonna have to pick up this week?" First there had been the dead eagle on Monday afternoon, then after trimming the bunkers yesterday he and Mark had picked up a dead goose over near the big pine trees on the side of the sixth tee boxes, now this. Usually finding dead animals happened only occasionally, but this week it was getting to be a regular thing. He sighed and drove on, hoping that this would be the last dead animal he would have to pick up for a while.

*   *   *

As it turned out, Ronnie came across yet another dead animal only a few short hours later. He and Mark had been sent to trim the long, shaggy grass around the lake on the thirteenth hole after lunch. Hole thirteen was a short little par-three on the western edge of the course. It had a kidney-shaped lake directly in front of the tee boxes, fed by three small waterfall pools that descended like round steps. The green sat just off to the left of those peaceful little pools and was partially shaded by a big old cottonwood tree. Ronnie and Mark had parked their cart out of the way and under the shade of the tree. They began trimming on the far side, going in opposite directions so that they would meet up in the middle somewhere near the tee boxes when they finished.

Ronnie had made it almost all the way to the far end. With his string trimmer in hand he stared down at a bloated dead fish that was floating five feet away from the rocks at the water's edge. Ronnie could see its white belly touching the surface of the water and the foamy froth around it. Some of the grass he had just trimmed had floated over and clung to it. This close he could even smell its reeking gassy, fishy odor. Ronnie squinted in disgust.

"Oh come on, really? Not another one." He held the back of his hand up to his nose and tried to take shallow breaths without having to smell that awful dead fish. He looked up and saw Mark on the opposite side of the lake, the side near the short fairway. Mark was facing the tee boxes and backing away from the lake, waving and nodding to a new group golfers, indicating that he saw them and it was okay for them to tee off. Without taking his eyes off them, he dashed back to their parked cart to get out of the way. Ronnie clicked off his own trimmer and began walking back as well. He wiped sweat off his forehead with the back of his forearm and took a deep breath, relieved to escape the smell of that dead fish.

Ronnie hopped over the narrow waterfall parts of the pools and joined Mark at their cart. They put their trimmers in the back and sat down, taking long drinks of water from their Indian Hill paper cups from the restaurant.

"It's hotter than fuck out here, man," Mark said with a sigh.

"Yeah tell me about it," Ronnie agreed. "And it's not even June yet. This ain't even the tip of the iceberg."

Mark groaned. "Awww, please don't say iceberg."

Ronnie laughed. The three old golfers finished teeing off, none of them even got close to the green so Ronnie and Mark had to wait. Farther back on the course, Mark saw Joe and Jeff riding across the twelfth fairway with a cart load of sandy old bunker edges.

"Hey, there goes Simon and Garfunkel," Mark said, keeping his voice low so he wouldn't disturb the golfers. They watched the golfers putt. One of them began pleading with the ball when it looked like it would fall short of the hole.

"Come on, get in there. Get it. Get it. Come on, get it."

"Come on, biggie. Git it. Act like ya want it," Mark said in a jivey funkadelic voice. He said it much louder than he had intended, and two of the golfers looked up at him. Both he and Ronnie quickly looked elsewhere. Through clenched teeth Mark whispered to Ronnie, "Was I really that loud?"

Ronnie covered his mouth with his hand, "Mmhmm."

"Shhhit," Mark whispered.

The golfers ignored them and finished putting. Both boys continued to look around casually in any direction but the green in front of them. Then suddenly Mark perked up in his seat.

"Hey, look who's coming."

Ronnie looked up and saw the silvery drink cart heading their way from the twelfth green. Behind the wheel was Tanya, Wendy's older sister. Tanya was twenty-three and drop-dead gorgeous, she easily caught all the men's attention out on the course. She had sleek, wavy, shoulder-length hair that was dark at the roots but bleached to a light brown in the sun. She had a tan, toned body and showed it off with her high-waisted athletic shorts and tiny T-shirt that showed off a smooth section of her midriff.

Both Ronnie and Mark ogled her as she drove up. Ronnie could hear "Anytime" by Journey blaring out of the headphones slung around Mark's neck and thought how appropriate it was. He knew Mark had it bad for Tanya.

The three golfers ordered a round of beers and Tanya walked over to the side-mounted cooler on the cart. She bent down into the cooler digging for beers near the bottom that were ice cold. As the boys watched, they had a perfect view of Tanya's butt peeking out from those tight athletic shorts. Mark let his mouth drop open and he pulled his Ray-Ban sunglasses down low, staring at her over the tops of the frames.

Mr. Hamilton knew all the golfers bought drinks from Tanya even if they weren't particularly thirsty, so he had her working in the drink cart most of the time during the summer months. She resembled her younger sister Wendy, but where Wendy was a meek and quiet girl-next-door type, Tanya was a confident and outgoing girl that looked like she belonged on a beach in San Diego. Just like every other guy out on the course, Ronnie thought she was definitely attractive, but if asked, he would've said he preferred her sister Wendy. Tanya was nice enough, but Wendy always seemed kinder and more genuine to him.

The golfers finished paying for their beers, gave her generous tips, and headed off toward the upper tee boxes for hole fourteen. Tanya spotted the boys sitting there and drove the drink cart over. Without missing a beat, Mark hopped out of his seat and ran back to the cart bed. He pulled out his trimmer and began lifting it up and down as if it were a barbell, breathing hard and making a big show out of it.

"Uh oh, here we go," Ronnie said sarcastically and began to chuckle.

Tanya pulled up next to their parked cart. She was about to ask them how it was going, but then she saw Mark "working out" near the back of the cart, and a strange look fell over her face.

"Uh...what are you doing?" she asked him.

"Oh hey, you caught me in the middle of my work out," Mark answered in a deep sleazy voice that no one could possibly take seriously. "I like to stay in shape while I'm waiting for these old fogeys to get off the green, dig what I'm sayin?" Tanya smiled and shook her head. Mark lifted up his sleeve and flexed his muscle for her. "Check that out."

"Oooh, look at you," she said humoring him, then giggled.

Ronnie shook his head and began cracking up. Suddenly Mark took a step back and a concerned look fell over his face. "Whoa, whoa, are you okay?" he asked Tanya.

Tanya gave him a confused look. "Uhh yeah. I could ask you the same thing."

"Oh I'm much better now that you're here," he said. Ronnie snorted out more laughter and Tanya rolled her eyes. "I'm only asking if you were okay because it must've hurt when you fell down from heaven."

Ronnie tipped his head back and howled with laughter. Tanya shook her head and grinned.

"Oh my God. Get outta here, you creep," she said giving Mark a playful shove on the shoulder.

Ronnie glanced over instinctively to see if there were any more golfers getting ready to tee off on hole thirteen's multi-leveled tee boxes. He didn't see any golfers, but he did see Joe and Jeff driving their way.

They rolled up alongside the thirteenth green and got as close to the drink cart as they could. Mark didn't take much notice of them, he was too focused on flirting with Tanya and trying to make her laugh.

"I was looking in the dictionary yesterday, looking for the right words to say to you, but--" Mark took his eyes off Tanya for just a second to see Joe and Jeff driving up near him, but it was too late. Ronnie also noticed the open cup in Jeff's hand right at the last second.

Jeff whipped his arm out and doused Mark with a cup of ice water just like Joe had done to Ronnie on Monday. The ice water completely soaked his blue and white baseball shirt and splashed up in his face. He stopped in mid-pick-up line and stood in shocked silence. Tanya let out a deep gasp and her hands flew up to cover her mouth. Then she and Ronnie both lost it.

"Aww come on!" Mark shouted at them as they drove away grinning and cackling.

"It's funny because I was just about to tell you to go take a cold shower," Tanya said between laughs.

"I'll give *you* a cold shower," he fired back and began flinging his wet arms, spraying her with droplets of water. She let out a scream, *"Noo!"* and ran back to the drink cart. Mark halfheartedly chased her, but she hit the gas and drove the drink cart away fast before he could reach her. Mark watched her go for a few seconds then walked back to the cart flinging his arms dry and shivering. "Whooo, holy shit that was fuckin' cold. That was more ice than water, let me tell ya."

"I'm sorry, man, but that was hilarious!" Ronnie laughed.

"I'm gonna get those motherfuckers back for that one. I don't know how, but I'm gonna get 'em back. You gotta help me think up a plan."

"Sure, sure," Ronnie agreed sarcastically.

Mark sighed and looked off toward the spot where Tanya had driven away. "That Tanya. Mmm mmm mmm," he said, biting his lower lip and shaking his head.

"Yeah she's pretty good lookin,' dude," Ronnie agreed.

"She's hotter than fuckin' fire, man. What I wouldn't give for one night with her."

"Well, if you like her so much, why don't you just ask her out and be serious instead of saying all that stupid junk about falling from heaven and working out and stuff."

Mark laughed. "You gotta make 'em laugh, man. You can't just dive right in. You gotta break the ice, know what I'm sayin'?"

"Maybe, *you* could. But I couldn't do that."

"Sure you could. It's not like it's hard work or anything. Girls love stuff like that."

Ronnie waved his hand. "Nah. Who'd want to go out with a skinny geek like me?"

"Aww, man, don't be like that. You are a very gorgeous man. I mean, you are a God!"

Ronnie shoved him. "Fuck you."

"Look, I'll tell you what, here's what we'll do. I'll ask Tanya out, and you can be my wing-man and take her sister out. We'll, like, double date, y'know?"

Ronnie grinned. The thought of himself on a date with someone as pretty as Wendy was a tantalizing dream, but he knew a dream was all it was. He wasn't dating material, he was Mark's sidekick, his wing-man.

"Seriously, let's go for it. I'll set the whole thing up."

"No, don't! Don't you dare," Ronnie fired back, suddenly feeling squeamish that Mark might actually go ahead and ask Wendy out for him. If she said no, he thought he'd die of embarrassment. Also he'd look even more pathetic for not just asking her out himself.

"Come on, what's the problem?" Mark asked.

Ronnie quickly tried to change the subject with the first thing that came to his mind. "Forget it, man. There's a dead fish over there in the corner that's starting to smell pretty bad. Let's go pull it out of there before those golfers get done on twelve and want to tee off." Mark glanced up and saw the golfers rounding the corner on the twelfth fairway heading towards the green.

"Okay," he relented, dropping the subject of double dates.

Ronnie drove them back over to the spot closest to the dead fish. He parked and yanked the spare shovel out of the cart bed, then they both walked over to the rocky edge of the lake. From here they could see the white bloating thing had now drifted out about seven feet from the water's edge. Mark took one whiff of the gassy stench coming off of it and had to turn his head away.

"Jesus! Gag me with a spoon. That's fuckin' awful."

"Yeah you can say that again," Ronnie agreed, taking only the shallowest breaths. "Keep an eye out for golfers for me, will ya?"

He stepped down onto the rocks, a few of them wobbling under his feet. He found sturdy places to stand, then held the shovel out as far as he could into the water. The metal spade splashed down about a foot away from the dead fish and he pulled it back towards him in a paddling motion. The dead white thing bobbed and slowly began drifting towards them. Ronnie tried to speed up his shovel paddling, but it only seemed to push the dead thing away. He forced himself to slow down.

Finally it came close enough that he was able to snag it with the tip of the shovel.

"Got it!" Ronnie said and pulled it through the water toward them. The closer it came, the worse the smell got. Ronnie glanced back at Mark and saw him wincing and covering his nose with his hand.

"Whatever you do, don't fall in with it," he said.

"Oh God, don't even say that," Ronnie replied.

He pulled it up to the water's edge. Up close it looked even more gooey and mangled than it had before. He tried scooping it up out of the water, but it only wanted to slide off the shovel. Squatting down low on the rocks, he tried to work the shovel up and under it. In one tricky maneuver he managed to get the dead thing just right and he lifted it up out of the water as quickly as he could. It threatened to fall back into the lake so he was forced to toss it backwards onto the grass. Mark had to jump back so no part of it, including the nasty water, would touch him. As it flopped down, a bunch of shredded entrails and gunk spilled out from inside it. The gassy stench seemed to explode around them. Both Ronnie and Mark gagged and turned their faces away from it. Ronnie dropped his shovel near the water's edge and felt his stomach lurch and heave.

"Oh my God!" Mark said between dry heaves. "That's the nastiest, most disgusting fuckin' thing I've ever seen in my entire fucking life."

"I feel like I'm gonna puke," Ronnie muttered. "I don't wanna puke, please don't puke." They both staggered and doubled over trying to ward off vomiting. After a few minutes they got themselves under control. The next batch of golfers were now heading off the twelfth green, making their way toward the tee boxes on hole thirteen.

"Come on, we gotta go take that thing down to the dumpster stat," Mark said. Ronnie nodded and reluctantly turned back to it. He picked up the shovel and scooped as much of it as he could off the grass. It threatened to fall apart under the metal spade. "Keep it on the shovel, don't let it touch the cart," Mark warned.

"If it falls into the cart, the whole shop will smell like that."

Mark hopped into the driver's seat and Ronnie held onto the shovel. As they drove back down to the shop, Ronnie faced forward, upwind from the stinking dead thing on the shovel. All thoughts of drink cart girls and double dates were further from his mind than they had ever been.

Once they reached the shop, they hastily tossed the dead thing into the dumpster and drove toward the wash bay to hose down down the shovel and the cart bed just to be safe. As Ronnie sprayed off the cart bed, he wondered just what the dead thing had been. It was white and shredded, looking almost like a fish belly, but it had no scales. Also, if it were a dead fish, as he had originally thought, then where was the head, or the tail? No, it probably wasn't a fish, and it was too big and too smooth to be a cat or a dead bird. If anything, it almost looked like a bloated, pruny human forearm that had been decaying and falling apart from spending too much time in the water. His stomach gurgled sickeningly again and he forced himself not too think about the dead thing they pulled out of thirteen lake.

*   *   *

Hours after Ronnie, Mark, and the rest of the maintenance crew clocked out and went home for the day, Wendy finished up her shift and was able to head home herself. She had the late shift on the drink cart and had driven around the course all evening in the fading daylight. Tips had been lousy and there hadn't been many golfers out there to begin with. She couldn't understand why the course was so deserted. By this time of the year, the back nine was usually crawling with golfers on a Wednesday night, and they all usually wanted to get hammered. Tonight though, she had counted only a handful of groups on both the front and back nines. Even the driving range seemed empty and lonely with only one or two guys quietly hitting a few small buckets of balls. She had quit driving the drink cart early, and parked it down at the maintenance yard where it was stored every night. Then she had walked back up to the restaurant to help the two others inside the clubhouse get their cleanup duties done.

Her sister Tanya had rolled up into the circular drop off lane at about 8:30 PM to take her home. Through the windows inside the round dining room, she saw her sister's sporty little Chevy Malibu sitting there idling.

"I gotta go, see you guys tomorrow," she called out to Mikey, the cook, as she rushed through the kitchen. Tanya hated to be kept waiting and would get extremely cranky if Wendy didn't get out to her car soon. Wendy slipped out the side-door, passed through the dark little alcove where they dumped their bags of trash into a big rolling bin, and cut across the little patch of grass outside the restaurant windows.

She could see Tanya sitting in the driver's seat with her hair pulled up in a ponytail and her smoked Aviator sunglasses on despite the fact that it was dusk and already way too dark for them. She probably wasn't wearing any makeup, Tanya hated to leave the house if she didn't have any makeup on, but she'd do it if she didn't have to get out of her car. Even with her doors and windows closed, Wendy could hear "Queen of Hearts" by Juice Newton on the radio inside the car. Tanya liked country music, but Wendy preferred to listen to the Top 40 hits.

Wendy opened up the passenger door and almost sat down when it hit her.

"Oh shit," she hissed. "I forgot to clock out.

Hang on, I'll be right back."

Tanya tipped her head back in elder-sibling annoyance. "Ugh. Don't I spend enough time at this place? It's bad enough we have to stay late on Friday and deep clean the stupid clubhouse."

"Will you just hold your horses? Let me run back in and punch out, otherwise Mr. Hamilton will have a fit. It'll take me five minutes."

"Hurry up then." Wendy slammed the car door shut on her sister in mid-sentence.

"Jesus," Wendy muttered to herself as she jogged back up to the building. "You'd think after twenty-one years, you'd stop being such a bitchy older sister and just treat me like a normal human being."

She ran back into the dark little trash-alcove and tried to pull the door open, but it thudded against the jam. Locked out.

"Shit," she whispered. Mikey must have locked the door while they were doing the clean-up duties. She pounded on the door with her fist, hoping he would hear it, but she knew how Mikey liked to turn up his radio at the end of the night and blast his eardrums while they cleaned up the kitchen.

The only other doors that might still be open were the glass double-doors around the back. Those were always the last ones to be locked so that employees could still get in and out, while other people who tried to come into the clubhouse through the front doors couldn't come in and try to hang around while they were closing up for the night.

Wendy ran around to the back of the building knowing that her sister was probably sitting in the driver's seat fuming. Looking west, she could see the last shreds of daylight on the horizon up above the seventh and ninth fairways. All the golfers were now gone, even the cart crew kids had pulled the last of the

116

carts down into the maintenance yard. The place was as deserted as a ghost town.

Every time Wendy worked the late closing shift, she always felt a pressing urge to get away as quickly as she could and not be the last person here. The clubhouse was fine during the day, but at night it was just plain creepy. It felt as if the course belonged to the dead after the sun went down, as if the living were trespassing on hallowed ground. She turned away from the dusky sunset, it only made her urgent need to get out of here worse.

That creepy feeling, plus the knowledge that Tanya would be bitchy and silent the whole tense ride home urged her to move faster. Their parents made Tanya drive Wendy to work and pick her up, and she hated doing it. All the guys on the maintenance crew and in pro shop thought her big sister was so pretty and so nice, especially that Mark guy. If only he knew the real Tanya, the cold, selfish girl she was at home, he'd think twice about declaring his love for her all the time. Wendy sometimes wondered if Mark or any of those other maintenance guys ever talked about her the way they talked about Tanya. She doubted it, but secretly kind of hoped they did. Mark was kind of short and stocky, but he was cute and funny, and he seemed like a really nice guy. He had even gotten his skinny friend, Ronnie, a job here.

As she approached the back doors, she glanced back out over the tenth tee boxes and across the lake. On the other side of the bridge that took golfers out to the tenth fairway, she thought she saw a man standing among the cattails, down in the secretive little cove of ten lake. He stood stiffly still with a cracked beige-yellowish face, his mouth turned down in a frown, and two colorful stripes painted diagonally across his cheeks.

The sight was so jarring and out of place that

117

Wendy stopped cold in her tracks and did a double take, forcing herself to look at him more closely. No, it wasn't a man, she could see that clearly now. Someone had moved that old wooden cigar-store chief statue down to that part of the lake. They had probably strapped him into their cart like a golf bag, drove him over near that pump house building, and walked him down the hill to stand in the cattails near the water's edge.

She shook her head and turned back to the doors. She would have to tell the guys in the kitchen or the old guy in the pro shop about what she had seen. They would have to go down to the lake, probably in the dark, and bring that creepy wooden statue back to the spot in front of the shop where it belonged. They might even have to hose it off too if it had gotten all muddy.

"Stupid drunk golfers. Got no respect for people's pr--"

Wait a minute. That Indian's still standing over near the pro shop doors. I just walked past it on my way over here only a minute ago. Also it had its face cut off by those vandal teens a few nights ago. So how the hell did I just see that?

Wendy spun around and looked back across the lake. The wooden chief statue wasn't there anymore. She scanned the water's edge and the entire steep hillside leading down into the water, but it was nowhere to be seen.

She narrowed her eyes suspiciously. *What the hell did I just see down there?* she asked herself. *Are my eyes playing tricks on me?* Surely she hadn't imagined that. It had been too real, and it had nothing to do with her original train of thought. Maybe if she had been thinking about that statue, she could've imagined she saw it down there, but she had been thinking about those young guys on the maintenance crew.

Now that she thought about it, the statue's stance

had been all wrong too. The wooden statue down at the pro shop doors stood with its arms crossed in a stern gesture. She could've sworn she had seen this one standing there with its arms at its sides.

Maybe he moved all by himself.

A chill wormed down her back with that thought, and she really didn't want to be out here anymore. She had an overwhelming urge to turn and run. To hell with Mr. Hamilton and his time clock. What if there really was a wooden chief statue running around out here at night after the sun went down?

"You forget something?" a voice called out to her. Wendy jumped and spun around. Mikey had just walked out the back door with his apron off and a cigarette jutting out of his mouth. Relief flooded into her and she felt her heart pounding in her chest.

"God, you scared me. I, uh, forgot to punch out for the night."

"Uh-oh. Can't forget to do that. Hamilton'll shit a brick."

"Yeah, I know how he gets." He held the door open for her and she rushed back into the kitchen. The time clock was mounted on the wall just inside the employees only door. She found her time card and punched it in the slot. Then she hurried out through the back doors again where Mikey was smoking, milking another few minutes out of his own time card.

As she came around the side of the clubhouse toward the pro shop again, she felt sure that the wooden chief statue would be gone. It would be out running around on the course somewhere. But no, it stood in its usual spot near the pro shop doors.

She ran back to Tanya's still idling Malibu and hopped in.

"Took you long enough," Tanya complained.

"Sorry. They locked the doors so I had to run

around the back."

"Maybe if you'd just remembered to clock out in the first place, we'd be halfway home by now," Tanya said icily.

"I said I was sorry, okay? What more do you want from me?" Tanya said nothing in response, only glared out the windshield and tore across the empty parking lot. Wendy locked the door and looked out her passenger side window at the course, scanning the fairways of the back nine for any wooden statues roaming around on their own. The only things she saw were the still and silent trees bathed in twilight shadows.

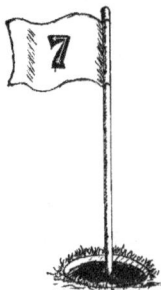

Thursday, May 21ˢᵗ, 1981

The fates had decreed that it was the golf ball's turn to die, and the maintenance shop was full of instruments of death. First they clamped down the ball in a vice, squeezing and flattening its round shape into a thick pancake. Its plastic white sides split under the pressure, revealing the yellow rubbery material inside. They pulled it out of the vice and examined the crumbling chunks of the inner rubber, it smelled almost like fresh bouncy balls right out of a supermarket vending machine.

Next they clamped it back in the vice and took a power drill to it, drilling three holes all the way through and pulling out more chunks of crumbling rubber. Then they freed the golf ball from the vice, and took it over to the electric grinder mounted to the corner of the cluttered tool bench behind them. They held it against the rough, gritty spinning wheel, sanding off one of the untouched dimpled white sides and continuing down into the rubber. The grinder left a deep trench that was perfectly smooth and hot to the touch. They ground it down so deep it began to look like some sort of white mutilated Pac-Man.

Finally one of them grabbed a handheld propane blowtorch off the shelf above the tool bench. With one experimental pull of the trigger, an intense blue flame blazed out of the nozzle with a deep furious hiss. They lowered the flame to the open Pac-Man mouth, and the plastic outer shell began to melt and turn black. A stinking burning plastic smell began to fill the air as the crumbling rubber inside also began to char and melt.

"What the fuck are you guys doing?" Mark asked. He and Ronnie walked into the shop to find Joe and Jeff giggling like trolls as they torched the golf ball. It was a little after one in the afternoon and Bill still hadn't come back from lunch to give them any orders. The rest of their jobs listed on the chalkboard for that day were done.

"We're making an art project," Joe said with a grin and Jeff lit the blowtorch again. He coughed and waved some of the burning plastic smoke away from his face.

"Yeah I can see that. It looks beautiful," Mark said sarcastically.

Jeff clicked off the blowtorch and suddenly looked over Mark's shoulder. "Bill's not back, is he?"

"No. Do you know where he went?"

"Out," Jeff said and went back to torching the golf ball.

"Him and Brian went to a meeting with Mr. Hamilton and some PGA douche bag," Joe explained.

"He wasn't too happy about it either," Jeff chimed in. "Said he had too much to do to be wasting his time with that shit."

122

Ronnie looked over his shoulder, saw no one, and suddenly got an idea.

"Oh shit, Bill's coming, you guys. Bill's coming," he said hurriedly.

Jeff quickly perked up and clicked off the blowtorch. He rushed over to the shelf where he found it and hastily set it back. Joe swept the mutilated golf ball off the tool bench and kicked it across the room, it rolled under one of the parked greens mowers.

"Just kiddin' he's not really back. Made ya look, fuckers," Ronnie said with a shit-eating grin on his face.

"Fuckin'-A! Good one, man! You even had *me* going," Mark said and cracked up laughing. He raised his hand and Ronnie slapped him an ear-splittingly loud high five.

"Goddammit, you made us lose our art project!" Jeff shouted, he was genuinely annoyed. "Get the fuck outta here!"

"Yeah. Get lost, kids," Joe said.

"Pch! Fine!" Mark spat back defensively. "We're goin.' Don't get your panties all in a wad."

Mark and Ronnie walked out of the shop and hopped into one of the newer work carts. It was still loaded with the trimmers they had been using before lunch to chop down the long grass growing up against the driving range fence.

"Umm, where are we going?" Ronnie asked as they drove off.

Mark shrugged. "That's a wonderful question, I'm glad you asked." Mark didn't elaborate any further. Ronnie chuckled and shook his head as they made their way out onto the deserted front nine. "Well, here are our options. We could just go around trimming around trees, which I'm sure is what Bill would be having us do if he were here."

"Ugh," Ronnie said in an exhausted voice. "I'm

so sick of trimming."

"Yeah, my thoughts exactly. Trimming bites the big one. *Or*...our other option is to go on an *Adventure!*" He said the word *Adventure* the same way an excited little kid would say they were going to Disneyland.

"What the hell is an adventure?" Ronnie asked laughing.

"It's an Adventure! Yay!" Mark repeated in that same little kid voice. He turned the cart toward the number two green and began heading up the sloped fairway. He drove into the tall wild grass on the west side of the rough. The trees began to grow thicker as the neared the perimeter fence on the north-western corner of the golf course behind the number two green. Mark brought the cart to a bumpy stop between the fence and a cluster of thick ferns and pine bushes where the cart wouldn't be visible to the golfers.

Mark stood up and looked around, double checking to make sure that Bill or Mr. Hamilton weren't around, then walked over to the green chain-link perimeter fence that was covered in vines and bindweed. One corner near a metal post was bent and pulled back, forming a secret opening out into the woods. Mark crouched down, pulled the corner of the fence up, and carefully slid through.

"Wait. We're going out there?" Ronnie asked.

"Yeah. I already told ya, it's an *adventure*," Mark said. "We're gonna go exploring, see some shit we ain't never seen before."

"Yeah but what if Bill comes back?" Ronnie asked.

"He won't. And even if he does, he won't see the cart back behind those bushes."

Ronnie remembered how Bill had yelled at them over the radio a few days ago. He did not relish the idea of Bill finding out they were doing nothing out in the woods west of the course while they were still on the clock.

"I don't know about this, man."

"Come on," Mark insisted. "It's not like we're gonna be gone for hours. We'll just go on a quick little adventure and come right back."

Ronnie finally gave in. "Okay, but I'm blaming you if we get in trouble."

"M'man!" Mark said in a low intense voice. He grabbed Ronnie's shoulder and gave him a friendly shake.

On the other side of the fence, the bushes and ferns were thick and wild, sprouting up out of the dry litter of pine needles and twigs that covered the ground. The trees all over the course were perfectly straight and kept neatly pruned by Butch and Pete, but out here they grew in wild clusters and strange angles. Thick canopies of fresh spring leaves overhead blotted out a lot of the sunlight. Ronnie saw the sun peeking through tiny gaps in the leaves as they walked. Even the grassy smell of the course was gone now, replaced by an earthy pine scent from the bushes.

Mark continued talking as he led them downhill toward the sound of a running stream. He kept reassuring Ronnie that they wouldn't get in trouble even though he didn't need reassurance.

"The course is slow, we've already trimmed pretty much every single thing there is to trim, except for maybe a few trees here and there. We've been busting our asses all week, we deserve a break."

Like little kids exploring, Mark led them on a winding path through little gaps between the trees and bushes. He looked back and caught Ronnie gazing up at the trees. For a second, Mark saw him as he looked when they were kids and he almost felt like they had traveled back in time ten years.

"I can't believe we're getting paid for this," Ronnie laughed, bringing Mark back to the present.

"Much better than trimming, right?"

"Hell yeah, it is. Speaking of which, how come JoeJeff gets out of this trimming crap? I mean, what the hell are they even doing besides wrecking golf balls in the shop?"

Mark laughed. "Y'know, that's exactly what I asked Bill the other day. He said he's leaving the rest of the bunkers for them to re-edge because he knows we did most of the work on the other ones. He's kinda evening up the score, if you know what I mean."

Ronnie shrugged. Trimming was no bed of roses, but it was a lot easier than cutting and heaving big sandy chunks of sod into a cart all afternoon. "Huh. Well, I guess I'm okay with that then."

"Yeah, Bill's a good guy."

"He's the best boss I've ever had. By far."

"Probably the best boss you ever *will* have too. I'm gonna miss working for him after we graduate and have to go get real jobs." Ronnie nodded in agreement. They fell silent and continued walking. After mentioning Bill, they both felt a twinge of guilt for being out here instead of working. Ronnie also felt a little sad at the thought of graduating college and having to leave this easy-going summer job behind. Thoughts of what life would be like *after* college rarely occurred to him.

They both stopped. The ground ahead opened up in front of them and they looked down into a deep ravine with a little creek babbling along at the bottom. They looked out over the edge of the ravine briefly. Mark casually picked up a small clump of dirt and tossed it into the water. Ronnie did the same and they continued their conversation.

"You still gotta help me think up a plan to get those guys back," Mark said. "I'll show them for pouring water on me."

"I thought you said it was so hot that it felt good."

"Yeah, but they made me look like a fuckin' idiot in front of my hottie, Tanya. And I can not let that stand."

Ronnie only laughed and tossed another dirt clod into the stream. *Plunk.*

"Okay, so here's what I was thinkin' we could--" Mark trailed off and turned his head back toward the golf course, Ronnie looked back too. Both of them heard a couple of faint, crunching footsteps in the underbrush farther back up the hill, but they couldn't see anyone through the thick trees and bushes. Then the crunching noises stopped. After a few seconds of waiting, they looked back at each other and Mark shrugged.

"So anyway, here's what I was thinking," Mark said. "You know how everyone leaves their keys in whatever cart they're using? Well, I thought maybe we could wait until Joe and Jeff are in the restaurant or at the shop or something, then we'll take their keys. Then we could get into their cars. and--"

"Take their car keys?" Ronnie asked doubtfully. "I don't wanna mess with their cars. That's taking it too far, man."

"Hold on, hear me out. We take their car keys and then we could maybe put some stink bombs in their cars, or maybe some nasty dead fish or something. I got the idea from that dead fish we pulled out of the lake yesterday."

"Where are we gonna get dead fish?" Ronnie asked, scrunching up his face in disgust. "That seems a little extreme, don'tcha think?"

"Okay, well what else could we do? *You* come up with an idea, smart guy."

"Shit, I don't know, man. Why don't you just

get a cup of water and splash 'em back?"

"Because they'll be expecting that. We can't just do the same--" Mark trailed off as they both heard the crunching footsteps creeping through the underbrush again. The footsteps fell silent as soon as they stopped talking. "Do you hear that, or is it just me?"

Ronnie nodded. "I hear it too." His mind immediately thought of that growling coyote he had scared off yesterday. He had run off this way, probably even went through that same hole in the fence. Ronnie felt better that he wasn't alone, but he still didn't want to have to fend off an aggressive coyote attack. Or what if it was that weird homeless guy they had run into on Monday morning, the air-guitar guy they thought had been lying dead up on hole seventeen? What if he had come back to the course feeling more alert and aggressive?

"Keep talking. Whoever it is will think we don't suspect them," Mark whispered. He cranked his hand, motioning for Ronnie to speak. Ronnie only shrugged.

"I don't know what to say," he whispered.

Mark rolled his eyes and began talking in a loud voice. "Okay, so if we take the keys out of their cart, then we could, I don't know, maybe put some firecrackers in their cars or something. Or maybe we could catch a snake and put it in there." Sure enough the footsteps started creeping towards them again, slowly and stealthily. They didn't sound like soft foot pads from a coyote, it sounded like a man's heavy feet. Ronnie clenched his fists, preparing himself for an attack.

"Yeah, or maybe just wait until they're coming out of the bathroom, then hit 'em with the water," Ronnie added when Mark urged him on again.

"Yeah, that would work," Mark said. "That's a good idea, man. Give those guys a taste of their own medicine."

128

Mark began creeping around the edge of the nearest tall bush. Ronnie could tell that the footsteps were now just on the other side of that bush. Mark's decoy-talking trailed off and he turned back to Ronnie. He counted up with his fingers and mouthed the words: *One, two, three.*

They jumped around the corner of the bush. "HA!" Mark screamed. Joe and Jeff looked up with mild surprise, they had been crouched down, laughing silently behind the bush and listening to them. Jeff had an open cup of water in his hand and he clumsily let it fly. Mark had seen the cup at the last second though and ducked out of the way of the water. It only caught the edge of his sleeve instead of drenching him like it had yesterday. The water sailed past Ronnie's chest and splattered on the ground.

"You motherfuckers!" Mark shouted. Joe and Jeff burst out laughing and hooting. They took off toward the golf course fence. Mark stumbled in the slippery pine needles and debris under his feet as he tried to chase them.

"Thanks for the ideas!" Jeff shouted over his shoulder.

"Run! Get to the cart!" Ronnie screamed. They awkwardly tore off after them.

"Goddammit! They heard our whole plan!" Mark yelled.

Joe and Jeff had a head start. They sprinted through the bushes, unmindful of outstretched limbs scratching their arms and legs. Mark and Ronnie chased after them as fast as they could, but the older guys were too fast.

Joe and Jeff slammed up against the chain-link fence and hurried through the hole at the bottom. Mark ran into the fence right as they let the loose chain-link spring back down over the hole. He fell to his knees and crawled through. Before Mark could get to his feet again, he looked up and saw Joe reach into their parked cart and snag his keys out of the ignition.

"Hey! Gimme back my keys, asshole!" Mark shouted. Both Joe and Jeff laughed madly and hopped into the older beat-up cart they had parked near Ronnie and Mark's. Jeff stomped down on the gas pedal, spraying up dirt and grass as they took off at full speed around the backside of the number two green.

Mark whirled around to Ronnie who was just coming through the hole in the fence.

"Please tell me you have your keys on you," Mark pleaded. The chain-link scraped against the back of Ronnie's white T-shirt as he let go. He dug in his pockets for his keys. "Come on, come on. They're gettin' away!"

"Here!" Ronnie turned his jean's pocket inside out and yanked his keys out. He nearly threw them at Mark. They jumped in and Mark rammed Ronnie's universal golf cart key into the ignition. He stomped down on the gas pedal before Ronnie even sat down, and he fell back against the backrest. They felt the trimmers in the back bed bouncing around as they swerved around boulders and trees following Joe and Jeff's wild path. Ronnie reached back and held them down so they wouldn't go flying out when they hit hard bumps.

Mark followed Joe and Jeff rolling through the same tire tracks they had left through the long grass. Luckily for him, he had a newer, faster golf cart, and was gaining on them. Up ahead, Joe and Jeff glanced back at them frantically as they closed the distance. Joe reached back into the bed of their cart where there were a few clumps of dirt and sandy sod left over from re-edging the bunkers. He threw the dirt clods back at Ronnie and Mark's cart. They bounced off the plastic hood, exploding into dust and spraying them in the face. Both

Ronnie and Mark ducked their heads and squinted their eyes, but they didn't alter course.

Mark laughed and yelled up at them. *"Oh you guys are dead. You're fuckin' dead! You hear me?"* As mad as he was, he could still see the humor in all of this. Ronnie also had a big grin on his face. In his head, he could practically hear raucous banjo music as a soundtrack to this ridiculous golf cart chase.

Both carts tore around the number two green, going up over the berms that rose around it, then through the narrow little stretch of grass between the tee-boxes to hole three and the perimeter fence. All four of them ducked under the low hanging branches from a tree standing in the decorative gravel island that separated two groups of tee boxes. There was a tight, steep little grass alley between the fence and a retaining wall that held up the tee boxes, and driving through here was tricky even at a slow speed. Joe and Jeff's cart dipped down low as they went full speed through the gap. Mark and Ronnie watched in amazement as Joe and Jeff's cart lifted up precariously on two wheels, threatening to tip over against the fence.

"Whoa! Jesus! Are they fuckin' nuts or what?" Mark shouted.

"They're out of their fucking minds," Ronnie agreed.

Joe and Jeff took a hard right turn onto the cart path that curved between the back of the fifth green and the tee boxes on three. Not far up ahead, the cart path went down a steep hill heading towards the number three green. Mark and Ronnie were almost close enough to pull up beside Joe and Jeff.

Suddenly there was a loud grinding noise as Jeff reached down to the gearshift behind his legs. He had switched the cart from forward into neutral. His slow golf cart—already at top speed—began to go down the hill even faster.

"Oh, so it's gonna be like that, huh?" Mark said. He reached down and pulled his own gearshift into neutral, their cart let out a harsh grind.

"What are you doing?" Ronnie yelled over the rush of the wind.

"You gotta put it in neutral, you go a lot faster that way," Mark answered. Once in neutral, the governor that kept the golf cart at a slow reasonable speed let loose. Since they were on a hill, their forward momentum and gravity carried them down much faster than usual.

They glided smoothly down the steep cart path, picking up so much speed that the wind began to roar against their ears. Both carts sped up to an insane forty-five miles per hour. Their tires whirring against the concrete were the only noises their carts made.

Mark tailgated them, pulling up dangerously close to their cart bed. In one hand he held the steering wheel tight, with the other he reached for his water cup in the cup-holder. He pried the lid off the top. The water inside sloshed around, he tried his best not to spill it on himself. He held the cup out, ready to pull up alongside Joe and Jeff and toss the water at them as soon as he got the chance.

They reached the bottom of the hill and began to lose speed as they approached the sets of tee boxes for holes four and six. Mark yanked the wheel to the right and pulled up alongside Joe and Jeff's cart. Joe looked back over his shoulder and saw both the water cup and the determined grin on Mark's face.

"Dude, brakes! *Brakes!*" Joe shouted.

Joe slammed on the brakes, their tires screeching and laying black skid marks along the concrete. Mark flung the water backwards as they careened past them. Joe and Jeff's braking maneuver saved their T-shirts from the worst of the water. It splashed against the cart's front hood, then up into their faces and hair as their momentum still carried them forward.

"Shit!" Joe and Jeff cried out as the water hit them in the face like a cold wet slap.

"Yes!!!" Mark screamed. *"We got 'em dude! We fuckin' got 'em!"*

"That was awesome!" Ronnie shouted laughing hysterically.

"Eat that you dumb motherfuckers!" Mark screamed back at them. He reached down and pulled his gearshift back into forward drive with another rough grinding sound. He hit the gas and fled for the back nine, tapping the horn with his foot. He and Ronnie both held out their middle fingers at Joe and Jeff, laughing and catcalling them.

Joe and Jeff smiled and wiped the water off their faces, but on the inside, their competitive, retaliatory nature was urging them for revenge.

"Okay," Jeff said pleasantly. "Okay, you guys wanna play this game, huh? This means war."

Joe turned to Jeff and gave him an evil smile. "What are we gonna do to them?"

"Tomorrow night, it's payback time." Jeff slammed his fist into his palm.

Jimmy Bloom of the cart crew was washing off the last few golf carts for the night. The other kid who usually helped him, Vic, had gone home early because he said he was coming down with a migraine, leaving Jimmy to wash the rest of the carts by himself. He had been partially relieved when Vic left because he didn't have to put on a smile and crack jokes and act like everything was fine. Nothing had been fine since Monday night. Though he couldn't show it to anyone, he had been living in a constant state of panic. Being here at the golf course made it worse. It felt like the course had come alive, like it was now a living, breathing thing with eyes that constantly watched him from the shadows. It felt like it had unfinished business with Jimmy and his friends. Or maybe that was only his guilty conscience.

That night, Travis had sped off down the road in the nick of time. Another thirty seconds and they would've been seen by the line of firetrucks and police cars that rushed over to Indian Hill after the big old hackberry tree was struck by lightning. Jimmy and Heff had both demanded that Travis slow the fuck down and take them straight home. He had complied, only arguing a little to keep up his tough guy appearance. Jimmy had walked back in through his front door as the hail gave way to pouring rain, trying desperately not to wake up his parents. He went straight to bed and laid awake for hours, his mind racing with a million questions.

What happened to Mack? If Mack is okay will he rat out the rest of us for leaving him? What will happen to me if they find out that I was one of the guys that broke the fence and vandalized the maintenance yard? And how bad will my father kick my ass when the dust settles?

The only way he had gotten to sleep at all was by repeatedly telling himself that they wouldn't find anything. Mack must have gotten away and he wouldn't say anything. And even if he did squeal on them, where was his proof? Travis would never admit to anything, and as long as they all denied it, it was their word against his.

Jimmy felt a little better Tuesday morning when he woke up around 10:15, but the panic rushed back in a few hours later when his mother called him downstairs to talk to the two policemen sitting in his living room. He saw them looking around the wood-paneled room with stern expressions on their faces. His mother looked furious and terrified at the same time. The question: *What did you do?* was plastered all over her face.

They grilled him with questions. *Where were you last night? When did you come home? What did you do last night? Why was the cart barn door open?* Jimmy gave them the shortest, easiest answers in his most casual voice as if he had no idea anything had even happened at Indian Hill last night. Their questions seemed to be drying up and only leading to dead ends. He felt like he was in the clear until one of them hit him with a bombshell: *Can you show us your golf cart key?* That almost knocked him flat on the floor. He had completely forgotten about the key he had handed to Mack. He stalled and then went up to his room to "look for it." To keep up appearances, he pretended to search through his piles of clothes and all around his messy room, knowing damn well that it wasn't really there at all. He had no idea if they had found the golf cart, or if Mack had driven it off somewhere, or what.

Just tell them you can't find it in your messy room. One look in this fuckin' pig sty and they'll have to believe that, right?

The skeptical looks on both of their faces told him otherwise. They didn't buy the *I lost my key* story for a second. They had him pinned down and he knew it, and they knew he knew it.

"Is there anything you'd like to tell us right now, son?" they asked. Worst of all, his mother repeated their question. She was turning on him and siding with them. Jimmy decided to hold out in the hopes that they didn't have enough evidence to pin anything on him. Luckily for his sake, they let it go and said they would be back with more questions later.

Jimmy had never felt more relieved as he watched the two officers drive away from his house. His mother tried to continue grilling him, but that was no big deal, he had years of experience handling her.

Later, he briefly talked to Travis on the phone while his mom was safely out of earshot using the bathroom. The police hadn't even been to Travis's house, but someone else had. Mack's mother had come looking for him at Travis's house this afternoon, she had been crying. Mack had never come home, and no one had seen him since he met up with Travis on Monday evening. Travis didn't spill the story to her though, not yet. He had told Heff and Jimmy to keep their mouths shut and not mention that they were at the golf course or that they had even seen Mack. Jimmy felt sick. This was getting too heavy. If there really was a missing person involved—not just a missing person, but a missing *friend*—he could bet that the cops would come back, and this time they would be a lot tougher on him. This had moved out of the realm of petty high-school vandalism and into scary territory. He had to hang up on Travis as soon as he heard the toilet flush in the other room.

That night at the golf course, Mr. Hamilton had stayed late to give him his own not-so-subtle line of questioning. Again Jimmy played dumb, acting as if it were purely a coincidence that he had lost his golf cart key. No one believed him, but what could they do? They had zero proof. Hamilton finished his lecture by giving him a new cart key, and telling him that he'd be keeping an eye on him.

Over the next few days he laid low, only leaving his house every evening to go bring in the golf carts at Indian Hill. He felt like there was always someone watching him, not Mr. Hamilton though, someone worse. He talked to Travis a few times and there was no change in the situation. Mack was still missing, and that made his sense of dread grow even deeper.

Jimmy was thinking about Mack, his mind only half focused on washing the golf carts with the high-pressure washer. He saw the goose shit, chunks of mud, and grass falling off the tire treads and plastic sides of the EZ-Go carts, but his mind was back on Monday night, replaying that lightning strike over and over again.

What the hell happened to Mack? he asked himself. They had all seen the lightning on top of that hill, if it could take out that tree, it easily could have killed him. But then where was his body? Even if he had tumbled down the hill after being struck and killed, someone would have found his body by now. Indian Hill was out in the country, but not that far out. Had Mack run away? Was he laying low somewhere, waiting for this whole thing to blow over? Jimmy doubted it, he felt in his heart that Mack was dead.

What if they find his body somewhere? Are they gonna blame it on me, and Travis, and Heff? What if he has my golf cart key with him? What if he's holding it in his cold, dead hand? He began to wonder if he should go up on that hill and look for Mack's body, or any sign of him. Maybe his golf cart key would be up there. That would be a relief. He could pretend he found it somewhere, show it to the cops and Mr. Hamilton, and his whole story would be a lot more plausible.

His mind lit up with brighter possibilities and he began to feel a little more hopeful as he backed the freshly washed cart into the dark cart barn. The only light in here came through a ventilation grate in the wall high up in one corner. A slowly spinning fan made the dim orange sunset light pulse in and out. Using that orange light to see, he carefully maneuvered the cart bumper to bumper against the next one in line. Out of the corner of his eye, he saw a movement toward the dark back corner of the barn. He turned.

Mack was sitting slumped over in one of the carts towards the back. Jimmy jumped off the cart seat and took an involuntary step back. He blinked his eyes, unable to believe what he was seeing. He squinted into the darkness, looking at the figure more carefully.

Taking a longer look, he could see that it wasn't Mack at all, someone had just left a big bag of trash and tree limbs sitting in that cart. Even in this dim light he could see how those branches had at first looked like arms. The shredded paper bag or whatever it was on top

138

of the pile had looked like a slumped head with wild locks of hair. He guessed that one of those big rough mowers probably ran it over.

"Jesus!" he sighed. He put a hand over his pounding heart and laughed a little at himself. "Scared the shit outta me."

As he walked back out to the spillway to wash the last two carts he mumbled to his absent coworker that had already gone home for the night. "Hey Vic, you're supposed to take the trash *out* of the carts, not just leave it there, ya moron. What are ya tryin' to do, give me a fuckin' heart attack?" He picked up the high-pressure spray gun and started washing the last two carts.

It was no wonder he thought he saw Mack back in the dark cart barn. He couldn't stop thinking about him and wondering where he was. His thoughts returned to his plan of looking for any signs of Mack's body. He considered pitching his plan to Travis and Heff. Maybe they would want to come with him. *No, Travis will never go for that. He'll just sit there and deny and deny and deny his involvement until he and only he comes up with a better plan. But maybe if I can somehow convince him--*

A flake of paint tore away from the side of the golf cart's wheel-well and began to flap under the high-pressured spray.

"Oh shit," Jimmy hissed. He let go of the spray gun's trigger. His mind had been so focused on his own thoughts that he had stopped paying attention to what he was doing. Since day one he had been told that you couldn't keep the boiling hot, high-pressured water on any one spot on the cart for too long or it would strip the paint off. Mr. Hamilton himself had told him to never ever start screwing around and spray each other with the spray gun, that thin blade of water came out so hard that it would cut through your skin like a knife.

Jimmy tried to put the flake of paint back in place, but it fell right back. "Oh great, draw more attention to myself. That's the last thing I need right now." He let out an exasperated sigh through clenched teeth. All he could do now was hope that Mr. Hamilton didn't notice it, even though he knew he probably would. That guy had eyes like a hawk.

Jimmy toweled off the windshields and backed the last two carts into the barn. Out of habit, he sat down in the shuttle cart to back it in, but it refused to move. He looked down at the ignition and suddenly remembered that Vic had taken the key with him when he left. "Sorry, man. Mr. Hamilton himself told me not to let you have the shuttle cart key. Jimmy had wanted to argue with him but only held up a hand and said, "Whatever." Then Vic had slunk off rubbing his temples. Now Jimmy put the shuttle cart in neutral and pushed it back into the barn manually, right in the front spot. All carts were safely in for the night, another day done.

He began rolling up the pressure washer hose and looked toward that heap of trash in the back corner again. In the deepening gloom, the trash looked human again. In fact, it looked so human that he almost wanted to call out *Hello* just to make sure it wasn't really some guy sitting back there, but that would be crazy.

What would I have done if Mack really had been sitting back there? A dead Mack all charred black from where the lightning had burned through his skin. The horror movie image in his mind gave him chills. He forced himself to turn away from the trash pile and focus on rolling up the hose.

Jimmy placed the spray gun in its holster on the side of the pump. At the garage door, he put one hand up to pull it down, but stopped himself. He wanted to just say the hell with it, slam the door shut, turn off the switch for the pressure washer pump (which was on the outside wall), lock up the gate, and get the fuck outta here. *Leave that bag of trash for the maintenance crew in the morning. So what if they tell on me to Mr. Hamilton, it was Vic's fault anyway.* His conscience was gnawing at him though. *Do you really want to draw more attention to yourself? Like Mr. Hamilton's so fond of saying: You're on thin ice as it is, buddy.* And he still couldn't shake that prickly feeling on the back of his neck, the feeling that he was being watched.

There was a row of fluorescent lights along the ceiling, but Jimmy had never used them. The cart crew was usually long gone before it was dark enough to need them. Though tonight, without Vic, he had worked slower and had to stay later than usual. He reached over and flicked the switch next to their towel rack. No luck, the cart barn remained dark except for that orange sunset flickering through the vent. With a resigned sigh, he gathered up his courage. It was just a little dark, that's all. Of course there was no one really watching him here, that was all just his guilty conscience.

He shuffled sideways in between the parked shuttle cart and the long horizontal rows of golf carts that stretched all the way to the back wall. There was a six inch gap between the two rows, only enough space for one of his legs at a time. Glancing back into the shadows, he could see that the cart with the trash heap was in the third row from the wall, maybe six or seven carts back. He side-stepped over to the third row, then climbed up into the carts to make his way toward the back. They bounced and sunk under his weight. He set one foot down on a footrest, then the other onto the seat of the cart in the next row over. It was such a tight fit in between the roll bars that he had to turn his chest sideways to squeeze past them. The farther back he went, the more the darkness seemed to press in around him.

141

In a few minutes he was there. He stopped in front of the cart with the trash, peering through its windshield. This was the closest look he had gotten at the heap sitting in the passenger seat. He had expected it to look obviously like trash now that he was up close and personal, but it looked more human than ever. The dead whitish tree limbs really did look like arm bones. Hanging down in the middle were ratty pieces of one of those tan leather fringe shirts like people wore back in the wild west. The sunken head wasn't a shredded bag like he'd thought, it was a tangle of long black feathers. Maybe one of those golfers had run over a goose or something and left it for the cart crew to clean up.

Jimmy wrinkled his nose in disgust. It smelled like old dirt and wood, but had a rotten, dead smell underneath, probably coming from the dead goose or bird or whatever it was. He wished he had brought gloves to pull it all out, but he didn't feel like squeezing himself all the way out just to get a pair, then coming all the way back in. Besides, he didn't think he'd have the nerve to crawl all the way back here in the dark again.

Just man up, grab that shit, and toss it in the fucking dumpster.

Jimmy leaned around the corner of the cart's windshield and wrapped his fingers around one of the tree limbs. He gave the trash pile a light, experimental pull, it felt much heavier than he'd expected.

A bony hand suddenly shot out from the other side, clamping down on his wrist. Jimmy screamed and jerked back, bumping his head hard against one of the metal supports of the cart behind him. The dead thing didn't loosen its grip at all. It sat up straight, limbs creaking and cracking. Jimmy could see now that it wasn't made of trash at all. It had a cracked wooden face that rolled up to meet him.

Jimmy bellowed and yanked his arm back,

somehow ripping himself out of that tight grip. He fell back clumsily into the cart behind him, the steering wheel dug painfully into his side and he almost fell into the gap between the two carts. In a quick burst of panic, he managed to untangle his feet and push himself back up with his hands.

The dead thing behind him began crawling forward. Jimmy scrambled back the way he came over the seats of the golf carts, the plastic rooftops bumping his head and the windshield corners scraping against his skin. He dared to glance back over his shoulder a few times and saw the thing crawling after him, wildly swinging some kind of blunt instrument. A tomahawk. Its sharpened stone end clanged against the support bars of the golf carts as it swung relentlessly.

The thing stumbled and Jimmy widened the gap between the two of them. He made it out into the little row between the shuttle cart and the long rows of parked carts, and shuffled sideways as fast as he could through the narrow gap.

The dead thing saw that he was getting away and, with an incredible amount of force, gave the two rows of golf carts in front of it a hard shove. One golf cart's bumper smashed into Jimmy's shins, crushing them against the metal edging on the side of the shuttle cart. Jimmy yelped in pain and instinctively tried to jerk his legs out from between the carts. The row of carts bounced back away from the shuttle cart, and Jimmy managed an awkward, panicked hop. He lost his balance and fell down into the gap, cracking his elbow against the concrete floor.

The dead thing gave the carts another shove, and this time Jimmy's head was smashed in between the bumper and the metal on the shuttle cart. The braces on his teeth cut into his lips and inner cheeks. His ears smashed and began to ring. His vision suddenly flared with the pressure, and he felt something like a huge migraine throb surge through his whole head.

In a painful daze he crawled forward, desperately trying to get away from the dead thing. It was crawling after him again.

Jimmy reached out into the dusky twilight trying to claw his way forward on the concrete, but it was too late. The dead thing had already reached him. The blade of the tomahawk slammed down in between his middle and ring fingers. Jimmy shrieked as his blood began to spurt out onto the wet concrete and run in little rivers. He could only focus on his hand, gasping and hitching in little breaths and trying to work his fingers between the sharp stone blade that had cut all the way down to the skin of his palm. The dead thing stepped over him in ancient, tattered moccasins that looked like they were over a hundred years old.

It walked up to the high pressure spray gun, stared at it for a second, as if examining some alien gun for the first time. Its skeletal fingers wrapped around the handle and yanked it out of its diagonal metal holster. It gave the trigger an experimental pull and a misty spray shot out of the nozzle. The pump and compressor thrummed even louder.

It looked back over its shoulder at Jimmy. He saw the silhouette of its wooden mask and its black feathered headdress. It turned toward him, holding the high pressure hose up to its shoulder as it if were a rifle. It pointed the nozzle directly at Jimmy's face and gave the trigger a quick squeeze. Jimmy squirmed away from the hot mist. Even at this close range he felt the high pressure spray bite into his skin. The thing walked up to him and pointed the nozzle right in his face.

"Please, please," Jimmy whimpered, flinching and squinting his eyes shut.

It pulled the trigger. The high pressured water

tore into Jimmy's face, slicing off his forehead and cheeks in little strips, leaving patches of bare red muscle and white skull. Jimmy felt it all, writhing and squirming. His shrieks became gurgles as water and blood filled up his mouth. All of his struggling sounds were drowned out by the harsh clatter of the compressor. Finally, it used the water to peel off Jimmy's scalp.

Long after the screaming stopped and Jimmy had finally died, the thing let go of the trigger. The skeletal hand lifted up Jimmy's dripping scalp and examined it for a moment. Then it dragged Jimmy's limp, steaming body back deeper into the cart barn and sprayed the water against the concrete. Jimmy's blood washed down the spillway, a harsh contrast from the green grassy water that usually ran off the mowers and golf carts. It slammed the garage door shut and eventually the safety stop shut the pump down.

The course fell silent except for a few faint shuffling noises from within the cart barn. The last of Jimmy's blood washed down the drain.

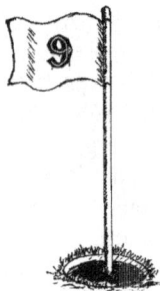

Friday, May 22nd, 1981

Bill had just drifted into a dream—something vague about the golf course in the moonlight—when the phone rang, jangling only a foot away from his ear. He jumped and his eyelids flew open. Whatever the dream had been, it burst like a balloon and dissipated like vapor. *God, I can't escape that place even in my dreams,* he thought.

He leaned over and glanced at the clock as he lifted the phone off its cradle. It was 10:45 in the morning, and even the thin curtains couldn't completely block out the bright morning sunlight.

"Yeah," he croaked.

"Bill, it's Harold. We've got a problem," Hamilton said. He sounded hurried, in urgent need of something. He always sounded that way whenever he needed Bill to take care of something at the course.

Bill let out a long irritated sigh into the phone. "What now?"

"I need you to come down here right now. There's something wrong with the pump house, it's making an awful racket out on seven fairway. You need to come down and take a look at it. It's disturbing the golfers."

"Oh they're disturbed all right," Bill retorted. Hamilton ignored the joke.

"Can you hurry?"

"Yeah, yeah. Be there in ten." He hung up before Hamilton could say anything else.

Bill sat up in bed, running a hand over his bald head and face. Everyday this week he had spent twelve to fourteen hours at work cleaning up the hail damage and trying to catch up on preparations for the tournament on Saturday. He had really only gone home to sleep. Now even *that* wasn't enough. In exchange for the crew coming in and working at night, he'd given them all today off so they could sleep. He'd taken the day off himself, hoping he could get some much needed rest before staying up all night. But here he was, getting out of bed to go down there yet again.

"Might as well just build me a little bedroom above the shop," he muttered as he pulled on an old Indian Hill T-shirt.

*   *   *

It was strange seeing the shop quiet and deserted like this in the middle of a Friday. It made Bill feel like he was in some apocalyptic *Twilight Zone* episode, or like Vincent Price in *The Last Man on Earth*. He opened up the main garage door in front of the hydraulic lift and backed out his maintenance cart.

147

As he drove through the half empty parking lot, he marveled at how few cars were there. On a typical Friday, the parking lot was full and the fairways were choked with old people and businessmen enjoying their early weekends. On Fridays it usually took longer for the boys to mow the tee boxes and the older guys to mow the fairways while they waited for the golfers to get out of the way. Today the course was so dead that it would've been a good day to get some work done. Too bad they were all at home sleeping.

Hamilton walked out of the pro shop doors as he approached, wearing a neat polo shirt and a sweater wrapped around his shoulders, the sleeves tied in a knot at his chest. Bill groaned inwardly. *Awww man, why can't you just leave me alone and let me do my job without hovering over my shoulder all the time?*

Bill pulled up next to him and Hamilton hopped right in on the passenger side. "Can you hear it?" he asked hurriedly, pointing his finger. "It's down there at the pump house."

"I know where the pump house is," Bill said making no attempt to mask the annoyance in his voice. "Look, just go back in there, sit down at your desk, and don't do anything."

"Very funny, wise-guy," Hamilton said. "I'm going with you. This needs to be fixed pronto. Or have you forgotten that we have the most important tournament of the year tomorrow?"

"Suit yourself," Bill said hitting the gas.

They had to stop near the seventh tee boxes and politely wait for a group of golfers to tee off.

"Do you hear it now?" Hamilton whispered.

Bill hadn't been paying attention, he had been lighting up a fresh cigar and staring down at the grass. He had to admit it looked pretty dry. Now he listened closely and could hear the thrumming thump of

148

something mechanical pounding away inside the pump house. To him it sounded rhythmic, almost like a tribal beat.

"Oh that?" he asked puffing out smoke. "Those are just the Indian Hill Indian drums."

Hamilton only frowned at him and casually scooted away a few inches. Bill smirked to himself. He knew that Hamilton didn't like the smell of smoke around him because it seeped into his neat, clean clothes and perfect, tight curly hair. Bill loved giving Hamilton a hard time whenever he could. The golfers finally began trundling their golf bags down the fairway, and Bill and Hamilton drove to the pump house.

They took a left onto the flat dirt road that began in the rough next to the seventh fairway. The cart bumped and bounced over the small dam that fed water from seven lake to ten lake. The short rectangular cinder block pump house building was just past the dam. It had no windows, only a locked metal door and a few ventilation grates.

Bill parked, stepped out of the cart, and unlocked the pump house door. The pounding, rhythmic machinery had been muffled out on the fairway and louder outside the pump house, but as soon as he opened the door the sound exploded out at them. *Ka-chunk, ka-chunk, ka-chunk.* Hamilton clapped his hands over his ears, and Bill reluctantly went inside the dark building, wincing at the noise. He turned to the rectangular electric box mounted on the wall near the door and pulled the safety switch down, killing the power to the pumps. The thudding noise quickly wound down to silence and left both of them with ringing ears.

"Whoa, wait, wait, wait," Hamilton demanded. "You can't just shut off the power. We've got customers in the restaurant."

"Relax. The pumps are on a different circuit

than the clubhouse."

"Oh. Well, why didn't you just say so? *I* could've done that. Why didn't you just tell me to do that over the phone?"

"Because I don't want you touching anything in here and messing up my whole watering cycle. You do that and this course will start looking brown instead of green." Hamilton had no reply for that.

It was dimly lit inside the pump house. The ventilation grates high up on the walls let in enough light that he could work during the daylight hours, so he had never installed any lights. There was the big well system and a huge configuration of pipes and pumping machinery in the middle of the room. Most of it was painted blue metal, and it was as big as a car. All along the sides of the massive pump, there were high stacks of boxes, extra fertilizer and chemicals, and old tools that weren't used very often. You had to squeeze past all the clutter to get anywhere in the pump house. Hamilton instantly felt uncomfortable as he looked around.

"Don't you ever clean this place out?" he asked.

"I got a golf course to take care of. I can't spend all my time cleanin'," Bill replied. The truth was he left it messy on purpose just to discourage Hamilton from coming in here and potentially screwing up the irrigation system. He knew Hamilton meant well but the guy was too headstrong. Bill didn't trust him not to come in here and start pushing buttons at random.

He pulled a small flashlight out of his pocket, he'd gotten it from the tool closet down at the shop. Walking all around the pipes and the well covers, he examined everything. It all looked intact, no wires had shorted out, there were no puddles on the floor. The control system seemed to be functioning normally.

"Control system's working. Pumps look okay."

"That's...a good thing, right?"

Bill grunted in agreement. He crouched down and lifted up one of the metal access hatches that covered the deep well, then shined his flashlight down at the water. The well was the size of a small room, descending twenty-five feet into the ground. If everything had been working properly, the water level would have been only about three feet lower than the pump house floor. Instead, the water level had sunk fifteen feet.

Bill opened his mouth to tell Hamilton what he saw, but then the smell wafted out at him like something out of a nightmare. It was a fishy lake smell mixed with putrescent rotting animals. It reminded Bill of when he had seen a dead cat in a sewer grate when he was a kid, only this was more intense. He turned his head to the side and winced, trying to breathe only through his mouth.

"Oh fuck," he uttered. He pulled the cigar out of his mouth and coughed.

The smell finally hit Hamilton, he pulled out a neatly folded handkerchief and held it to his mouth as he also began to cough. He backed out of the pump house and into the fresh air.

Bill forced himself to turn his flashlight down into the well again. The rippling black water was dark and murky.

"What's down there?" Hamilton asked.

"I can't see anything. The water level's too low. We've got a blockage somewhere." He looked up, trying to think of possible explanations for the blockage. "If I had to guess I'd...."

Something caught Bill's eye and he trailed off. For a split second, it almost looked like he had seen the shadow of someone creeping behind one of the stacks of boxes, then they had slipped farther back into the shadows. He shined his flashlight at the boxes but could see nothing out of the ordinary.

He began to get that same prickly feeling on the back of his neck like he had the other day in the old abandoned pump station. It felt almost as if he were being stalked, like whatever it was had followed him out of that small pump station and moved into this big one. Maybe this whole pump incident had just been a ruse to lure him inside.

"Can you fix it?" Hamilton asked. Bill nearly jumped as Hamilton's words brought him back to reality. Bill shrugged off his prickly, creepy feelings and stood up. He let the metal hatch cover fall back down with a loud slam, and walked back out of this dingy pump house into the sunlight.

"Not today."

"Well, won't that ruin your watering cycle or whatever?"

Bill threw out his cigar in the tall grass, that nasty smell had made him lose his taste for it.

"Look, I'd love to fix it, but I just don't have enough time today. I might be able to take a look tonight, but I'm not sure. Right now the tournament is my top priority, and we can let the course run without water for a day or so. Besides, it's supposed to rain tomorrow anyway. It'll keep 'til Monday."

"If you say so, I don't want this place drying up between now and then."

"It'll be fine. Relax."

"I won't be able to relax until this tournament is over and we get back to normal."

"Yeah, you and me both."

Bill locked up the pump house door and they drove off. On the ride back, Hamilton explained that he may drop by sometime tonight, he hadn't fully decided yet. Bill thought, *Oh, the guys will just love that.* He dropped Hamilton off at the pro shop doors again.

After Bill's cart was parked back in the maintenance shop again, he closed up the garage door and was muttering to himself. "Jesus, one more thing added to my never ending--"

"Have you seen Jimmy?" a woman asked from directly behind him. A cold, thin hand fell on Bill's shoulder right as she said it. He jumped in surprise, falling back a step and whirling around to take a look at her. She wore a purple house dress and her hair was still done up in curlers. Looking at her drawn, haggard face with dark circles under her eyes, Bill guessed that she'd been up all night.

"What?" Bill exhaled, his voice full of both relief and confusion.

"My son Jimmy. Have you seen him?" she repeated her question almost desperately.

"Jimmy?" Bill asked. There was no one currently on his crew named Jimmy, he mentally scanned backwards over the last few years. There had never been anyone named Jimmy on his maintenance crew.

"He works with the golf carts in the evenings."

"Oh, one of the cart crew boys. I'm sorry, I don't know them very well. I'm the superintendent so I run the maintenance--"

"He was here last night working. Then he never came back home. He's already in trouble with the p-p-police. I'm afraid to call them." Her voice began to crack with sadness, but her eyes remained dry. She looked too wiped out to cry. Bill tried to offer her a sympathetic look, but he was still recovering from the fright she'd given him.

"Ma'am, you might wanna go up to the pro shop, see that big building up there?" he pointed to it and she glanced over her shoulder. "Go up there and talk to a man named Mr. Hamilton. He's the head pro, and he's in charge of those cart crew boys. I'm sure he'll straighten this whole thing out for you."

After a long pause in which she stared over at the cart barn, she finally thanked him and walked slowly up to the pro shop. Even the way she walked looked kind of eerie to Bill, like she was sleepwalking. Bill finally put the pieces together in his mind, that Jimmy kid must have been the one who opened up the cart barn on Monday night. Now it seemed he'd run away. This woman—his mother—looked like she was in a state of shock.

"Ma'am," Bill called out to her. He'd thought to offer her a ride up to the pro shop in one of the carts, but she didn't turn around. She sleepwalked out of sight behind the dumpster fence. Bill looked over at the cart barn as she had, and wondered why it gave him the same prickly feeling he'd had back in the pump house.

He forced himself to look away, turning to the deserted shop and the half-empty parking lot. It felt too quiet, like an old ghost town. "Maybe this place really is cursed."

He thought of those old stories he had heard a long time ago, the ones about the Tomahawk brothers and the massacre. Chief Tomahawk had supposedly put a curse on old Indian Hill before he died. Maybe it was all true. For a fleeting second, he thought about calling in tonight and just telling Hamilton he was violently ill.

Let him deal with the curse. If the stories are true, it was partially his family's fault anyway. I'll just stay home in my comfy bed, shutting out the world, and dreaming about anything but Indian Hill Golf Course. It was a nice thought, but an impossible one. The golf course was his responsibility and he would have to see this night through, curse or no curse.

When Ronnie's phone rang at eight o'clock that Friday night, he was so disoriented that it took him a full minute to figure out just where he was and what was going on. He jolted awake at the sound of the harsh jangling on the night table next to his bed. Instinctively, he rolled over and lifted the phone off the cradle, a knee-jerk reaction.

"Hello?" he answered loudly, forcing his voice to sound more alert than it actually was.

"Hey, man. You awake?" It was Mark.

Ronnie looked out at the window, it was filled with the orange light of the sun near the horizon.

"Oh shit, I slept in. I slept in again, didn't I?"

"Guess that depends on your definition," Mark said vaguely.

Ronnie narrowed his eyes in confusion. *What the hell did that mean?* He squinted at his clock, but without his glasses, he couldn't see anything.

"What the fuck time is it?" Ronnie asked in a mumble.

"It's about eight."

Eight o'clock in the morning? Oh fuck, I've gone and missed my alarm clock again. I already missed two hours of work. Bill's gonna kill me for not doing the cups.

"Eight? Fuck. Is Bill pissed?" Ronnie hissed.

"What? What the hell are you talkin' about?" Mark asked. "Bill's fine. Remember, we said we'd call each other at eight to make sure we were awake and ready to go work?"

Ronnie's brain sluggishly refused to cooperate. This felt like Monday morning, it had to be. He tried to remember just what the hell was going on and what he was supposed to do. On the other end of the line, Mark realized what Ronnie was thinking.

"It's eight at *night*, not morning. It's Friday night. We gotta go in and work all night, don't you remember?"

That finally jogged Ronnie's memory, and all at once the world made sense again. "Ohhh. I'm sorry, man. I literally just woke up from your call. I'm way out of it. My brain just crapped out on me."

"Jeez, I was worried about ya for a second there, pal. I thought you were having a stroke or something. Remember last year when that old guy had a stroke out on the course?"

"Yeah, I remember."

"Okay, well I won't hold ya up. See ya in about an hour, alright?"

"Okay, see ya." They hung up. Ronnie groped for his glasses and put them on. He walked over to his window and looked out at his street. The little neighbor kids were riding their bikes around in circles. He could even smell the smoke from someone's barbecue seeping through the window. It was a fine, warm Friday evening in late May.

How could I have ever thought it was morning? he wondered. This was the first time he'd gone to work in the evening in two years, not since his grocery store bag boy days. *Well, I s'pose,* he thought. It was a phrase Butch and Pete used when it was time to quit dilly-dallying and get to work. *Better pretend like it's morning and start getting ready for work.* He shook his head at the strange thought and went downstairs. Maybe he would turn on the TV and catch a little bit of *The Incredible Hulk* while he heated up some leftovers, or a TV dinner, or whatever he could find.

*   *   *

Forty five minutes later, Ronnie walked out the door with a half empty bag of Cheetos, a can of Pepsi, and his Walkman loaded with fresh batteries. It was warm out now, but he wore an old gray sweatshirt and long jeans instead of shorts, he figured it would probably get much colder out on the course in the middle of the night. He felt refreshed, he'd gotten about six hours of sleep starting just after two that afternoon by forcing himself to watch boring daytime soaps on TV. At some point he'd woken up for a few seconds to turn off the squawking TV, and gone right back to sleep until Mark called. At first, he hadn't thought he would be able to sleep during the day, and that he'd be giving Mark the wake up call, not the other way around. Now he thought it was a good thing they'd made that pact, otherwise he might have slept right on through until the next morning.

Driving out to work at sunset, and knowing that he would be out all night felt like an adventure. He wondered what it would be like out on the course in the dark, probably super creepy, but he didn't really know

157

what to expect. Out of habit, he flipped on the radio, tuned to his country station and caught "Sundown" by Gordon Lightfoot. He smiled, Gordon Lightfoot was good, mellow road-trip music.

As he drove and sang along with the song, he marveled at how different everything seemed to look going to work at this time of night.

"Hunh, it's all backwards," he said aloud. And it was: all the shadows, all the reflections of light, the sun in his eyes instead of at his back, it had all flipped around. The bright orange glare of the setting sun made him squint. He pulled down his overhead visor, but it didn't help much, the sun was halfway below the horizon at this time of night and still glared right in his eyes.

He passed by the empty farmland and saw the old Wentworth barn on the left. "God, that place looks even creepier at night than it does in the morning." In the morning, silhouetted against the rising sun, it just looked cold and unused, kind of lonely. But in the reddish waning daylight it looked more shadowy, like it was full of secrets and bad memories.

On Old Wentworth road he could see the last shreds of sunlight flashing through the trees on his right side instead of his left. Straight ahead, the patches of scrubby grass and hunks of sandstone cast long shadows up on Hackberry Hill—or was it Indian Hill? After his history lesson from Zeke he found it hard to call it by its new name. In the place where that tall, old hackberry tree had once stood, he could see the purplish twilight sky and the first faint twinkling stars.

The totem poles and the Indian Hill Golf Course sign on the side of the road, which usually sat bathed in golden morning light when he pulled in, were completely dark, covered in shadows.

As he coasted down into the parking lot, the sun disappeared over the horizon, and Ronnie saw the golf course under a dim, dusky sky. There were a few scattered cars left in the parking lot, most of them owned by golfers trying to beat the sunset and get a last couple of holes in before going home for the night. A few of the golfers were at those cars, packing their golf bags away in their trunks. He pulled his old Mercury into a parking spot between Butch and Pete's two big trucks. As he got out, carrying his chips, Walkman, and big headphones, he was surprised to see that he was one of the last guys to arrive. He looked down at the clock on his dashboard, saw that it was getting close to nine, and hurried in.

Inside the maintenance yard, Ronnie saw two of the younger cart crew kids washing off a half dozen golf carts and joking around with each other. Old Zeke stood near the main garage bay door to the maintenance shop, leaning against the wall. He held a Styrofoam cup of coffee in one hand and a smoldering cigarette in the other, and stood looking out at the western horizon.

"Hey, man," Ronnie said.

"Mahnin.' Or is it evenin'? Kinda hard t'tell, ain't it?"

Ronnie laughed and Zeke gave him a casual, sideways grin. "Yeah, you can say that again." He passed through Zeke's cloud of cigarette smoke.

Everyone except Joe and Jeff were already there. They were all standing around between the hydraulic lift and the open garage door just shooting the shit. Ronnie noticed that they were all in sweatshirts like him, or warm plaid hunting jackets. Bill stood at the chalkboard writing down everyone's jobs for the night. He glanced over as Ronnie walked in and pointed to a big blue plastic cooler sitting on the floor near the board.

"Hey, once you get punched in, help yourself to sodas in the cooler," Bill told him. "We also have coffee brewing in the office if you'd rather have that."

"Aww, you should've told me. I wouldn't have

brought this from home," Ronnie replied, holding up his can of Pepsi. He rushed into the office, pulled out his time card, and punched in. *Ka-chunk.* He pulled a radio off one of the chargers and clipped it into one of the pockets of his jeans. Then he turned around and joined the other guys near the open garage door. They were all drinking cans of soda or cups of coffee, so he pulled his own Pepsi can out of his pocket and cracked it open.

Pete noticed him walking over. "Hey, your little sidekick made it after all," he said to Mark. As usual, Mark was goofing around, hanging from a rolling winch that clung to the underside of a beam above the hydraulic lift. He was trying to swing back and forth on it without touching the ground.

"Look who it is, it's Rip Van Winkle," Mark teased. Ronnie grinned.

"'Bout time you showed up, ya goofy little fucker," Butch teased.

"What? I'm still on time," Ronnie said. "I'm not used to driving over here at night, so cut me some slack, okay?"

"Plus, you had to pull the curlers out of your hair and put on your face," Mark added.

"That too," Ronnie jokingly agreed, and they all shared a chuckle at Ronnie's expense. "How much sleep did you guys get?"

"Shit, not much at all," Mark said. "Maybe two hours, if that."

"How about you guys?" Ronnie asked the others, trying to engage them in the conversation a little more. Brian, clad in a warm black leather jacket, said he had only gotten a few hours. Pete had about six hours, the same as Ronnie.

"Couldn't get more'n an hour or two," Butch said. "The wife wouldn't stay on her side of the bed." Then he made a sexual kind of grunt noise, further driving home his point.

"Yeah, way to go, man. Get down on it," Mark joked to him, then he turned his back to Butch and made a puking, gagging face at Ronnie. At the thought of Butch and his wife "not staying on their sides of the bed," Ronnie pulled a look of disgust himself.

Bill finished writing jobs and joined the group. Ronnie looked over at the board and caught a glimpse of his scheduled jobs for the night.

Ha, even the jobs are backwards, he thought to himself. He had to mow the greens first, then the collars and approaches, then do all eighteen cups by himself. At the end of the night they would all get together and pull the carts up in special designated lines for the tournament. It was completely backwards from a normal Friday schedule.

"Yeah, no one wants to hear about which side of the bed you were on, Butch," Bill said.

"You'll be lucky if you get half as much as I do when you're my age there, Billy boy," Butch bragged. Bill winced.

"God! Please! I can't take anymore!" Bill protested, and they all laughed. Joe and Jeff sauntered in behind them and went into the office to clock in.

"How much sleep did you get today, boss man?" Brian asked, spitting tobacco into the drainage grate near the open door.

"Shit, I didn't get any sleep at all. Had to take a couple of No-Doz. I'm running on pure caffeine tonight. I've got a story for you guys." He glanced around behind himself toward the spillway where the cart crew kids had just finished up parking the last carts in the cart barn.

"First, I had to come by here because there's some shit caught down in that fuckin' pump again...ugh..." he shuddered.

"What's wrong with it now?" Brian asked.

161

"I don't know. I have to look at it tonight when Hamilton's not hovering over my shoulder. I swear, we've had more shit go wrong this past week than we did all of last year. I think this place really is cursed."

Ronnie noticed that Zeke, who mostly stayed out of the conversation, had now looked over at the mention of the word *curse*. Bill glanced out the open garage door again and saw that the cart crew kids had slammed the cart barn door shut and were now walking toward the parking lot. Once they were safely out of earshot, he continued the story.

"You remember how the police thought that one of the cart crew kids had something do with all that vandalism on Monday night?"

"Yeah, what about it?" Brian asked.

"Turns out the kid's gone missing now."

"No shit?"

Bill nodded. "Kid's mom is worried sick." He told them the story of his odd encounter with Jimmy Bloom's mother this afternoon. "God knows where he is now. Probably ran away to try to get out of all the trouble he's in. Hamilton's about ready to shit a brick over the whole thing."

"I don't blame him with everything he's been through with this tournament."

Old Zeke had watched Bill the whole time while he told the story. He was so quiet that none of the other guys noticed him, except for Ronnie. The old guy's story from a few days ago at lunch still hung heavy over his mind.

"That's fuckin' crazy," Mark chimed in.

"I'm tellin' ya, it's this place. Cursed. You young guys better watch out when you're out there. Whatever took that cart crew kid will probably come looking for more fresh meat."

"Yeah, you never know what you're gonna find

162

out there in the dark," Brian teased in a spooky voice.

"...when you're all alone," Pete chimed in. Both of them directed their ominous comments at Ronnie and Mark. The boys humored them.

"Uhh, I'm gonna go to the store," Mark said in a quavering scared voice, and all the guys broke up.

"Yeah, I'm gonna go see if the Colonel's hiring," Ronnie added and pretended to start walking back to his car. They laughed even harder.

Bill looked out the garage bay door. "Get a load of that, you guys. It's full dark now. Oooooh." Ronnie and Mark looked out toward the course. The fairways seemed to be as dark as mine tunnels. There were no lights out on the golf course whatsoever.

"Whoa. It looks spooky out there," Ronnie said.

"Just wait till you get out there in the dark. It's gonna be pitch black and quiet like you've never experienced before. There's only nine of us out here tonight. Ten if you count Mr. Hamilton, he said he might show up later."

"Ten little Indian Hill maintenance workers," Mark joked. Ronnie was again reminded of Zeke's story from Tuesday, Mark had made that same joke about the ten guys that were involved in that Indian Hill massacre. *Ten little Indian killers,* he had said. It was only coincidence, but something about it sent a little chill down Ronnie's back.

Bill glanced at the clock and saw that it was getting on towards nine-thirty. "All right, get to work. Hope that Indian Hill curse doesn't get you, and you don't go missing like that cart crew kid," he taunted the younger guys in that eerie voice again.

They all muttered a few last words, "Yeah, I s'pose," and "Better get to it," then walked off to their respective mowers or golf carts. None of them really said much, they all felt a kind of tension in the air. They had known about this night of work for the past few days, but now it was finally here, and somehow it didn't seem real. Ronnie and the other young guys backed the carts out of the shop to get them out of the way of the mowers. Since he had to do cups later, Ronnie decided to leave his keys in the ignition. One by one they boarded tee mowers, greens mowers, fairway mowers, and golf carts. Mark, assigned the job of raking out the bunkers, got onto the bunker machine. They fired up the engines, flicked on the headlights, and pulled out of their parking spaces one after the other.

Bill had set them in motion like little wind-up soldiers. His last taunting words echoed back in his mind and he remembered the worried look on that poor Bloom woman's face. Guilt washed over him as he associated those two things together. *I shouldn't have said that. I took it a little too far.* He couldn't take it back now though, the words had already been spoken, and words had power. By saying a few words you could either bless someone or put a curse on them. *What if I just cursed these guys?*

"Hey, be careful out there," he impulsively called out to everyone. "We've got all night so take your time, okay?" It sounded kind of lame in his ears, but it was the best he could come up with. A few of them turned back to look at him. Ronnie was one of them, Zeke was another. They both seemed to recognize something subtle, either it was the worry in his voice or on his face. The reassuring grins that they gave him didn't do much to reassure him.

They formed a line like a funeral procession, and drove out through the maintenance yard gate. Out in the parking lot they all branched off and went their separate ways. If anyone had been up on the roof of the maintenance garage looking out toward the parking lot, the line of mowers with their headlights on breaking

164

apart might have resembled a slow-motion firework. Bill stood just outside the main maintenance bay door watching them go.

He was not the only one watching.

*   *   *

On his orange Jacobsen greens mower, Ronnie drove toward the number one green, leaving the lights of the clubhouse and the parking lot in the dust. The darkness fell over him like a blanket, and seemed to grow thicker and thicker the farther out he went. *Holy shit*, he thought. *Now this is dark.* All the trees around him were indefinable black blurs. Only when the small sphere of the greens mower's headlight fell on them could he make out any kind of details.

Just as an experiment, he turned the headlight off and drove in complete pitch black darkness. It felt like he was driving while wearing a thick blindfold. He began to laugh out loud, feeling the hairs on the back of his neck prickle.

He hadn't even bothered to turn on his Walkman yet, his big headphones still hung unused around his neck. He was too busy taking it all in. The darkness was so tight that he almost felt claustrophobic. In his mind, he began to consider all kinds of frightening images. So many *what if* questions frantically rushed through his mind: *What if I see someone out here? What if they come towards me? What if this mower breaks down and I have to walk all the way back to the shop in the dark? What if, what if, what if?*

His hand hovered over the console switch for the headlight, but he hesitated to turn it back on again. What secrets would that light reveal? Did he even want to see what was out there in the dark now? He sensed the green was approaching and forced himself to flick the

165

switch.

There was the number one green about twenty yards ahead of him, lit up by the bouncing headlight. He quickly scanned the entire area around the green for any signs of people, animals, or any of the blood-curdling things he had imagined out there in the dark. There was only grass and trees, all the same stuff that was there in the daytime.

Ronnie drove onto the green to the flag in the middle. Even after a year of working out here, he wasn't quite as comfortable on a mower as the other guys were. Usually the others could reach over at full speed and pick up a flag stick on the first try, then drop it back in the cup perfectly on their next stripe. He had seen both Joe and Mark do this, but the one time he'd tried it himself, he had bent the flag stick and almost completely yanked the cup out of the green. Then, when he had let go, it sprung back against the mower, banging into the buckets and causing them to gouge a rough divot in the perfect smooth surface. He hadn't tried it since. Now, as usual he played it safe, he brought the mower to a complete stop and pulled the flag stick out carefully, then drove to the edge of the green and tossed it aside until he was done mowing.

Dropping the blades down, he let his eyes settle on whatever distant landmark was straight ahead of him, and mowed the straightest lines he possibly could diagonally across the green. Driving back and forth like that made him wish that he had put his music on now. Soft lonesome country music wouldn't do though. Tonight called for some rock'n'roll, something fast and uplifting to keep those creepy thoughts at bay while he worked in the dark.

When all the diagonal stripes were done, he mowed his clean-up pass around the circular edge of the green, then drove back toward the spot where he had dropped the flag stick. He throttled down, hopped off the mower, picked up the flag stick, and carried it back over to the cup where it belonged.

Down at his belt he heard a staticky squawk coming from his radio and he listened for a response from someone. There was no response, only silence. Was Bill trying to call him? He unclipped the radio from his belt, and pressed the *TALK* button on the side.

"Ronnie to Bill, did you just try to call me?"

There was a few seconds of silence. Ronnie almost put the radio back on his belt, then a harsh whispering voice spoke.

"The trees have eyes."

It was unmistakably Bill's voice. Ronnie started laughing, but he quickly realized something. *One of them is gonna pop out and scare me. Of course they will, I'm the youngest one here, and everyone picks on the youngest. It's like a national law or something. Maybe Mark has something to do with it, maybe he planned this out with Bill.*

"Where are you?" Ronnie asked into the radio. No answer.

Oh fuck, here it comes, he thought. He spun around waiting for someone to pop out screaming from behind a tree or a bush and make him jump out of his skin. No one did though. He sensed Bill laughing somewhere.

"Ronnie to Bill," he tried again into the radio.

After a moment, Bill answered. "Go ahead."

"Are you planning on jumping out and scaring me?"

"What?" Bill asked.

"That was you on the radio just now, wasn't it?"

"I have no idea what you're talking about." Just before Bill clicked off the talk button, Ronnie heard Brian's high-pitched laugh in the background. Bill even sounded like he was grinning and trying to suppress his own laughter.

"Uh huh, sure you don't." Bill didn't respond. Ronnie shook his head, climbed back up on his mower, and took off toward the number two green. He kept one hand on the steering wheel, and with the other he put on his headphones and started up his Walkman. He kept one paranoid eye on the trees around him though. After all, the trees had eyes.

There she was. From his low vantage point, he watched Tanya washing the windows. She was in the curved corner of the clubhouse at the end of a long hallway that led from the front doors to the banquet rooms. In the darkness outside, he watched her bending and flexing, wiping the window up and down with a wad of paper towels in both hands. She hadn't noticed him yet though, she was too focused on the glass itself, not what was creeping up outside. Even if she had looked out, she would've only seen darkness, her eyes were adjusted to the light from inside.

He approached, crouching low so the bushes that lined the lower half of the building would cover him. He watched her with growing lust, the skimpy pastel pink cheerleader's tank top barely hung low enough to cover the bottom curves of her breasts, and she was wearing no bra. A loose lock of hair hung down alongside her cheek.

Moving through the gap between the two bushes, he came closer. The bushes shook a little and finally caught her attention. She noticed the motion and took a step backward nervously. Her eyes went wide for a second, then narrowed suspiciously, searching the bushes for some kind of animal—a raccoon maybe—that was prowling around.

He inched forward trying to make as little movement as possible, ignoring the way the prickly bushes scratched his arms.

Something is moving out there, she thought. It moved slowly but those shifting branches were undeniable. She stepped close to the window, squinting her eyes. The glare off the glass made it nearly impossible for her to see what was out there. The branches fell still and she dared to press her face up against the glass, cupping her hands over her eyes to block out that damned glare.

"RAAAAAHH!" Mark suddenly sprang up from his spot deep between the two bushes uttering a mad, raging scream. Tanya jumped back, her feet slid on the smooth tiles and she fell on her butt. Mark laughed wildly and doubled over slapping his knee with one hand.

"Mark!" Tanya shouted. As she clambered to her feet, he began drumming his fingers on the window pane and mimicking a creepy 1950s horror movie theremin with his mouth. She gave him a frown and cranked the circular latch to open the window. The sound of chirping crickets and croaking frogs from the small lake just across the eighteenth fairway immediately filled the hallway.

"Goddammit, Mark! You scared the shit out of me!"

"I'm sorry. That was mean of me. But I couldn't resist. You shoulda' seen the look on your face!"

He imitated her look of surprise and fell back. Her hand shot out through the window and she tried to smack him. Letting out a cry, he flinched back just in time. "I know, I'm really a dumbass. I'll make it up to you though, maybe later tonight if you're not too busy." He waggled his eyebrows at her. She reached down into her bucket and threw out one of her wet paper towels all covered with dust and Windex.

"Get lost, Mark," she said. He cried out again as he ducked away from the paper towel.

From down at the other end of the hallway near the front doors, Wendy called out. "What was that? What happened?"

Tanya quickly thought of an idea to scare him off.

"Nothing, Mr. Hamilton. Just one of the maintenance boys messing around outside."

At the mention of Mr. Hamilton's name, Mark said, "Oh shit," and leaped back out of the bushes. He scampered back down the hill toward the bunker raking machine he had parked next to the oval-shaped sand trap alongside the eighteenth fairway.

"Huh?" Wendy asked. She looked around for Mr. Hamilton, but they were alone. "Mr. Hamilton's not here." Tanya closed the window and explained to her sister what happened.

Mark started up the bunker machine and drove off up the fairway. He had originally meant to rake the bunkers in order so he could stay near Ronnie and joke around with him all night, but as soon as he'd seen Tanya's car in the parking lot, he changed his plans. He thought that maybe she would still be in the restaurant cleaning up and he could enjoy a couple of quick glimpses of her before getting on with his work for the night. *God, she's so hot*, he thought. *Even a quick glimpse is better than nothing*. Then he had spotted her washing the windows and gotten the bright idea to pop out and scare her.

He knew he acted like a creep whenever she was around, but hey, he had to get her attention somehow. Maybe he would rein it in a little after tonight and try to lay on some genuine charm. He knew he probably didn't have a snowball's chance in hell with her, but he felt that he had to at least try.

Now that he had already started raking the bunkers on hole eighteen, it was too late to go back to the front nine and meet up with Ronnie again. He decided to continue in reverse order, making his way backwards toward the front nine and the north side of the course. With his trusty Glen Campbell mixtape blaring in his headphones, he put himself on autopilot.

Sometime after eleven thirty he had finished up almost all of the bunkers and was making his way up the fairway towards the number two green. This hole had five bunkers on it, and most of them were big. During the day, he hated raking the bunkers on this hole because it was usually choked with golfers, but tonight it was kind of nice. It was a relief to not have to constantly be looking over his shoulder for golf balls flying at his head. He figured he would start on the big cashew-shaped bunker that butted right up against the hilltop green and work his way back downhill as he went along.

A few times tonight, he had gotten a strange feeling that someone was nearby, watching him. It reminded him of the way that he had felt yesterday afternoon when Joe and Jeff had snuck up on them out in the woods. Now that he thought about it, he wasn't far from where that had happened either. The hole in the fence behind the number two green was only about twenty yards away. Now that feeling of being watched was getting stronger. Maybe it was just the memory from yesterday that he was feeling. If anyone else were around, he surely would've seen their headlights by now. All the carts and mowers had some kind of light, even his own bunker machine had one big headlight mounted just under the steering wheel.

What if JoeJeff is planning something? Maybe it's them out there somewhere watching me right now. What if they want revenge for the ol' water treatment that I gave them yesterday?

"Fuck them if they can't take a joke," he said aloud. "They've gotten me with that old gag half a dozen times. About time they get a taste of their own medicine." If he hadn't been riding the bunker machine, he wouldn't have been talking out loud, but the roar of the motor drowned out his voice enough that he felt comfortable talking to himself. Talking seemed to help shake off that feeling of being watched. He decided to take it a step further and sing along to "Rhinestone Cowboy" that was playing on his Walkman.

He drove over the lip of the bunker and into the sand. In the glow of the headlight he could see three of the bunker rakes lying in the middle of the sand trap. They had probably been casually tossed in by either the golfers or the old-timers mowing the rough, and now they were right in his way.

"Goddammit," he grumbled, shaking his head. "Can't you just leave them on the side of the fucking bunker? How hard is that?"

He throttled down, got up off the bunker machine, and walked through the soft sand toward the rakes. Kneeling down, he tossed the first and second rakes out onto the grass, but the third one looked like its long handle was buried deep in the sand, with only its wide rake teeth exposed.

"What'd you do, step on it as you walked out?" He grabbed it by one of its upturned plastic teeth and pulled. It came up more easily than he had expected. Its handle, which was normally four feet long, had been reduced to about eight inches, ending in a sharp broken point.

"Fuckin' golfers." A little stream of sand cascaded out of the rake's hollow broken shaft. He plunged his hand down into the sand digging for the handle and came up with nothing.

"What the fuck did ya do with the handle? Bury it or throw it off into the woods somewhere? Probably had some drunk assholes fucking around out here tonight."

What about JoeJeff? Would they do anything like this? he wondered. He looked around once more but couldn't see any other carts or mowers around. *No, it probably wasn't them. What would be the point of a prank like that anyway?*

With a shrug, he tossed the broken end of the rake into the little plastic basket that was mounted just behind his seat on the bunker machine. He swung his leg over the steering column and sat back down. With his left hand he throttled all the way back up, and with his other he pressed forward the two levers on his right side. The wide center rake below his seat dropped down into the sand, and the metal drags on the back dropped with clanging sounds. He hit the gas and started driving around in circles, smoothing out the sand in the bunker again.

He always started from the outside and worked his way in. Once the first full circle was complete, he faced the green and moved inwards toward the middle for his next circle.

Something thumped hard under the middle rake and the whole machine bounced violently. He felt the center rake under his feet being pulled off the mechanical hooks that raised and lowered it. The rake fell backwards, caught under the machine's wide tires, and began to bounce and jerk under them. Mark immediately lifted his foot off the accelerator and let the bunker machine abruptly jerk to a halt. All three of its tires sprayed sand forward.

"What the fuck?" he cried out with clenched teeth. Sometimes if he didn't raise the middle rake soon enough before exiting the bunker it caught on the edge of the grass and was pulled off the hooks like this. It also happened if he took a turn too sharp. Getting the center rake back on its hooks was always a pain in the ass.

Peering down into the darkness below his feet, he saw the center rake jutting up out of the sand at an awkward angle, it almost looked like a sinking ship. It had definitely caught hold of something buried in the sand, something that looked like trash or dead leaves.

Mark tipped his head back and yelled up at the stars in complete annoyance. *"FUCK! Are you fucking KIDDING me?!"* He slammed his fists against the steering wheel in frustration.

Just what the hell were these golfers doing burying something in the sand like this?

Mark throttled down and hopped off the mower. He knelt down in the sand and examined the heap caught underneath the machine. A big mass was tangled up between the center rake and the tires, it was much bigger than he had first thought. He still couldn't tell what it was though, in this darkness he could hardly see a thing. One thing was sure, whatever he had run over was still partially buried in the sand.

He began to dig, hoping to uncover the buried thing and dislodge it so he could get back to work. At about eight inches down, he was able to get his hand under it and pull. It came up a little, it was....

He jerked his hand back, suddenly disgusted and afraid. Whatever was down in the sand felt like shoulders covered by a cotton T-shirt, and cold skin.

Dear God, there can't be a person down there. I did not just hit a person with the bunker machine. At once, he imagined some mafia mobster type guys burying one of their victims in this bunker just before the sun went down. He hesitated, not wanting to know, but needing to.

Slowly, he started to brush sand away with his fingertips. His heartbeat raced in his chest as he began to uncover terrible, but familiar, shapes all caked with sand. First there was a mangled, pointy chunk that could've once been a nose. Then there was the brow ridge of a forehead, two round cheekbones, and sinking orbs that could've been eyes. He gave it one more brush with his bare hand and saw the only part of it that wasn't caked with sand: white teeth covered in metal braces shining in the moonlight. Mark knew Jimmy Bloom in passing, and he had seen these braces before.

For once in his life, Mark was stunned into terrified silence.

Then he heard the soft hiss of sand falling away from something. He whirled. Less than three feet behind him, another body was slowly rising up, the sand streaming off of it like water. The top of its head was covered in a ratty headdress made of black feathers and a leathery dead bat. Its chest was a bony wreck, scraps of leathery flesh clung to its ribs, and all of it was barely covered by a tattered frilled buckskin shirt. Its shoulders and upper arms were like tree branches, brownish and scarecrow thin. Its face was the worst though. It was the face of that old wooden cigar-store Chief that had once stood outside the pro shop, now sawed off. A cracked stern frown and hooked nose came into view after the sand tumbled out through the punched-out eye-holes. It was looking right at Mark.

Without warning, it threw a handful of sand into Mark's eyes. He fell back screaming, his lower back crushing Jimmy Bloom's dead face farther down into the sand. He cried out and blinked desperately, catching only blurry glimpses of the dead thing scrabbling through the sand toward him.

Mark tried to crawl backwards, then scrambled to his feet. He blindly mounted the bunker machine, and floored it. The center rake bumped a few times under the tires, then broke off.

Behind him, the Chief rose up out of the sand and followed the bunker machine. It was lanky and taller than Mark, standing well over six feet. Mark tried to look back at it, but everything was blurry. He wiped at his eyes, the dry grains of sand grinding against them. He tried to reach for the radio clamped to his pants pocket, his fingers wildly searching for the *TALK* button.

Gotta call someone. Ronnie. Bill. Anyone! Gotta--

He pulled the radio up to his mouth. *"Hel--"*

It swung the tomahawk hard at his skull. He heard it knock into his head and tear away a piece of his scalp. His head was tossed to the side with the force of the blow, forcing another tortured scream out of him. His hands clamped onto the steering wheel, yanking it hard to the left.

The radio flew out of his hand and landed in the sand. One of the bunker machine's tires drove over it, pushing it down deep. Then the drag rakes pulled a layer of sand over it like a blanket.

The chief tossed the tomahawk down in the sand and pulled up another weapon in both of its skeletal hands. It was the sharp, broken end of the bunker rake.

The bunker machine swung around in a circle, heading straight for the dead thing in the mask. Mark regained his balance on the machine, just as the chief reared back with the bunker rake. Before Mark could let out another scream, the killer jammed the bunker rake down into his open mouth. It knocked Mark backward against his seat. He gagged and felt the tender skin of his throat rip open.

The chief ripped the rake end out of his mouth and stabbed down furiously again and again. Mark struggled to grab for the sharp end of the rake, but only succeeded in getting his hands sliced open. He quickly weakened, slumping over the steering wheel and trying to turn his head away from the rake's vicious point. In one last moment, he saw his own blood dripping down the side of the bunker machine, clumping up as it hit the sand.

*   *   *

Ronnie was the only one who heard Mark's brief scream for help over the radio. He had been setting a flag in the twelfth green. By coincidence, he had been far enough away from the mower, and one song on his tape player had just faded out, allowing him to hear the radio. He pulled his big headphones off and held the radio closer to his ear. Was Bill playing another prank on him, like that thing with the "trees having eyes?" Or was someone else playing a prank on him, someone like Mark?

"Hello? I didn't quite catch that, can you repeat?" Ronnie asked into the radio. No reply. Ronnie narrowed his eyes and clipped the radio back onto his belt. As he walked back to the mower he wished that Bill had sent him and Mark out together tonight. Maybe if he had been with Mark, he wouldn't have felt so creeped out or so alone.

Something flashed past the glass doors at the other end of the long hallway, catching Tanya's eye. She looked up from the black floor mat she was vacuuming and stared down the hall at the back doors. Through the glass she could see only darkness outside.

"God. Give it up, Mark," she muttered under her breath. She shook her head and went back to her vacuuming. Mr. Hamilton would accept nothing less than spotless perfection, even on dirty old floor mats.

Once she finished with that, she went into the restaurant and vacuumed the floor mat at the cashier's corner of the bar. Her sister Wendy was in here with a broom sweeping up crumbs around the tables. They finished at the same time. Tanya switched off the vacuum and Wendy brought the dust pan back behind the bar to dump it out into the trash. She could hear Roseanne Cash's "Seven Year Ache" blasting from the radio in the kitchen, Wendy must have turned it on at

179

some point.

"Vacuum's all yours," Tanya said.

"Thanks." Wendy let out a large yawn and covered her mouth with the back of her hand.

"And when you get done in here, bring it over to the pro shop. We gotta vacuum and wash all the windows in there too."

"I know."

"And hurry up, will ya? I wanna try and get out of here before old man Hamilton shows up and adds more crap for us to do."

Wendy nodded and opened up the door to the pantry at the far end of the bar. She stowed the broom and dust pan away behind the door and turned back to the restaurant rubbing her temples, she was getting a headache. The door swung shut and there was a loud crash from inside the pantry. Tanya—already out in the hallway again—heard the crash and whirled around.

"What are you doing?" she cried out, it was more of an accusation than a question.

"I didn't do anything," Wendy yelled defensively. She turned back to the pantry door and opened it up. All the shelves on one of the walls had collapsed spilling their contents onto the floor. Soda and beer cans, chips, candy bars, and other various restaurant items cascaded out around her feet. Tanya leaned over the bar, took one look at the mess, and her mouth dropped open.

"Now look what you did," she accused.

"How did *I* do it?"

"You slammed the door too hard."

"All I did was let it shut by itself. I didn't slam it at all."

"You *had* to have slammed it."

"I'm barely half awake, why would I slam it shut?" Wendy looked down at the damage. "You know

180

what it was? It was that curse I heard those maintenance guys talking about." Yesterday when she brought Butch and Pete their lunches, she had overheard them talking about a supposed curse that hung over the golf course. "They were right. This place really is cursed."

Tanya rolled her eyes. "Give me a break." she muttered. She began making her way toward the kitchen entrance to help her sister clean up the mess.

"No. You know what? Just stop right there. Get out of here. I'll clean it up."

"You can't get it all by yourself."

"I don't want your help if you're gonna be getting all cranky at me every five minutes. So go away, I got it."

"Oh sure, leave me to clean the pro shop by myself," Tanya protested, but Wendy ignored her. She went into the pantry, clicked on the light from the pull switch, and slammed the door shut.

From behind the door, she heard her sister yell back, "See, now *that* was me slamming the door."

Tanya shook her head, threw her hands up in the air, and walked out of the restaurant.

She knew she was being too hard on her little sister. It was probably only because it was after midnight and she was tired and ready to head home. Letting out a huge yawn, she glanced in at the dark banquet rooms across the hall from the restaurant. She had walked through those rooms in the dark hundreds of times and they had never bothered her before, but that had always been during the day. Now, in the dead of night, the banquet rooms gave her the craziest sensation that they were haunted, as if the shadows themselves would reach out and try to pull her in if she didn't hurry past.

Oh, knock it off, she thought, forcing herself not to hurry past the dark doorways. *This place isn't haunted and there's no stupid curse.*

She reached the end of the long hallway and turned right to head into the pro shop. Her tennis shoes crunched in something. She stopped and looked down, her shoes briefly sliding to a gritty stop. A light trail of sand led in from the outside. On the floor mat in front of the glass doors—the one she'd just vacuumed fifteen minutes ago—she could clearly see sandy footprints. They seemed to dissipate into indistinct shapes on the tiles.

"What the fuck?" she whispered to herself. "I just vacuumed this. Who--"

Mark. He was raking the sand traps and probably got it all over his shoes. Apparently he thinks he can scare me twice in one night. She spun around in a circle, hoping to catch sight of him peeking around a corner, but saw no one. Mark had to be in here somewhere, the sand told her that. Sand was not sticky like mud though, he hadn't left a definite trail, but she could tell he was somewhere in the building.

Maybe he was hiding just behind the door to the men's restroom, waiting to pop out screaming as soon as he heard her footsteps go squeaking by on the tiles. Maybe he was back in the dark banquet room, and that was why she had gotten that creepy feeling when she passed by. Or maybe.... She turned and faced the open doorway leading into the dark pro shop. That was it, had to be.

"You wanna play hide and seek? Okay, Mark," she said in a low voice. *And if you get punched or kicked in the balls when you jump out, it'll be your own fault*, she added internally.

Tanya began to creep forward, taking the softest footsteps she possibly could. All the lights in the pro shop were off except for a small desk lamp on the corner of the long curving cashier's counter. It gave off a glow about as bright as a child's nightlight. All the blinds were open and the floodlights on the outside of the building (left on for the maintenance guys) let in some light too. There was just enough light to see, and also enough to cast crazy shadows everywhere.

The pro shop was like the identical twin of the main dining room in the restaurant: a long curved room like a quarter of a circle, but it was filled with golf merchandise instead of tables and chairs. It had wood-paneled walls and a matching ceiling that sloped up to a high center point, making the room feel like a cross between a log cabin and a giant tepee. The cashier's counter and a little hallway that led to Mr. Hamilton's office were in the main corner of the room, covered by a high curved ledge that jutted out from the wall. Up on the ledge there was a small taxidermied buffalo on display to break up some of the dead space.

One of the jobs Mr. Hamilton had assigned for them tonight was to replace two of the burned out bulbs in the track lighting that illuminated the buffalo. Bill, the superintendent, had brought an extension ladder from the maintenance shop earlier. He had propped it up against the ledge near the end of the counter, and left a box full of fresh light bulbs next to it.

The merchandise was on display in front of the curving wall and all the windows. New golf bags, racks of polo shirts, golf shoes, sets of shiny new clubs, boxes of golf balls, and all sorts of other golf paraphernalia had been painstakingly arranged by Mr. Hamilton.

Tanya peered around all the merchandise, looking for Mark crouching down. Her shoulders were tensed, she was ready to let out a blood curdling scream when he jumped out. She would scream so loud that he would probably wind up more scared than she was. Every now and then she checked over her shoulders to make sure he wasn't creeping up behind her.

She jumped suddenly, thinking that she had

finally noticed him, but it was only a mannequin wearing an Indian Hill golf shirt and hat.

Halfway along the curve of the cashier's counter, she began to feel impatient. Where the hell was he? She had already passed the taller rows of shirts and golf bags, and it would be much harder for him to hide on this side of the room. Then it hit her. He was probably hiding behind the counter, maybe even planning on reaching out and grabbing her shoulder. The idea made her whip her head to the right to look over the counter, but he wasn't hiding there either.

Her eyes wandered down the length of the curving counter and stopped on the extension ladder. *He wouldn't go up there, would he?* She took a long look at that high overhang, considering the possibility that he was hiding behind that buffalo. *Better make sure he's not.* She stepped silently to the far end of the counter. Looking up at the little bit of space between the buffalo and the wall, she could see that he wasn't up there. The tension eased in her shoulders. She almost turned to walk over to the light switches, but a new idea popped into her head.

What if I climbed up there and hid behind the buffalo myself? Then when he comes in to try to scare me, I can give him a taste of his own medicine. Yeah, that would really get him back for that little stunt at the window earlier.

Using those same soft footsteps, she climbed the ladder. It was even slower going than it had been just walking through the pro shop because the aluminum ladder kept wanting to creak and clatter, bouncing with every slight movement.

Up near the last few rungs, she stopped. Soft stealthy steps grating against the tiles were echoing down the hallway. She could hear his shoes, still caked with sand, getting louder and louder, coming toward the pro shop. She panicked, not wanting to let him see her climbing up the ladder, her prank would be ruined. Hastily, she hurried up past the last few rungs, making more noise than she wanted to, and hopped onto the overhang. The ladder gave one last bounce, relieved that her weight was off it. She gritted her teeth. *Fuck, I'll bet he heard that.* She squeezed around the buffalo's wide dusty head and crouched down, using its burly chest as cover.

Those gritty footsteps crept into the pro shop a few moments later. He was being very quiet, but his sandy shoes were a dead giveaway. She peeked around one of the buffalo's legs. The overhang blocked the lower ground level from view but the desk lamp on the counter cast his shadow against the far wall. His head looked bigger than usual, his normally shortish hair looked bouncy and teased out in crazy strands as if he were a rock star like David Lee Roth or Robert Plant. *What the hell is he up to? What kind of tricks does he have up his sleeve?*

Tanya dared to lean over and peek out from behind the buffalo's chest. Just for a split second, she saw what looked like wild black feathers bouncing up and down as he slipped out of sight.

Oh, I get it now. He's got some kind of weird Indian costume on with a full feather headdress and everything. Well, that's elaborate. He and his little friend with the glasses must have been planning this all week.

She scooted closer to the buffalo, hoping he wouldn't see her if he looked up when he reached the end of the counter like she had a minute ago. She waited, listening as his footsteps slowed and came closer. In her mind she debated whether or not he had actually seen or heard her up on the ladder. His footsteps seemed to have an unsure quality about them, or maybe that was only wishful thinking. He stopped and silence spun out for a full minute, it felt like forever to her crouched, aching legs.

A faint whispering floated into her ears from below. She caught a few of the harsh, punctuated sounds: *sh...ch...ka-teh...ah....* Tilting her head, she strained to hear was he was saying, but she couldn't pick out any words, at least not any words that she knew. It almost sounded like he was speaking in another language, but there was also a rhythm to it. *What the hell is he saying down there? Is he singing or something?* She held onto the buffalo's leg for extra support as she leaned out even farther to hear what he was saying.

The whispering chant rose to a crescendo and then abruptly stopped, leaving the air thick with silent tension. Tanya froze. She expected him to jump out, or maybe run up the ladder at her. All was silent, so silent that she could almost feel like no one had ever followed her in this room in the first place.

Then something twitched under her hand. She jerked it back, her first impression was that a snake had crawled under her hand. That was absurd though, there were no snakes in here. She scanned the buffalo and all around the overhang with her eyes and saw nothing wriggling around.

It twitched again and this time she saw it was the buffalo. She could clearly see its muscles and tendons worming around under its skin as it leg began to spasm and jerk. Tanya recoiled, pressing her back flat against the wood paneled wall. Right before her eyes the buffalo's other legs began to flex and twitch, its hips and shoulders rolling around. The buffalo's head began to sway back and forth in creaky movements, and its mouth opened and closed like a fish. A dry, gravelly moan blatted out of that mouth.

186

Tanya watched in growing disgust and horror at the buffalo's resurrection. It looked like every part of it was writhing and twitching in agony, as if its unnatural life brought it nothing but pain.

She awkwardly stood up from her hiding place and inched away from it, going straight for the ladder, but when she glanced at where the aluminum rungs had been, she couldn't see them anymore. The ladder suddenly clattered loudly as it hit the floor. She was trapped up here.

"Hey!" she cried out. She tried squeezing past the writhing buffalo carcass's head but it nudged her bare midriff with its fur and snapped at her with its dry lips. She yipped in terror and backed into the corner. There was an opening near its back end, and she scrambled past its twitching tail, panting in terror.

Now looking down from the edge and standing as far away from the buffalo as possible, she could see the ladder lying diagonally across the floor, one end blocked the main front doors into the pro shop. It had even knocked over a basket of golf balls and they were all bouncing on the tiles. *"Mark! Put the ladder back! Put it--"*

She barely heard the tight creaking of wood and leather over the buffalo's dry bleating. Standing between two sets of golf clubs stood a tall man, bone thin with the stern, carved wooden face of the old cigar store statue. He wore a ratty old buckskin and a headdress made of black feathers. She could tell he was far too tall and skinny to be Mark. He held an old bow with an arrow drawn back, pointing right at her.

Before she had time to react at all, he let the arrow fly. Its heavy carved end sliced right into her throat and stuck. She stumbled back into the wormy hide of the buffalo. Her first thought was that she'd been hit in the throat with a heavy rock. Her hands flew up and felt the rough arrow shaft jutting out of throat. Excruciating pain, shock, and disbelief hit her all at once. She tried to scream as her throat began to throb and bleed, but she could only manage a gargling noise. Her eyes bulged in pure panic as blood filled up fast in her mouth and began to ooze out between her lips.

Another arrow slammed into the bare skin on her stomach just above her waist. She hadn't even seen him load this one, she'd been too focused on the first. She staggered and tried to back away, but she was caught between the open air and the horrible reanimated buffalo. As she tried to look down at this fresh wound, the first arrow scraped painfully against something inside her throat.

A third, fourth, and fifth arrow flew in: two more in her belly and another in her tan thigh. Every time another one hit, she felt like she was being hit with a thick rock, then the pain rushed in accompanied by the ugly sensation of something underneath her skin that didn't belong there. It was like having a giant splinter in your finger, only a hundred times worse.

Tanya looked down at the strange dead man in the mask and held out her pleading bloody hands. Tears streamed out of her eyes and blood ran out of her mouth. His only response was another arrow into her chest.

She thumped a bloody fist against the wall, wanting to cry out for her sister to help. *Wendy! Help me! I'm sorry!* her mouth formed the words, but she could only manage a bloody gargle. Wendy would never hear her on the other side of the building, and even if she could she was probably ignoring her. She briefly regretted being so mean to her younger sister.

A wave of dizziness washed over her and made her legs buckle. Clouds of gray were swirling in at the corners of her vision. She sank to her knees right on the edge of the overhang, tottered, then everything went gray. Tanya fell forward off the overhang and didn't even feel it when her skull cracked against the hard wooden cashier's counter.

The Chief waited. The buffalo fell silent and motionless again, he had let it return to its death. He expected the other girl to come running in any moment, she had probably heard at least some of the commotion. The thumping beat of the radio was the only sound in the entire clubhouse.

Leaving the pro shop he began to walk toward the kitchen for the other girl, but he stopped when he heard the roar of one of the big fairway mowers finishing up a stripe outside. Rage boiled within the chief's old bones as he looked over his shoulder, watching the mower turn and go back up the fairway toward the green again. He decided that the other girl could wait.

It was a quarter past one in the morning and Butch, Pete, and Zeke were almost finished mowing all the front nine fairways. Pete was mowing his last few stripes down the long straight fairway toward hole nine, lifting the mower blades every so often when the curvy outer edge of the rough swooped in. He saw that Butch had finished mowing the seventh fairway a few minutes ago and was now parked over on the grassy berms behind the eighth green, presumably taking a piss in the trees along the edge of the lake. Zeke usually liked to go off on his own, so they left him to mow the long par-five fairways for holes four and five by himself.

Butch and Pete were a team. They had both started working here shortly after they retired from the same trucking company, and they pretty much stuck together all the time. Butch was the taller and burlier of the two, and, with his strong-willed personality, he naturally led the way. He always came up with a plan, and Pete always filled in the gaps, reminding him of little things he might have forgotten and coming up with easier ways to get their jobs done every once in a while.

As soon as Pete finished up this fairway, he would go over to meet up with Butch and figure out their best plan of action for mowing the back nine fairways. He already knew what Butch would say: *Okay, I say we go do ten and eleven, and let ol' Zeke take care of twelve and fourteen.* Then Pete would add: *Yeah, he likes mowin' them long ones anyhow.* They would plan out exactly who would mow which fairway so there would be no confusion.

He began his clean-up pass around the outside edge of the ninth fairway, working his way from one side of the green all the way up to the tee boxes, then back down the other side to the green again. With careful steering, the mower blades on the right side hugged the fairway's outer edge perfectly. As he rounded the curve near the tee boxes, he glanced up and saw that Butch was still parked on that berm back in the trees behind the eighth green.

"Christ, what's he doing back there?" he asked aloud, his voice drowned out by the roar of the mower's engine. "He's gotta be taking one hell of a leak." He had mowed three long stripes and started his clean-up pass since he first saw Butch parked back there, and that had been over ten minutes ago. He shrugged, maybe Butch had been waiting for him to finish up and had fallen asleep on his mower. "He better hope Billy don't catch him sleepin' on the job." They were both retired, so it wasn't like they really needed this job, but Pete didn't like the idea of getting reprimanded by a boss at his advanced age. Bill laid down the law, and Pete respected him for that. He guessed you had to lay down the law when you had goofy young punks like Jeff and that smart-ass Mark kid working under you. If those kids were this country's future, then America was in deep shit. As far as he and Butch were concerned, both those kids needed a good swift kick in the ass.

Pete rounded the last curves onto the collar of the ninth green, and pulled back on the switch that lifted his mower blades. He took a wide U-turn to avoid tearing up the grass, and headed back toward Butch. Usually Butch would meet him halfway and they would discuss their next plan of attack, but this time Pete saw no headlights approaching. *Maybe he really is asleep*, Pete thought. *Shit, I'd better go wake him up before Billy catches him sleeping. Night shift or not, Bill won't stand for that.*

He drove up the short eighth fairway along the edge of the glittering lake. The headlights on Butch's mower had been turned off. It had been sitting there in the same spot for the last twenty minutes. As he rolled over a few of the smaller berms toward Butch's mower, he began to get the strange feeling that he wasn't alone out here. Maybe Butch had stopped to talk to Bill or someone else in a cart that he hadn't been able to see from down on the ninth fairway. Or maybe his mower had broken down and Brian was out here working on it.

Pete pulled up beside Butch's mower and saw his dark silhouette sitting slumped forward with his head down and his chin resting on his chest. A drop of drool even hung down from his open mouth, sparkling in the moonlight. Pete throttled down and cupped his hands over his mouth.

"Ay!" he barked out loud enough to be heard over both idling mowers. "Rise and shine, soldier!" Butch should have jerked awake, but he didn't stir. Pete tried again in a loud but more serious voice. *"Hey, Butch! Wake up!"* Butch still didn't move.

An icy feeling of dread suddenly froze Pete's heart. *Oh Jesus, what if he's had a heart attack out here?* Butch had suffered a very minor heart attack a few years ago. The doctors had told him that he was susceptible to having another one and he had to be careful.

Pete quickly stood up and climbed down off his mower, stumbling on the little steps that rested above the blades. Getting in and out of these things were a bitch when you had a stiff back and pain in your hips. He rushed over to the front of Butch's mower, terrified of what he'd find. In his mind, he was already trying to figure out what to do if Butch really was having a heart attack. First thing was to get Bill on the radio if he could. Then what? Squeeze in next to him and drive down to the shop? He didn't know.

With shaking legs, he stepped over the mower's blades. "Come on, Butch. Not tonight. Not tonight," he mumbled repetitively. "Come on, ol' buddy. Don't do this to me right now." He hauled himself up onto the mower deck and gave Butch's shoulder a hard shake. "Hey, wake up, fella. Wake up." Butch's head bounced with each shake, but he offered no reaction. "Oh dear God, please don't do this to me right now."

Pete reached out with two fingers and felt Butch's neck for a pulse, but his fingers slid into something wet and slimy. It was like sticking his fingers into a cold Thanksgiving turkey. He jerked his hand back and examined his fingers. Even in the dim moonlight, he could see that they were covered in dark liquid: Butch's blood.

He stared gape-mouthed at his friend for a few seconds, trying to figure out what happened. Butch's head still hung down low, and Pete had a sudden strong urge to lift it up and take a look at his face. He had to know for sure what he already suspected. With a trembling hand, he grasped the bill of Butch's trucker hat, it was also soaked with that dark, sticky liquid. As

Butch's head rose, Pete saw the jagged line slashed across his throat, and the blood dripping out between his grimacing lips. Then the hat came free in his hand, and Butch's head flopped forward again. Gleaming white bone from Butch's skull was exposed. He had been scalped.

"Holy Jesus!" Pete gasped. Butch was dead. No, not just dead, but *murdered*. The murderer was probably still around here too. Maybe he was even watching from behind one of the trees.

Pete spun around and took two giant steps off the mower. He landed awkwardly on the grass and fell forward. His back and hips flared up in pain, but the pain didn't distract from the panic. Scrambling to his feet, he ran for his mower.

"No. No. No no no," he repeated. "Oh Christ no."

Get on that radio, call Bill. No, he had to get out of here, had to put the pedal to the metal before whoever killed poor old Butch got him too. He clambered up the steps as fast as his aching hips would allow. *Goddammit I wish my fucking hips would work. I wish was ten years younger.*

Behind him he heard the swish and thud of footsteps running through the grass, running straight for him. Too late, the murderer was coming. Pete practically jumped up face first into his driver's seat. He felt the mower bounce as something leaped up onto the mower deck behind him.

Hard fingers grabbed the back of his head and slammed it forward into the metal screen that was there to protect him from flying golf balls. He groaned as his nose and forehead mashed into that hard grating. The hand pulled his head back and slammed his face forward again two more times. He saw a fresh wave of colorful stars twinkling in front of his eyes. Reaching back, he tried to grab hold of something, and his elbow hit the throttle. The engine began to roar under them. His head felt all swimmy as if he were drunk and his legs gave out. Those rough hands caught him under the shoulders, spun him around, and threw him back into the driver's seat.

The stars in his vision cleared and he looked up at what he first thought was a black demon. It had a wide head covered in wild black feathers, and an impossibly thin, wiry body. Then the moonlight glinted off the cracked wooden mask, and the grim face suddenly reminded him of all those cowboy stories and comic books he had read as a kid.

That's no demon, it's an Indian, he thought.

It reached back and pulled an arrow out of the quiver strung on its back. It held the chiseled stone point of the arrow toward Pete like a knife in its right hand. The other hand flung Pete's arm up against the metal mesh screen behind the seat. Before Pete's arm had a chance to fall forward again, it stabbed the arrow through the soft skin of Pete's wrist and all the way out through the hole on other side of the metal screen. Pete let out one hard scream, then another yelping one as it gave the arrow shaft a quick twist.

He writhed in the seat, trying to pull his arm forward but the rough arrow shaft tore against the nerves in his wrist. The arrow's barbed points caught against the screen just like a fishing hook caught on a fish's gills. He stared at his pinned hand in bug-eyed horror while the dead thing threw his other hand up against the mesh. Pete turned a moment too late and watched the arrow tip jam into his other wrist. The dead thing gave the new arrow another agonizing twist.

Pete struggled against his wounds and tried to kick the dead thing away, but it was too strong. He knew he could probably pull his hands free, but he would have to suffer through two feet of thick splintery arrow shafts tearing the insides of his wrists to shreds. His brain was firing off too fast for him to think. All he knew was that there was excruciating pain in his wrists and he had to make it stop somehow.

The dead man crouched down near the accelerator. Pete caught a terrible glimpse of the dead man's mask from the glow of the mower's headlights, and he recognized it as the face of that wooden statue that used to stand in front of the pro shop. It examined the gas pedal slowly tilting its head. Then it pulled another arrow out of its quiver, this one with a fatter stone head, and jammed it down between the accelerator pedal and the gap in the mower deck. The accelerator stuck down tight and the mower jerked forward. The dead thing jumped off the mower, leaving Pete to careen out of control.

The steering wheel turned madly as the mower flew over more berms. Without any hands to steer, the ground level decided where the huge mower would turn. A berm rose on the right, making the wheels turn to the left. It picked up speed as the wheels rolled downhill toward the lake.

"Noooo!"

Pete screamed as the rippling water rushed toward him. He tried to kick away the arrow that was jamming down the accelerator pedal, but he only succeeded in breaking off the wooden shaft. His mower bounced up over the rocks lining the edge of the lake, roared in midair, then came down into the water with a huge splash. Its heavy front end dipped forward as the mower began to sink. The water in this lake was easily twelve feet deep. Something short-circuited and the engine died. Pete felt the ice cold water soak into his shoes and pant legs.

Oh Jesus! I'm going under. I'm going under!

He desperately tugged at his pinned wrists as the water rose up over his waist, they tore forward another few inches but the pain was unbearable. He felt his veins and ligaments stretching horribly with every tug. Nevertheless, he continued trying. He screamed in pain and terror as the water rose up to his neck. His screams became gurgles as the water filled his mouth and covered his head. It didn't take long for him to lose all his air. He had used up too much of it from screaming.

Up on the grassy berms behind the eighth green, the chief watched the mower sink into the black depths until its roof was completely submerged. Then he turned and looked back over his shoulder toward the north side of the course. Another one of those big mowers was still running.

*   *   *

For the past hour Zeke had that spooky feeling of being watched prickling the back of his neck. Being out here at night made him nervous and he couldn't figure out why. He had worked out here at night many times over the last thirty years and had never felt this way. All week though, and especially tonight, there had been bad omens. It seemed that everywhere he turned he was reminded of those old stories of the Tomahawk brothers and the massacre up on Indian Hill. Even though he was in his seventies, he had spent his entire life in the twentieth century and always felt detached from those long dead wild west days. Tonight he felt that the past was somehow more real.

Earlier, he had heard Bill's crack over the radio about *the trees having eyes,* and he had shaken his head. His father had always told him, *You shouldn't joke about dark spirits boy, they may come right out of the shadows and bite your ass.* At the time, he had considered saying

197

that to Bill over the radio, but he kept it to himself. Billy was a good kid, and Zeke knew he didn't mean anything by it.

Tonight he had been more than happy to mow the long fairways on the north side of the course and leave the south side for those other guys. He wanted to stay away from that damned old Indian Hill, and mowing the fourth fairway, like he was doing right now, was as far as he could possibly get while still staying on the course. As he turned the mower around in front of the fourth green and began another southward stripe, he saw the hill looming high over the golf course, its peak visible above the clubhouse's roof. He ignored it and focused his vision on one of the thick metal poles that held up the tall net at the back of the driving range, trying to make his stripe in the fairway as straight as possible.

Hole four was a long par five that curved off to the left halfway down the fairway. In the crook of that curve stood the decorative tepee in a thin stretch of ash trees that separated the fourth and fifth fairways. Zeke had started out near the green and worked his way backwards mowing stripes back and forth toward the tee boxes. Now that he was halfway through, he took a long swig of coffee from his Styrofoam cup. It felt like it went straight to his bladder. He needed to stop and take a piss, and he needed a cigarette. His coffee cup could use a refill too, but that could wait. He decided that he'd pull over by the tepee after the next stripe and take care of some business.

Within two minutes he parked near the tepee, shut off the engine, and slowly climbed down off the mower. With every precarious step his stiff back protested and his bladder threatened to let loose. As he stepped down into the tall grass between the two fairways and began to relieve his aching bladder, he heard thunder rumbling off in the west. He could feel the chilly breeze of a storm blowing in. That being-watched feeling was also creeping back in. He tensed his shoulder and stretched his neck from side to side as if to ward off that feeling. He thought he heard gravel crunching nearby but figured it was only the wind.

He finished and zipped back up, instinctively wiping his hands on his pants even though they were dry. Turning back to his mower, he pulled his pack of Lucky Strikes out of the breast pocket of his plaid work shirt and tapped out a fresh cigarette against the heel of his hand. He scraped a fresh match against one of the trees, brought it up to the cigarette in his mouth, and cupped his hands over the flame to block the breeze.

That gravel crunching sound came again. It was louder this time, coming from the direction of the tepee. Zeke stopped puffing and looked up. For a second he saw one of the tight canvas sides of the tepee bulge, as if something or someone had leaned against it from the inside. The gravel crunching noise abruptly stopped.

Someone was in there. Even if he hadn't seen the side of the tent bulge he would've felt that someone was in there. He briefly glanced around for other golf carts. Maybe one of the boys was in there, slacking off and trying to avoid the boss. There were no other carts around though. He should have been completely alone.

Slowly, he began walking toward the dark opening near the base of the tepee. He tread as lightly as he could, wanting to hear any slight noise that might come from inside. As he approached, he felt like he was moving dangerously close to some wild animal's den, or something even worse. He stopped a few feet from the circular entrance hole.

"Hello?" he called in a loud voice, the corner of his mouth clamped around the cigarette. "That one of you boys in there?" He waited for a response but found none. "I don't care one way or th'other, but you oughta' know that Billy's apt to lose his temper if he catches ya in there."

Zeke inched closer to the opening, pulling out another match without looking at it. Pinching the tip between two of his long, yellowed fingernails, he popped it alight and held it out to shine some light in the pitch black interior. There was a little decorative campfire and two log benches. From outside, everything looked like it was exactly in its place except for the gravel floor. Normally it was perfectly smooth, but he could see footprints as if someone had been walking around inside.

The flame crawled down to his fingertips and began to burn. Ignoring the pain, he shook it and pulled out another match, lighting it the same way as he had with the last one. With the fresh match ahead of him to light the way, he stuck his head in to get a closer look. He looked to the right, wanting to see the side that had bulged a few minutes ago. Other than those footprints in the gravel, everything was fine. The tepee seemed to be empty.

He turned to the left and came face to face with a grim wooden mask. The chief grabbed Zeke's head with both clawed hands and threw him to the floor. The match fell to the gravel and burned out. The smoldering cigarette flew out of his mouth and landed in the campfire, starting to catch some of the kindling. Zeke groaned and writhed in pain as one of the campfire rocks dug sharply into his lower back.

The chief rose up from his squatting position near the opening and lifted one of the heavy log benches. Zeke saw what was about to happen and turned his legs away at the last second. The log dropped down right onto his shin and he let out a scream as he felt his brittle old bones snap.

In the flickering light of the fire that was

catching behind his head, he saw the chief lunge forward, black feathers bouncing on the top of his head. The fangs of the stiff dead bat mounted on the top of the headdress gleamed. One leathery, decayed hand shot out and yanked Zeke up by his wavy white hair. With his other hand, he reared back his stone tomahawk for a fatal chop. In that instant, Zeke knew exactly who he was.

"No! Please, Thomas! No!" The hand holding the tomahawk faltered, and the fingers in Zeke's hair loosened. "Please, Chief. Thomas. Don't! I beg you."

The chief cocked his head curiously and lowered his weapon. Zeke gasped for breath, watching the chief with huge staring eyes.

Behind the wooden mask came an inhuman, gravelly whisper.

"How you know my name?"

Despite the flaring pain in his broken leg, Zeke struggled to stay focused and answer the question. "Y-you're Thomas Foutuer. Chief Tomahawk of the Tomahawk brothers. M-my f-father told me all of the Kikawa legends, all the stories about you."

The chief let go of his hair and leaned in closer, examining him through the dark gaping pits that served as eye holes in the wooden mask. Zeke resisted the urge to shrink away from that intense glare.

"You are Kikawa?" it asked.

Zeke hesitated for the tiniest moment, trying to figure out the right words to say to this dead thing.

"My...m-my f-father was Kikawa. I'm...half Kikawa. Just like you."

The chief looked away, as if he were thinking about something, considering what his next move should be. Zeke watched him paralyzed with fear, wondering if he had said the right thing, wondering if the chief would kill him anyway for his white blood.

Finally the chief leaned down again, grabbed a

handful of Zeke's shirt, and hauled him up. He yanked Zeke forward, so close that his face was only inches away from that mask.

"Do not get in my way."

He threw Zeke roughly back to the ground. His back hit several of the campfire rocks again and he writhed in pain. When he looked up again, the chief was gone.

Ronnie thought he heard thunder rumbling through his headphones so he looked up from the medium-sized collar mower he was washing. Dark purple thunderclouds flickering with lightning were lumbering in from the west. He could even feel a breeze coming from that direction, blowing some of the mist from the high pressure washer back in his face and covering his thick glasses with tiny droplets. It looked like it was going to rain a lot harder than the light drizzle the forecast had predicted. He grimaced at the thought of being out in both the dark and the rain, and hoped he would have time to finish changing all the cups. Shaking his head, he hurried to finish washing all the mud and grass off the mower.

Five minutes later, he drove his dripping wet mower off the spillway and parked it just outside the open garage doors to the bright, warm maintenance shop. Normally he would've parked it back inside the mower storage garage, but since the older guys still had their fairway units out, he would have to wait for them. He killed the engine and walked back inside, glad to be back in the light again. After being outside for so long, it took a minute for his eyes to adjust to the bright rows of fluorescent lights. Yawning, he went to the cooler and grabbed a fresh Pepsi.

Brian was sitting on a low rolling stool in front a tee mower that was up on the hydraulic lift. With his sleeves rolled up, he was tinkering with some metal part on the outside of one of the tee-mower's blade reels. It was a silver metal cylinder about the size of a soda can with two hydraulic hoses attached.

"Aww, what? What'd ya do to it?" Ronnie teased. This was usually the line Brian used whenever Ronnie or anyone else brought him some piece of equipment to be fixed.

"Oh, y'know. Fuckin' dipshit was going too fast and hit something. Broke the reel motor off." He spit tobacco into an oil pan at his feet.

"And which dipshit would that be? There are four of us you know, well, six if you count Butch and Pete."

Brian snorted out laughter. Ronnie had never made Brian laugh before and he hadn't expected that his last joke would be the one to make it happen.

"Joe is the dipshit this time. And I'm gonna tell Butch and Pete you said that, hope that's okay."

"Please don't. I can just hear it now," Ronnie switched his voice over to a southern drone that sounded vaguely like Butch's real voice. "You goofy little fucker, I'mma cut yer nuts off 'n feed em to the cat, I tell ya what." Brian let out his full high-pitched laugh and dropped the wrench he was using to the concrete floor. "I'm just kiddin.' Those old guys are okay."

"Ugh, they piss me off sometimes," Brian

grumbled, his laughter trailing off.

"Really? Why?"

"They talk big, but I'm constantly having to fix their mowers. They break shit all the time, probably more often than you young guys."

"No kiddin'?"

"Mm'hmm."

"I did not know that. Glad to know we're not the only fuck-ups around here." This was the longest conversation he'd ever had with Brian. He was usually so quiet, and Bill, with his loud voice, usually stole the spotlight. Now Ronnie wondered what other useful tidbits of information he might have.

Bill pulled up in his work cart outside. He had just finished spray-painting all the drop zones and out-of-bounds lines around all the lakes. The legs of his coveralls were wet with dew all the way to the knees and the sides of his work boots were bright with red and yellow paint. He pulled the spray paint gun and a box of unused spray paint cans out of the back of his cart and walked into the shop.

He turned his attention to Ronnie. "What are you doin' down here? Slackin' off?"

"No, man. I just finished mowing collars, like, five minutes ago. I was about to go do my cups."

Bill gave him a skeptical, "Uh huh."

Brian jumped in on his defense. "He's literally the first person I've seen back here since Dipshit brought this thing back in," he said pointing to the broken tee mower. "That was two hours ago."

"Thank you," Ronnie said to Brian, then turned back to Bill. "See? I'm not the one slackin.' I'm the only one getting anything done around here."

"Okay, okay," Bill relented, dropping the stern boss act. He looked out at the course. "What the hell is taking those guys so long? You'd think without golfers in the way, they'd be cruisin.'"

"Yeah, cruisin' for a bruisin'," Ronnie joked in a threatening voice. Bill raised an eyebrow at him as if to ask *What the hell does that even mean?* Ronnie grinned sheepishly. "Okay, so I'm not as good as Mark at making jokes. I admit it. But hey, at least I tried."

"Get to work," Bill laughed, shaking his head. "Wait, on second thought..." he dumped the spray paint cans and gun into his arms. "Take that stuff to the back room for me, would ya?"

"Yessir."

"And don't worry about the flag sticks. I had Jeff switch out all the flags for these ones made specifically for the tournament."

"Copy that."

Bill turned to Brian as Ronnie walked off toward the back room. "So how bad is it?"

Brian lifted up the silver reel motor to show Bill. "Well, I'll have to bend these edges straight again and put on new bolts. It should be fine for now. But the blades are the real problem. I mean, look at this shit." Brian pointed to several rough dings and chips where the blades should have been a straight sharp edge. "It's like he broke off the reel motor, and then mowed over it. Look, you can even see the scratches." He pointed out several diagonal scars along the tough metal casing of the reel motor. "We're gonna have to order a new set of blades."

"Fuck. Can you grind out those chunks?" Bill asked.

Brian shrugged. "I won't cut that great, but I guess it's better than nothin.'"

"Do it then. I really don't want us to lose a good tee mower, especially not right at the beginning of the summer."

"You got it. Anything else I can do for you,

206

sir?" he asked sarcastically.

"Not unless you wanna help me pull a dead animal out of the irrigation pumps."

Brian grimaced. "Ooh, yeah, you know, I'd love to help out with that, but I'm really busy over here. I just...." he said in a sarcastic, regretful voice and finished with a shrug.

"Sure, sure. I see how it is," Bill laughed.

Ronnie caught the tail end of their conversation as he walked out from the back storage room with his bucket of cup changing tools and metal cup cutter. He walked out of the shop and past the few carts that were still parked outside. Squinting into the darkness, he looked for his set of car keys that he'd left dangling in the power switch when he had backed his cart out of the shop earlier. The keys weren't in any of the parked carts. He checked again, looking around the whole maintenance yard in case someone had moved his cart to a different spot.

"Hey! What the hell? Who took my cart?" he asked out loud. He called back to Bill who was rummaging around in the back of his own cart for something. "Hey Bill, what's the big idea? Someone stole my cart."

"You mean they took off with your keys in it?"

"Yeah."

"It was probably Jeff. I sent him to change out all those flags for the tournament. He's probably out there somewhere."

*   *   *

High overhead, up at the top of the sloped roof of the maintenance shop, Joe and Jeff were crouched down, peeking over the edge and laughing into their fists.

"Oh, I'm sorry. You looking for *these* keys?"

Jeff whispered pulling Ronnie's set of car keys out of his pocket. He gave them a little jingle.

Joe suppressed a mad attack of the giggles and nudged him with his elbow.

"Shh shh. Shut up, dude. They'll hear that," he whispered. Two hours ago, Jeff had snagged both Ronnie and Mark's keys out of the carts while Joe was explaining to Brian how he had accidentally hit the retaining wall on the number one tee as he drove by, snapping off the reel motor in the process. Hitting the reel motor had been an accident, but Jeff took the opportunity to go with Joe back down to the shop. Stealing those keys had been Phase One of their big revenge prank. Now it was time for Phase Two.

About a half hour ago, they had ditched Joe's replacement tee mower over at the storage bin area near the fourth green where no one would see it, and drove back to the maintenance shop in Jeff's cart. They took the long way through the trees on the north side of the driving range so Brian wouldn't hear them, and then parked up against the short cinder block wall on the back side of the shop. Back here they were uphill from the parking lot and maintenance yard, at about the same level as the road coming in. Even though the lowest edge of the roof was easily twenty feet high from down in the maintenance yard, it was only about five feet off the ground back here. Both of them had climbed into the cart's back bed and hoisted themselves up on the roof. They crawled to the highest edge and looked down into the yard. It was lucky for them that they had made sure the coast was clear up here, because Ronnie had pulled up to wash his collar mower right as Jeff was about to begin Phase Three.

From down below they heard Bill say, "Why don't you just take Mark's cart?"

Right on cue, Jeff pulled Mark's keys out of his

pocket and gave them a little jingle. Joe laughed even harder.

"His keys are gone too," Ronnie explained.

Bill walked out of the maintenance shop and examined the carts for himself. Then he shook his head. "Goddammit. Those guys can't go fifteen minutes without pissing me off."

"Well, like Mark always says, we're the best two workers you've got."

"Shit, I don't know about that. But you're a hell of a lot better than those other two idiots."

Up on the roof, Joe frowned. "Pch, best workers my ass." Jeff tore a corner off one of the shingles on the roof and threw it down at Ronnie. Joe saw what he was about to do, and tried to stop him at the last minute.

"No, wait. Don't--"

Too late. The shingle fragment bounced off the metal edge of the cart bed behind Ronnie and fell to the concrete. It made a little ding noise that caught both Ronnie and Bill's attention. Both of them looked at the cart, then up at the roof. Both Joe and Jeff quickly ducked down, grimacing in fear.

They clearly heard Ronnie say, "Is it starting to rain already?"

"God I hope not," Bill said. "Hang on, let me go find you a key. Unless you wanna take the picker cart..."

The picker cart was a metal monstrosity. It was basically a regular golf cart that had a metal mesh cage all around the cab. The people that worked in the little shack on the edge of the driving range usually used it. They hooked up the wide picker machine to the cart's trailer hitch and drove around the driving range, picking up hundreds of golf balls with its circular reels. From time to time, Ronnie and Mark had used it as a shield if

209

they had to dig up a broken sprinkler head out on the driving range. When it wasn't in use, it was parked near the cart barn, right next to the drink cart.

"Meh, I'd rather not take that one," Ronnie said. "Whenever I'm in that thing, the doors always get stuck. I'm always afraid I'm gonna get trapped inside it."

"Okay, one sec."

Bill disappeared inside the maintenance office and came back out a minute later with both a fresh new cart key and the picker cart key on a white golf ball shaped key chain. "You sure don't want the picker cart?" Ronnie shook his head. "All right, well don't lose this one. It's the only spare we've got left at the moment."

"I won't."

"If you need me I'll be down at the pump house trying to figure out what's wrong with the irrigation system."

Ronnie thanked him and took off in his cart. Bill spent another minute inside the shop talking to Brian, then also drove off. Joe and Jeff dared to stand up and watch Bill as he crossed the mostly empty parking lot.

"Okay, I'm gonna go head over to Ronnie's car. You take Mark's," Jeff said. "Brian should start working any second now. Let's go." He began walking carefully down to the lower edge of the roof.

Joe hesitated. "Umm, I don't know, man. Maybe I'd better not. I'm already on Bill's shit-list for breaking the mower."

"Bill don't scare me. I could go get a job with my uncle tunin' up cars anytime I want."

"Good for you. But if I get fired, I'm up shit creek, y'know?"

"He won't do anything. Come on."

Joe still looked unsure running his hands through his spiky shag hair. "Ummm, I can't. You go."

"You pussy."

"Why don't I just keep an eye out in case someone comes back?"

"Alright fine, you fuckin' chickenshit. Make me do all the work."

"I'll signal you when Brian starts using the grinder or turns on that mower or whatever. That way he won't hear the car start up."

"Yeah, yeah."

Jeff hopped down into the bed of their parked cart, then down into the grass. Joe faintly heard Jeff's footsteps crunching through the underbrush as he made his way toward the main entrance driveway. When Jeff reached the pavement Joe could no longer hear his footsteps.

Joe crawled along the roof about halfway from the top, heading in the same direction as Jeff, toward the parking lot. He stopped five feet from the far left edge, directly above where the office would be. From here he had a perfect view of Ronnie and Mark's parked cars.

Jeff came creeping down the road a minute later, hunched over like he was in some kind of cheap spy movie. He hopped over the parking lot median, being careful not to step in any of the gravel. Then he crouched down beside the driver's side door of Ronnie's Mercury and waited for Joe's signal.

Even in the dark, Joe could see the gleam of Jeff's grinning white teeth hiding between the cars. Joe grinned back and held up one finger.

"Wait! Hang on," he whispered, even though he knew Joe couldn't hear him from this far away. He listened for the sounds of Brian's tools. The guy had started up some music down there, it was some song by Led Zeppelin that he didn't recognize. While they waited, Joe sat down on the roof. Jeff carefully unlocked Ronnie's door and sat down in the driver's seat.

What felt like ten minutes slipped by, then finally Joe heard the harsh whine of the hand-grinder starting up. He immediately stood back up and signaled Jeff with a thumb's up and a wave of his arms.

"Go go go!" he whispered, waving his arm in the direction of the exit.

Jeff started up the engine, and Joe kept an eye on the rest of the parking lot for any approaching mowers or carts. Keeping the headlights off, he slowly backed out of the parking spot, drove the car up the exit driveway, and pulled out onto Old Wentworth Road. Following the car, Joe ran back to the spot where they'd been before. Through the trees that grew alongside the road, he saw the headlights turn on. Jeff drove north toward the little dirt access road that led to the storage bin area.

Once the Mercury's red taillights were out of sight, Joe crawled to the lowest edge of the roof and hopped down into the cart. He would rather sit and wait on the soft cart seat than those flat shingles. After tipping his head back to let out a long yawn, he folded his arms across the steering wheel and rested his forehead against them. He had planned on letting his eyelids rest for a minute or two, but dozed off almost immediately.

*   *   *

Metal sparks flew as Brian ground down the chips and dings in the mower blades. Ordinarily, he would have used the big bulky automatic blade sharpener machine that sat next to the lift, but these blades were in such terrible shape that he decided to use the hand-grinder instead, saving the machine from the extra wear and tear. Once the blades were sharp again, he turned off the grinder and the shop fell quiet. Led Zeppelin's *IV* album was playing low on his little portable tape player, but for the moment, the ringing in his ears was too loud to hear it.

Next, he opened up the little closet that stood next to his tool bench, and pulled out his heavy rolling tool chest. He selected a flat heavy sledge hammer from his hammer drawer, and brought it over to the silvery motor reel with the bent edges that he had left sitting on the vice. Loud metal on metal clangs rang out as he slammed the bent corners back into place with the sledge hammer. When it looked about straight, he held it up into the light and examined it with one eye closed.

"Is that straight enough?" he mumbled to himself. He tilted his head back and forth, trying to decide whether or not he should give the bent corners a few more whacks with the hammer.

From outside there was a metal ding and the tinkling of glass. Brian stopped what he was doing and looked out the open garage door. Was someone out there breaking into people's cars? He narrowed his eyes suspiciously and listened for the sound of a car door, but heard nothing. After a moment he shrugged and went back to work.

It only took him a few minutes to reattach the blades, bolt down the reel motor again, and reconnect the hydraulic hoses. Now to inspect the blades and make sure they were working correctly. He reached over and turned the key ignition. After a few struggling cranks the engine caught.

With his hand, he pressed down the foot pedal to lower and spin the blades. All three blades dropped, the one he had just fixed sluggishly dropped after a short delay. *Probably just have to work some more hydraulic fluid back into the reel motor,* he thought. He raised and lowered the blades three or four times, trying to work that strange delay out of the system. It began to even out, the blades dropping and spinning at the same time.

Then the lights began to flicker and dim. Brian looked up surprised as the rows of fluorescent lights overhead went in and out sporadically, they almost looked like they were doing some kind of weird slow-motion strobe effect.

"What the fuck?" Brian said aloud. He stood up and looked around the room. It wasn't just the row of lights above his head that were going in and out, it was all the lights throughout the shop. Even the lights in the office were doing the same thing.

Without bothering to shut off the mower, he walked out into the maintenance yard. The floodlights mounted high up above the shop's front door were flickering in and out too. As he walked forward toward the parking lot, he saw the red and green lights that illuminated the outer walls of the clubhouse flickering in the same way. The lights inside the restaurant windows too.

"Fuckin' power outage or somethin'," he said. His mechanic's mind was already trying to diagnose the problem. He wondered if there was a problem with the transformer, or if one of the power lines was faulty.

Brian walked toward the main driveway, wanting to get a look at the splintery old power pole that stood across the road from the main entrance. Like the rest of the course, the parking lot was pitch dark. All three of the streetlights that usually kept it well lit were out. The maintenance shop and the clubhouse were two flickering islands of light floating on a sea of black.

Why aren't the streetlights flickering like everything else? he wondered. He walked directly underneath one and looked up, trying to see if they had blown out or something. Broken glass crunched under the soles of his work boots. He looked down and saw curved shards of glass that looked like light bulb fragments underneath his feet.

"What the hell's going on around here?" he asked. Had the light bulbs shorted out and exploded?

Something is wrong here. Something bad is happening. Gotta tell Bill.

His mind suddenly flashed back to Bill talking about this place being cursed as the guys had gone out on their mowers. *That was just stupid talk. Curses aren't real. Something's wrong with the power transformer, that's all. Or maybe there's some kind of weird blackout happening all over town. Just get over there and take a look at that power pole to make sure before you go disturbing Bill over nothing.*

With his hands in his jean pockets, he hurried toward the main entrance. As he came around the thick pine trees that stood in the parking lot island, he began to see blinding blue sparks flickering high up in the air and raining down onto the pavement. He could hear the faint crackle and sizzle of electricity. In that harsh blue shower of sparks, he could see that something was sticking out of the metal cylindrical power transformer. It was right at the source of those sparks, a blackening, smoking husk that looked like a three-foot long twig. He thought that he could see the dim shapes of a half dozen other twigs sticking out of the electrical and phone line connections higher up, but, just like with the streetlights, it was too dark to tell.

No, those aren't twigs, they're as straight as arrows. Arrows. Someone shot a bunch of arrows up into the power pole.

It was an absurd thought of course, but that was just what it looked like. Another absurd thought branched off from that one. *If I went back to those burned out streetlights and shined a flashlight up at them, would I see arrows sticking out of them too?*

Something is wrong! You've got to call Bill over

215

the radio and tell him what's going on. Hell, you've got to call all the guys back in. Right on cue, thunder rumbled again from the west, the direction of the course. Brian had a crazy urge to run, but he forced himself down to a fast walk.

Back inside the shop, it was dimmer than ever. The flickering lights seemed to be drawing even less power than before. Brian hurried past the still running mower and snagged the radio off of his cluttered tool bench.

"Brian to Bill," he said. No answer. Brian knew that the radio reception was shitty inside the concrete and cinder block walls of the pump house, and Bill frequently left his radio in his cart instead of bringing it with him. "Bill, come in." He noticed the panicky way his voice sounded on that last transmission, and knew he needed to suppress that. Bill still didn't respond.

Brian looked around the shadowy shop trying to figure out his next move. Should he just call all the guys in? If this did amount to nothing, Bill would be mad that he pulled them away from their work. No, he had to talk to Bill, had to drive over to the pump house if Bill wouldn't answer.

He pulled his own cart key out of his pocket and almost walked over to the carts parked outside, but he stopped himself at the last minute. *On second thought, it might be a good idea to bring a flashlight just in case.* There was a thick black Maglite in the closet where he locked up his tool chest. He walked quickly over to the closet and flung open the door.

The dead thing in the wooden chief's mask sprang out of the darkness. It wildly swung the heavy stone tomahawk at Brian's head before he even had time to scream. He let out a choked little cry and stumbled backwards. It felt like a heavy rock had hit him in the

216

head. The tomahawk chopped diagonally across the side of his forehead, piercing the skin down to the bone and splitting it open. It even cut off a few locks of his long wavy brown hair.

Brian fell back onto the flat little mechanic's creeper lying near the hydraulic lift. His back landed perfectly against the padding, but the fall knocked the wind out of him. The back of his head bounced hard against the concrete floor. Gasping for breath like a fish out of water, he writhed in pain. A bright explosion of stars flared over his vision and his head throbbed. He was dimly aware of a thin trickle of blood running down into his hair from the open gash on his forehead.

Thin dead legs covered in ragged frilled buckskin pants walked forward out of the tool closet toward him. As Brian writhed around in pain trying to catch his breath, one moccasin-clad foot pressed down between his legs on the edge of the creeper and rolled him forward under the running mower. The stars in his vision began to fade and he looked up at the spinning blades directly overhead. His aching head and breathless lungs made it hard to think, but he knew he had to move, had to get out from under those blades. He slowly rolled off the creeper and it slid away a few inches.

A bony hand slid over the support pole of the lift, examining the controls mounted to the side. There were two buttons, one with an arrow pointing up to raise the lift, and an arrow pointing down to lower it. Most modern machinery was completely alien to the dead thing, but it understood arrows perfectly. It slammed a fist against the down arrow.

Right on cue the mower began its slow descent to the concrete floor. As Brian crawled forward, he felt it lowering over him and glanced over his shoulder. The hot wind from the spinning blades blew his hair into his face. They were inching closer to his back and

217

shoulders. Little by little his breath was coming back, but he needed air, it was so hard to move without air. He lowered himself flat against the floor, trying to do his best army crawl out from under the descending mower.

Brian thought he was going to make it until he felt the blades start to rip and tear at his clothes. It was quickly pinning him down. He shot a desperate, clutching hand out from under the left reel, trying to dig his nails into the concrete floor. Then the blades began to slice at the back of his head and shoulders. He shrieked as it pulled him in.

Blood began to spurt and spray out from under the mower as it tore into him, the roar of the engine drowned out his short choked screams. The mower bucked and bounced, the blades slowed, struggling to chop up such a big object. Only his clawed white hand, shaking and convulsing against a widening puddle of red could be seen sticking out from the blades he had just sharpened.

* * *

Joe suddenly jolted awake. *Was that a scream?* He still sat in the cart, listening for anything else, nervous to move. There was a series of bumping, jostling sounds from somewhere down in the shop. Now that he thought about it, that almost sounded the same way it had when he accidentally mowed over that broken metal part earlier tonight. Then the mower engine sounded as if it the blades were being bogged down on something and the engine died.

"What the fuck is he doing down there?" he whispered to himself. There was no clanging of metal tools, no grunts, and no more screams (if a scream was even what he'd heard in the first place). He thought he heard an electric crackling as if Brian were welding.

Maybe I should go see what that was, he considered. *What if Brian needs help?*

Joe hopped up out of his seat and stood on the metal edge of the cart bed with his back to the roof. Placing his hands down on the shingles, he hoisted himself up and scooted backwards until he could get his feet under him.

As he crawled up the roof on all fours, he heard the sound of footsteps crunching through the underbrush somewhere down below. It had to be Jeff coming back from parking Ronnie's car at the storage bin area. Joe stopped and turned around for a second to wait for Jeff, but he was still too far away. Joe couldn't see him through the thick trees yet, but he would get here eventually. For now, he had to see what was going on down at the shop.

He continued crawling up toward the top edge of the roof, slowing down for the last few feet. It would've been stupid to just pop his head over the edge and possibly give himself away to anyone that was down there. As the pace of the crawl slowed, his heartbeat sped up. He had no idea why he felt so nervous peeking over the edge like this. He felt the strangest sense that he was he was in big trouble, much worse trouble than breaking a piece off the mower.

Slowly, he craned his neck to peer over the edge of the roof. Of course, the mower was too far inside the shop for him to see anything. At this angle, he could only see the first few feet just inside the doorway. The light was all wrong. Everything down in the shop and the yard was too dark. In fact, the entire parking lot looked much darker than it had before. He blinked and squinted his eyes, trying to make sure it wasn't just the bleariness of sleep that was blurring his vision. No, there was nothing wrong with his eyes. The lights were flickering in and out as if a little kid were playing with a dimmer switch that controlled the lights of the entire golf course.

Over his shoulder, he could hear Jeff walking closer. Joe only gave a brief glance backwards to whisper to him.

"Hey, man. Come look at this. It's the weirdest thing. I think something's wrong with the power."

Joe turned back to his view of the maintenance yard, barely listening to the footsteps that softly shook the cart below. He looked back into the doorway of the shop and saw a dark puddle running from back toward the lift. It poured into the little drainage grate that ran along the base of the garage door. At first he thought the liquid was just some spilled motor oil, but then he squinted his eyes again. No, it was much too bright to be motor oil. Too red.

"What the.... Is that what I...?" he asked with his mouth dropping open.

Behind him, there came a scratching against the shingles, the sound of someone climbing up on the roof. Joe paid it no attention. He felt his face going pale and he had to turn back around to tell Jeff what he saw. As he turned around and spoke, the other person up on the roof began to run towards him.

"Dude, come here. Is that--"

As he turned, the bony thing with the head full of black feathers and the cracked wooden face ran up the roof straight for him, his ancient moccasins stomping on the shingles.

"Wh—*FUCK!*" Joe whirled around, slipping on the shingles. He didn't have any time to scramble away from the thing as it tore towards him at full speed. Joe screamed and shakily got to his feet. He tried to run off to his right, but the dead thing was too fast. It stretched its skeletal tree branch arms forward and gave him a hard shove.

Joe flew backwards into the air, his calves scraped against the roof's top edge. He tumbled backward, spinning in a crazy circle. His arms flailed wildly as he fell to the maintenance yard thirty feet below. A scream ripped from his throat as the concrete rushed up to meet him. Everything went black the second his skull cracked against the concrete.

*   *   *

Jeff came out of the woods twenty minutes later. That damn storage bin area was farther away than he originally thought. The hike back had taken him much longer than he expected, and it had been darker and creepier out in those woods than he cared to admit, but at least he'd finally made it back. He could see the maintenance shop up ahead, its slanted silhouette materializing out of the trees.

He crept around the back side of the shop to the spot where they had parked their golf cart, and looked around for Joe. The cart was still there, but the guy was nowhere in sight.

"Joe," he stage-whispered with his hands cupped around his mouth. He half expected to hear Joe's footsteps crunching on the shingles from the other side of the roof, but he only heard crickets and the pop and crackle of electricity. Like Joe, he assumed that Brian was welding something in the shop. "Joe, where the fuck are ya, dude?"

Jeff imagined Joe getting all scared up on the roof while he waited. Maybe Joe had chickened out, walked back down to the shop, grabbed another cart, and went back to work.

"Fuckin' pussy better not be ratting me out to Bill," he muttered to himself. He called out for Joe a few more times as he continued walking around the back side of the maintenance shop. Taking the same route as he had before, he hurried out to the main entrance driveway and walked softly against the pavement. The parking lot ahead was dark now, and that made him cautiously slow his step. He felt left out, like he had missed something big while he was off parking Ronnie's Mercury and walking back to the shop.

He briefly wondered why the parking lot lights were out now. *Maybe they're on some sort of timer and they only stay on until a certain point at night.* He was in such a hurry to finish this prank and get back to work that he didn't give it much more thought.

Instead of going straight to Mark's van, he wandered toward the maintenance yard and peered around the corner of the dumpster fence, wanting to make sure the coast was still clear. He expected to hear voices talking loudly in the shop, and see Bill's cart parked there. Other than that electric crackle, there were no other sounds. From what he could tell, no other carts or mowers had pulled up in the half hour that he'd been on the other side of the course either. He noticed the flickering lights and assumed that Brian's welder was draining the power.

Well, better get out of here while Brian's still welding or whatever it is he's doing, he thought.

If the two rows of work carts and mowers hadn't been parked outside the garage door, he would have seen the ruin of Joe's body lying sprawled on the concrete.

For an instant, he considered just giving up on the whole prank and leaving only Ronnie's car out there at the storage bins. It was still a good prank, but it was no fun without someone else to laugh along with him. He had originally thought that Joe would ride out to the storage bins and walk back through the trees with him. They would've talked and laughed about how dumb those kids would would look when they found out their

222

cars had disappeared. But of course, Joe had chickened out and disappeared. Joe was an okay guy, but he was all talk. Jeff thought he had no balls to back up what he said or did, he mostly just stood back and laughed while other people did all the work.

Fuck him. I still can play this prank on those little doofuses if I want. And I probably won't get in as much trouble with Bill if it's both of their cars. If he thinks I'm singling out just one of them, he'll be pissed. But if he knows that they both got a fast one pulled on them, he'll just laugh it off. He had known Bill for years. He had worked here much longer than any of the other young guys, and knew Bill liked a good practical joke as much as anyone. If he got mad though, Jeff didn't really care. He had an idea that this would probably be his last summer working here anyway. At twenty-five, he was getting too old for this minimum wage, college-kid job.

Jeff pulled Mark's keys out of his pocket and silently thanked himself for having the foresight to hold on to both sets. He unlocked the driver's side door to the Chevy van, hopped in and started it up. As he backed out of Mark's parking space, he noticed that one of the back doors had swung open.

"Jesus," he muttered to himself and put the van in park again. He walked out to the back door and closed it quietly, glancing cautiously at the maintenance shop after he did it. "Fuckin' kid doesn't even know his doors are open. He's lucky he doesn't get this piece of shit stolen...well, stolen *more often.*" He grinned and chuckled to himself as he added that last thought, then he climbed back in.

With the back doors shut, he backed out of the parking space quickly. He checked his rearview mirror frequently as he drove up the exit driveway. He was so focused on the dark parking lot behind him and looking for any headlights of one of those golf carts or mowers

223

that might be coming back from the course, that he didn't even notice the sparks from the power pole falling down right in front of the van.

After he pulled out onto Old Wentworth road, he finally hit the switch for the headlights. The dark, empty farm road stretched out in front of him as he headed north toward the storage area. The old Hamilton barn passed by on the right, then the intersection that Ronnie and Mark usually turned onto when they were heading home blurred by. The traffic on this road was usually fairly sparse, but at this time of night it was completely deserted.

A little ways farther down the road was the turnoff to the dirt access road leading back into the course. It was so neglected and overgrown with low hanging tree limbs and weeds that if he didn't know what he was looking for, he would have missed it entirely. Without bothering to signal, he pulled the van in.

A marshy area filled with cattails blurred by on the right, and he felt the weight of the van squelching in the mud on the right side of the dirt road. If it had been daylight he might have been able to look to his left and see the driving range fence through the trees.

The storage bin area, just east of the fourth green, was where Bill kept a huge pile of extra sand to refill the bunkers, extra top soil for filling in divots and low spots, and various other items in three big concrete cubicles. Everyone called these cubicles storage bins. All the junk that couldn't fit down in the maintenance yard ended up here. Just north of the concrete storage bins, was also a big messy area where Jeff and the other young guys had dumped off all their loads of overgrown sandy bunker edges.

The access road leading to this area was outside the main perimeter fence of the golf course, and to get back onto the course he had to drive through a chain link gate, and up a curved dirt driveway. He had left the gate open and unlocked when he pulled Ronnie's car in. Going up that dirt driveway always reminded him of this creepy old house out by an old baseball diamond that he and his friends had dared to venture into once when they were little kids.

Jeff flicked off the van's headlights as he went through the gate and up the winding road. Now the green glow from the dashboard was his only source of light. He looked back in the rearview mirror on impulse, just to make sure that no one had followed him in and--

A man sat in the backseat directly behind him. His silhouette was clear in the rearview mirror, a grim wooden face and outstretched skeleton hands reaching toward him were visible over his shoulder in the green glow.

"Whoa! Fuck!" he screamed. Its hands grabbed his hair and roughly yanked his head back. It pulled his hair so hard that he felt himself being lifted up out of the driver's seat. It was tearing his dark spiky-shag hair out by the roots. Instinctively his feet shot out, one foot hit the gas pedal and they zoomed forward the rest of the way up the dirt driveway. He couldn't see the road in front of him as he struggled against the dead man's tight grip. The van bumped along into the grass and back onto the dirt road.

The chief swung his bloodstained tomahawk down at Jeff's head. He screamed and yanked the wheel hard to the right. The chief lost his balance and stumbled against the back of the passenger seat. The heavy tomahawk chopped into the headrest mere inches from Jeff's right ear and tore out a chunk of foam padding. The hand gripping Jeff's hair loosened enough for him to plop back into his seat. Through the windshield, he saw that he was about to smash into Ronnie's parked Mercury. He yanked the wheel hard to the left toward the sand pile in the middle storage bin, and jammed on the brakes. The van spun out of control, dirt spraying up from the locked wheels.

The dead hand yanked his head back again and chopped down. The sharp edge bit into Jeff's scalp. He shrieked as he felt it being peeled off the top of his head.

The spinning van slammed sideways into the huge pile of sand and stalled. A tidal wave of sand flew into the air and over the top of the concrete storage bin wall. Joe felt himself being thrown forward into the steering wheel as they came to their violent stop. The rest of his scalp tore free in the dead man's hand.

In a wild panic, he lifted himself off the steering wheel and touched his own skull with his bare hands. Blood ran into his eyes as the chief crawled into the front seat to finish him off. He groped for the door handle, found it, and pulled, but the door wouldn't budge. It was held tightly shut by the heavy wall of sand that reached all the way up to the window.

Joe turned, screamed, and weakly struggled against the tomahawk as it chopped down into his flesh again and again.

Five minutes later, after Joe was dead, the two back doors of the van were kicked open. The chief stepped out into the night with blood spattered all over his buckskins and wooden mask. He walked serenely back onto the course, drawn by the faint echoes of a rubber mallet hammering into a metal cup cutter off in the distance.

The course was quiet, too damn quiet. Ronnie
had taken off his headphones halfway through changing
the cups, partly to give his aching ears a break, and partly
because the long curly cord got in his way when he
swung the rubber mallet. He listened for the sounds of
the big fairway mowers roaring away in the darkness but
heard none. One machine was moving out there, but
maybe that was just a car on the farm roads nearby, he
really couldn't tell. Not only hadn't he heard anyone, he
hadn't seen anyone either.

*Maybe they're just taking a break down at the
shop*, he thought. *That's it, has to be. But God, I feel
like the last person on Earth out here.*

"Okay, don't get carried away with that stuff,"
he said to himself. Talking out loud, even to himself,
somehow made it not so damn creepy out here.
"Everyone is probably down at the shop taking a break,
that's all. Or maybe they're over on the front nine

somewhere. Who the hell knows?" He tried to talk to himself the way Mark would've talked to him if he were here.

Come to think of it, where the hell is Mark? I haven't seen or heard from him in hours.

It was all too easy to imagine that everyone had gone home and left him behind to work out at this dark, creepy place all by himself. In his mind, he saw some huge natural disaster happening or the start of a nuclear war, and all the guys running for their lives without bothering to give him any warning. Of course, with his big Koss headphones on, he wouldn't have been able to hear news of any nuclear disasters anyway.

He considered calling Bill over the radio to ask if everything was okay, but decided against it. Bill had seemed kind of cranky when he saw him a little while ago at the shop, it was probably just the stress of the week piling up on him. Maybe it was better to just get his work done and leave Bill alone.

Ronnie stuck the flag down in the fresh new hole on the tenth green and walked back to his cart.

"Maybe I'll just take a little ride over to the front nine and do those cups first. Anything's better than being out here by myself."

The number one green wasn't too far away. All he had to do was drive down the dog leg curve of the seventh fairway, cross over the ninth fairway, and he was there. After seeing the other guys and confirming that World War III hadn't broken out, he could come back and change the last few holes he'd skipped on the back nine.

As he drove across the ninth fairway, he looked over his shoulder toward the pump house trying to spot Bill's cart, but it was too dark to see it. Even over the clattering golf cart engine, he heard the rumble of thunder, the storm was closing in from the west. He saw a few flickers of lightning. The wind was picking up too, a large gust tossed his wild black hair as he approached the number one green.

Maybe that's the reason I can't hear the big mowers. Sometimes the wind carries the sound away out here.

Ronnie drove straight up to the number one green, the cart's headlights illuminating most of the grass. Standing up in his cart, he listened for other mowers. The wind died down a little and he could now clearly hear one machine that was definitely out on the course. From the faint clank of the metal drags, he recognized it as the bunker machine. Mark. Ronnie let his eyes wander in the direction of the sound, and he even saw Mark. His one center headlight spun in lazy circles in one of the bunkers up on the hill near the number two green.

Ronnie let out a sigh of relief. Mark was still out here, and that meant that everyone else had to be too. He stretched and let out a yawn. It was getting close to three in the morning, and even after two Pepsi's he was beginning to feel the effects of staying up this late. His eyes felt dry, his eyelids didn't want to open all the way anymore, he was yawning too much, and every time he sat down, it was harder to get back up again.

With a big sigh, he slammed the cup cutter blades into the ground in what he hoped was a nice fresh spot. It was hard to see the exact condition of the green in the dark, even with his cart headlights on. In a hurry to get over to Mark, he rushed through changing out this cup.

The number three green was closer to him than number two, where Mark was, so he drove down the hill to change that cup first. He predicted that when Mark saw his headlights, he would drive down to meet him. After pounding out the new hole, he looked up at Mark. The guy was still on the same bunker up by the number two green just going around in endless circles.

"What the fuck is he doing?" he asked out loud, squinting his eyes.

At this distance he could just barely make out Mark's silhouette slumped forward and leaning over the steering wheel. Then it hit him. He remembered their fake sleeping-on-mowers routine from the other day and began to laugh. Mark must have seen him coming and decided to do it again.

"You idiot," he laughed shaking his head. He put the plug into the old hole, and pushed the cup and the flag into the new one. On his way back to the cart he looked up at Mark again, he hadn't changed positions. Apparently he was going to string this joke out as long as possible. "Come on, man. Give it up already."

As Ronnie approached the number two green, he leaned back, closed his eyes, and let his mouth hang open. He drove around in a few circles in the fairway doing his own fake sleeping routine. Finally, he looked up laughing and Mark was still slumped forward on the bunker machine.

Oh shit, is he really sleeping? he wondered. He pulled the cart up in front of the green, lighting it up with his headlights, and stepped out facing the bunker. Crossing his arms impatiently over his chest, he waited for Mark to pretend to wake up.

"Hey! Wake up, you moron. Bill's gonna be pissed if he sees you doing that again. Remember how pissed he was on Monday?" The smile slowly melted off Ronnie's face as he stared at Mark going around in circles. "Okay, you got me, man. Enough's enough."

The longer Ronnie looked at Mark the more uncomfortable he felt. Something about how Mark was slumped forward with his face in the steering wheel didn't look right. He looked too limp, his head and shoulders just barely holding on. Another rough gust of wind blew and Mark's arm slid limply off the steering wheel. Dark red streams were dripping down the white underside of his forearm. It dripped off his fingertips and fell to the sand only to get raked over by the machine a second later.

"Mark?" Ronnie stepped forward into the sand. He felt his heartbeat ramp up and his mouth go dry. "Hey, man. You okay?" he called loudly, as if he could somehow wake Mark up if he made his voice as loud as possible. Up close, he noticed more of that dark liquid spilling down the sides of the bunker machine. "Seriously, man. If this is some kind of joke, you got me. Stop foolin' around." He realized that this was no joke.

Don't just stand there like an idiot. Do something. What if he's really hurt?

Swallowing a dry lump in his throat, Ronnie approached the machine, dreading every step. He didn't want to see Mark's face, but he had to. His palms felt slick with sweat as it circled towards him again. Here it came. Ronnie bent his knees, ready to jump.

He took a few steps with it, then jumped aboard on Mark's right side. His shins collided with Mark's and knocked his foot off the accelerator. The bunker machine came to a halt and Mark's body slumped backwards against the seat.

Ronnie looked directly into the staring glazed eyes of his best friend. His throat and chest were a red dark ruin, filled with ragged puncture wounds and sticky, drying blood. Some of that blood smeared on Ronnie's hands as he grabbed the steering wheel and Mark's shoulder. Ronnie let out a scream and fell back off the bunker machine.

"Ohh shit!"

He landed awkwardly on his butt in the sand and instinctively crawled backward from the gory sight in front of him. He felt sick and nearly sobbed as he stared at his dead friend.

"Jesus Christ!" he wheezed. From down on the ground he couldn't see Mark's face, but the stab wounds in his bloody chest and neck were all too visible. *"No, no, no. Oh God, no!"* Ronnie whispered repeatedly. He had to call someone, had to do something.

Bill will know what to do.

Ronnie scrambled to his feet, sand filling his shoes and caking onto his bloody hands, but none of that mattered. All that ran through his mind was that he had to run, had to tell Bill. He took two steps toward the cart, then stopped dead in his tracks.

Standing there in the headlights of the cart was the coyote again. It had a wild, rabid snarl on its face. Its sharp little needle teeth were bared and runners of foamy drool dripped down from its muzzle. Its beady black eyes seemed to squint with malevolence but its pupils glowed reflectively against the headlights, giving it a demonic, possessed look. Ronnie could hear it growling, a low rumbling punctuated every so often with little angry yips that made him flinch.

Don't make any sudden moves. Just get over to the cart and grab the cup cutter.

A crazy question flashed into his mind: *Did that thing kill Mark?* No, it had no blood on its mouth, but maybe it had come out of the woods to start chewing on Mark's body. The image his mind formed of a coyote gnawing on Mark's dead limbs made his stomach lurch. The coyote seemed to sense it and gave another one of those yipping barks.

Ronnie panted. "Easy. Easy there. I'm not gonna hurt you." Ronnie took a few tiny, tentative steps toward the cart, and the coyote advanced a few steps toward him. Ronnie stopped.

It doesn't want Mark at all. It wants me.

Suddenly it sprang forward, snarling and galloping toward him at full speed. Ronnie dove toward the cart, but had no time to grab the cup cutter. He jumped into the driver's seat. The coyote slammed into his left leg, its teeth gnashing and its claws digging at the denim.

Ronnie let out a hoarse scream and frantically batted at it with his hands. Pure panic wouldn't allow him to make a fist. He kicked furiously and felt its teeth pinching at his leg, trying to tear out a chunk of flesh. It reared its head back and clamped down on Ronnie's ankle. He shrieked and kicked it hard with his other foot. The coyote let go and Ronnie didn't hesitate to kick it squarely in the snout with his injured foot. It fell back only a foot or so. Ronnie stomped down on the gas pedal just as it leaped forward for another bite.

The cart surged forward onto the number two green. He quickly thought, *Shit I'm on the green. Can't drive on the green, Bill will be pissed.* The coyote still snapped and snarled as it ran alongside the cart. Ronnie steered with one hand and desperately beat at the coyote's head with his other fist as it nipped at his knuckles.

He drove up over the berms around two green, yanking the wheel back and forth and taking wild turns. He and the coyote separated for only a few brief moments as Ronnie tried to get control of the wheel. Then it came back, trying to jump into the cart and bite at Ronnie's arms and legs. Ronnie leaned to his right, trying to protect his head and face.

Get him against the fence, it'll be too tight between the fence and the left side of the cart for the both of us. He steered the cart toward the upper tee boxes on hole three, coming dangerously close to the wrought iron fence. The coyote came within a few inches of being smashed between the cart and the fence, but it ducked back at the last second. Ronnie glanced back a few times and saw its head and hindquarters bouncing along behind the cart.

Why didn't I take the picker cart like Bill said? Goddammit, why didn't I take it when I had the chance?

Yipping and barking, it chased the cart toward the tight, steep alley between the fence and the retaining wall at the edge of the tee boxes. He was vaguely aware that this was the same path he had taken yesterday when he and Mark chased Joe and Jeff.

They blasted through the alley, the cart's metal bed scraping against the fence with a xylophone ring. Ronnie took a wild right turn at full speed, tires skidding and screeching onto the concrete cart path just below the retaining wall. The coyote tried to cut him off. It jumped off the top of the retaining wall, diving right for Ronnie's head. He looked over at the last second and saw the open mouth filled with gnashing teeth inches away. Ducking down, he flattened his head against the steering wheel. Rough paws scraped against his back as it flew through the air over him. It tumbled and rolled gracelessly as it hit the grass.

Ronnie gunned the cart toward the steep downhill stretch of the cart path. If he could make it to the crest of the hill, he could pull the gearshift into neutral like he'd seen Mark do, and gather more speed. For now, the cart kept a painfully slow pace. The coyote got to its feet and sprinted toward the cart again.

Ronnie steered with his left hand and reached down for the lever, preparing to switch to neutral. Just as he reached the downhill stretch, he felt the governor kick in slowing the cart down. He pulled the gearshift to his left, switching over to neutral with a harsh grinding of gears. The cart's engine went silent and he began to pick up speed.

He sat back up and the coyote dived at him,

clamping its jaws around his forearm. Needle teeth sawed into his bare skin and he screamed. He madly flung his arm back against the metal side of the cart, repeatedly slamming the coyote's wiry body against it. Its scraggly tail caught under the back wheel on the third slam, and with a yelp it let go. It rolled off into the grass whining.

Ronnie looked back, watching it go and feeling the wind blasting against his sweaty hair. He looked down at his arm and saw blood oozing out through the jagged teeth marks. Wincing, he glanced back at the cart path.

A nightmare apparition walked into the glow of the headlights. It came toward the cart with its arms outstretched, ready to grab Ronnie and pull him out of the driver's seat. It was wearing tattered, dirty buckskin clothes like an old Davy Crockett costume that had half rotted away over time. Perched on its head was a tangled headdress of black feathers and a wooden cigar-store chief mask over its face.

"FUCK!" Ronnie screamed and jammed on the brake pedal with both feet. The rear wheels locked up, and he felt the back end of the cart fishtailing off to the right. The cart spun away from the dead man in the cart path. Ronnie felt it tip up on two of its wheels and for a terrifying second, he was convinced that it would flip over. The locked tires dug long twisting grooves in the grass as he spun around three times, came to a standstill, and slammed down again.

The cart was facing off to the left of the cart path now, in the direction of the driving range. Ronnie adjusted his crooked glasses and looked back over his shoulder. Higher up on the path, the dead man was walking toward him. Without the headlights pointing at it, Ronnie could barely see its silhouette in the darkness. It pulled something off its back, some kind of weapon but he couldn't tell what it was from here. With a fresh surge of adrenaline, he stomped down on the accelerator pedal. The engine revved but the cart sat still.

Neutral. It's still in neutral!

"Shhhit, *shit!*" he screamed and groped blindly for the gearshift. Something small and hard knocked into the cart just behind the small of his back. He pulled the gearshift into forward again and stomped down on the pedal. The cart took off and something whistled past his ear. He finally realized the masked psycho was shooting arrows at him. He crouched forward as he drove, not daring to look back. Another one of those sharp arrows slammed into the seat next to him and he could see the stone chiseled arrowhead poking out a fresh hole in the upholstery.

He continued to drive, never letting his foot off the pedal for anything and felt the wind from another four or five sharp arrowheads flying at him. A few of them hit the cart, Ronnie was pretty sure one punctured one of the back tires. Then they slacked off. Ronnie finally dared to sit up straight and look over his shoulder. In the darkness, and with all the bumping and jostling around at full speed, he couldn't make out anything.

Mark! Gotta c-- No, Mark's dead, he suddenly reminded himself. *Bill! Gotta call Bill! Gotta get help!*

The radio was thankfully still hooked to the belt of his jeans. He pulled it off his belt, it still had some sand on it from when he fell into the bunker in front of Mark's corpse. He jammed the talk button down and screamed into it.

"BILL!!!"

*   *   *

Twenty minutes earlier, Bill had gone into the dark pump house with a flashlight and lifted up the hatch cover to look down into the deep pump house well. The water level was still low, about fifteen feet lower than the hatch cover. That smell wafted up from down there again too, just like it had this afternoon, that gassy, dead smell.

He let out an annoyed sigh. "What the fuck?" he said out loud as he shone the flashlight down into the black water, scanning for leaves and debris from the lake outside. Now he could definitely see that something was floating down there, but a thin scum of yellowish foam covered the surface of the water, obscuring his view. "Ugh, please don't tell something got sucked up in the intake screen again."

There was a long eight inch pipe that went down into the low part of the number seven lake outside, sucking in water to feed the deep well at his feet. The water in this well was then sucked up into three huge turbines and supplied the main sprinkler lines throughout the entire golf course. Of course there was a thick screen covering the mouth of that intake pipe, and it was supposed to filter out a lot of the crap, but occasionally something big like a tree branch or a dead animal got caught up in it and would block the water coming into the well. If there wasn't enough water flowing into the pump house, the sprinklers wouldn't have enough pressure to water the grass. It had happened a few times before.

Bill elected to try the lazy solution first: turning the pumps on and off, hoping that the changes in pressure against that intake pipe would dislodge whatever was caught in the screen. If that didn't work, then he was stuck with the hard solution: diving down into the water or taking a row-boat out into the middle of the lake and trying to scrape away whatever was blocking the screen with a long metal pole. Bill did not relish the idea of a boat ride in the moonlight.

While Ronnie was over on the number three green changing the cup, Bill walked out of the pump house, scanning the ground with his flashlight for the first valve box he could find. He finally spotted one near the edge of the seventh fairway, opened it up, and turned on the little bleeder valve. This normally would've immediately started up the sprinklers, but since the pumps were off, it did nothing. Bill left it on so that he would be able to look out of the open pump house door and see that the heads were spraying at full pressure once he fixed the problem.

Back in the pump house, Bill got ready to turn the pumps on again, but stopped himself. He pointed the flashlight at the open hatch around the back side of the pumps again.

"Maybe I oughta find out what's down there, get an idea of what we're dealing with here," he said to himself.

Bill walked out to his parked cart, grabbed a metal rake that was hanging out the back, and took it inside to the open hatch. He took a long look down in the well, bracing himself to descend the metal rungs down into that cavernous concrete pit. A bad feeling was nagging at him. It wasn't the darkness down in the well that bothered him. It was just as dark in the pump house, and also just as dark outside for that matter. It was that smell. Something about it reminded him of the other day when he'd gone into the old abandoned pumping station next to the lake beside the twelfth fairway. When he was lying in bed struggling to fall asleep, he had tossed that little experience back and forth in his mind. *There was something in that pumping station. No there wasn't. Yes there was. Nope. Yes, and now it's down here.* Then he had thought he saw something in here earlier today, something in the back corner--

"Nope, we're not gonna think about that.

M'mm." He shook his head, put the flashlight into the belt loop of his jeans, tucked the rake under his arm, and forced himself to climb down into the well before this jumpy feeling would let him waste any more time.

Bill descended to the lowest rung above the water level. Everything down here echoed maddeningly off the thick concrete walls. At the bottom, he hooked one arm into the rung near his chest for safety, and turned around. Still holding the rake pinned under his elbow, he pulled the flashlight out with his free hand and pointed it out in front of him.

The three massive turbines sat still in the water. He always liked to think that they were what a wood screw would look like to an ant. They were giant metal corkscrews that sucked the water up out of the well and into the main sprinkler line.

Pointing the flashlight down into the water, he could see a dark mass floating next to one of those turbines. Down here the smell was even stronger. There was no question that it was coming from that thing under the water. Bill stared at it for a second, not wanting to touch it with the rake. He had a quick crazy vision of it grabbing the rake and yanking backwards, pulling him down into the water with it.

"I know this week's getting to ya, but come on. Soonest begun soonest done." He took a deep breath, then awkwardly used the hand holding the ladder rung to secure both the flashlight and rake together in his free hand. This way he could see exactly what he was doing. He gave the rake and flashlight combo a little shake to make sure they were as steady as possible, then reached out with them.

The metal teeth slapped into the water, parting the mucky yellow foam. The shape of the thing under the murky water was clearer now, it looked like some kind of knobby tree branch with its bark stripped off. It had one bulbous end that made him think it might even be a full tree stump. He poked and prodded it with the rake's metal teeth, but it didn't feel solid like a tree branch, it felt...squishy.

"Shit, maybe it's some kinda dead animal," he said out loud. He pulled it a little closer and saw that it was covered in some sort of fine black algae that even looked like hair. Maybe it really was hair. He had to flip it over, had to see what was on the underside of it. He sunk the rake down into the water underneath the floating thing, then lifted with all his forearm strength.

A white stump with a ragged, chewed up end lifted out of the water. It looked like an arm severed just above the elbow, but Bill refused to believe that was what it was. Before he could talk himself out of it, Bill flipped the limb over, and the bulbous thing that looked like a stump rolled over too. It bobbed up and down, and the water parted and slicked back that fine black algae that looked like hair. Despite the sick, dreadful feelings rolling in his stomach, Bill leaned out even farther to get a closer look.

Now he knew it definitely wasn't a tree branch. It was a severed head, neck, and arm. Puffed gray facial features were clearly visible, they were pruney and wrinkled like hands in a bathtub. Its eyelids, nostrils, and lips were swollen shut with water. Bill had never seen Mack Rosenberg in his life, but he instantly knew it was him. He knew the police were looking for two missing boys and the dark hair that he'd mistook for algae matched the description the police had given him. The unsettling encounter with Jimmy Bloom's mother this afternoon popped into his head, and he wondered if that boy was floating down here somewhere too.

Everything fell into place at once in his mind, and he began to breathe in shuddery little gasps. This swollen corpse had been what was clogging the intake screen. The pressure from those spinning turbines had probably broken the screen and pulled these chunks through. The rest of the body was probably still out there in the lake. And speaking of still out there, who killed him, and where was he now? What if the killer was here in this pump house?

"BILL?" Ronnie's wavering voice called out. It echoed loudly against the concrete walls of the well, and made Bill cry out. He jumped so hard that he almost dropped both the rake and the flashlight in the water. "Bill, i-is that you?" Finally, he recognized who it was.

"Uh, y-yeah, Ronnie. I'm in here," he yelled back, his voice echoing even louder.

"BILL! Thank God. Thank God!"

Bill shoved the flashlight into this belt loop again so that it shined up toward the open hatch. He tucked the rake under his elbow again and rushed up the ladder rungs, temporarily relieved to have the company. Ronnie appeared at the open hatch, and when Bill saw the pale, terrified look on his face, he felt sick all over again. Even the kid's glasses were crooked on his face, he looked too freaked out to notice. At first, he thought Ronnie had seen the dead body floating in the water down there.

"Don't look at it," Bill said. Ronnie kept frantically glancing back at the pump house door, and didn't respond. As Bill reached the last few rungs of the ladder, Ronnie grabbed him by the arms and pulled him up to the ground level again.

"It's Mark! He's dead! *Dead!*" he yammered in a panicky whisper. "The guy's still out there, he might be following me. We gotta get outta here!"

"Wait, what? What did you just say?" Bill asked. His own voice had a panting, nervous waver that he couldn't control, the sound of it shocked him even more. Bill noticed the blood and bite marks on Ronnie's arms. "What is this? What happened to you?"

"Mark is dead," Ronnie shuddered. "I found him out on two. He's all bloody. That guy in the Indian mask killed him. I know it. He's fucking crazy! He shot at me with arrows. I just barely got away."

With shaking hands Bill unclipped the radio from his front jeans pocket. "Brian, you there? This is an emergency. Call the police."

"I already tried. I tried to get Brian and everyone else on the radios, but no one's answering me. What if he got them? Fuck! He's out there, he's probably headed this way!"

"Brian! Butch! Pete! Zeke! Joe! Jeff! Mark! Anybody!" Bill shouted into the radio.

"They're all dead. Fuck, they're all dead!"

Bill stared intensely at the radio, as if he could make them answer by force of will.

You sent them out there tonight. This is all your fault, he thought.

"Anybody! Answer me goddammit! This is an emergency! Someone please answer for the love of--"

The door to the pump house thunked closed. Ronnie and Bill whirled around. Bill pulled the flashlight out of his belt and shoved past Ronnie to get around the huge pumping machinery. Ronnie went dead silent and shrank back behind Bill. He shined the flashlight at the front door. Holding up the rake protectively, Bill crept forward, pointing the flashlight frantically at every square inch of the pump house. He wished he had a gun or a knife or anything better than a fucking rake. Ronnie peered over his shoulder with his hands cupped over his mouth.

"Who's in here?" Bill shouted. His voice was loud and commanding but his knees were shaking. With every dark spot the flashlight illuminated, he thought he'd see some crazy man covered in blood. *"Whoever*

the fuck is in here better come out right now."

Every corner between the old boxes and around the big pumping machinery was empty. They waited in silence for a second, Bill forced himself to stop breathing so he could hear any tiny sound. Despite the pounding in his heart, he heard nothing; no shuffling around, no footsteps besides his and Ronnie's, no other breathing. It was just them. Bill dared to consider the possibility that there was no one else in here besides Ronnie, that maybe the wind outside had pulled the door closed.

"Maybe the door just closed on its own," Bill suggested in a low voice.

He heard Ronnie bump into a piece of machinery, it gave a metallic clank. Bill turned the flashlight on Ronnie to see what he was doing. Ronnie was standing still behind him, but behind Ronnie a ragged, western scarecrow with a black feathered headdress and grim-faced wooden mask rose slowly up out of the shadows. It raised a blood-spattered tomahawk in both hands high over Ronnie's head.

Bill let out a guttural scream and stepped back. Ronnie whirled around at the shocked look on Bill's face and stepped aside just before the sharp end of the tomahawk came slamming down onto the curve of one of the thick metal pipes with a loud clang.

Ronnie crowded into Bill, screaming and trying to squeeze around him. Bill was also screaming, swinging the rake down onto the ragged masked man repeatedly like some mad farmer. He knocked the dead chief down and pinned it to the floor with the rake. It thrashed and uttered guttural hissing noises like a wild animal. Bill could barely keep it held down.

"Ronnie! GO! Get help!"

"BILL!" Ronnie shrieked. He had already yanked open the doorway to the pump house, and stood staring back.

"GO!"

The chief lashed out with the tomahawk, its sharp stone edge sunk into his Bill's shin and chipped the bone. He howled. With its other bony arm, it knocked the rake away. It stood up as Bill collapsed to a kneel clutching his bleeding leg. The flashlight fell out of his hand and bounced against the concrete floor at their feet.

The chief shot a knobby hand forward and grabbed Bill by the collar. It yanked him off the floor and he felt the toes of his work boots dragging against the concrete behind him. In the dim light, he stared straight into the dead, wooden face of what had once been their cigar store statue outside the pro shop. The chief dragged Bill backwards, then suddenly threw him to the side. Bill thought he was being thrown down against the concrete floor, but to his surprise he plummeted down into the open well.

First his screams, then the splash echoed off the walls. The well was twenty-five feet deep, and even though the water level was low, Bill was completely submerged. Ice cold water shocked his face and arms, then the rest of his body felt the cold sting as it soaked through his clothes. Bill kicked madly for the surface, feeling the weight of his heavy work boots pulling him down. He came up gasping for breath and the gassy, dead smell rose in thick, nauseating waves. Oily body parts bobbed in the water around him. He looked up into the open hatch, it was now his only source of light.

Up above, the chief stormed toward the exit door, but stopped when he noticed the electric safety switch mounted on the wall. Earlier today, as he had been creeping behind the boxes in the shadows, he had watched Bill operate this. It looked simple enough. Pulling up on the lever would turn on the machinery, and pushing it down would turn it off. The chief wrapped its thin fingers around the switch and in one quick movement yanked it upwards.

Sure enough the electric whine started up and the turbines began to spin. Bill was pummeled with greasy body parts that got sucked through the broken intake screen, then the water level began to rise. He felt himself being sucked toward them, his heavy work boots leading the way.

"NO!" He coughed out water and paddled to the ladder rungs on the side wall, grabbing onto them just before the turbines got gong too fast. He held on for dear life and let out an agonized wail as it pulled him nearly horizontal with hurricane force. In his darkest daydreams he had imagined being in a situation like this, but he couldn't believe it was now happening in real life. The turbine began to beat at his legs and he shrieked in terror. He looked up and saw the silhouette of the chief in his wild black-feathered headdress staring down from the open hatch. It was the last thing he saw before the turbines began to chop him up. He screamed one last time as his wet fingers slipped off the metal rung.

*   *   *

Panting, Ronnie ran out to his golf cart, threw the gearshift into reverse, and floored it. He heard the pumps winding up but that didn't matter. The only thing that mattered was getting away from here, getting away from that murderous freak in the wooden mask. The cart bounced over the dam between the lake on hole seven and the little waterfall that fed the lower lake on hole ten. He yanked the wheel to the left, tapped on his brakes in the long grass, then threw it into forward drive before the cart even came close to a full stop. The gears crunched loudly as he floored it again.

Ronnie tore out onto the seventh fairway, glancing over his shoulder every other second. His eyes kept returning to the pump house to see if the masked man was chasing him, but he only saw blackness. The dead thing had chased him here, it would follow him wherever he went.

Then the sprinkler heads on the fairway spurted to life, spraying out water in powerful seventy-five foot streams that rained down on him. He swerved, dodging the streams as they popped up all around him. Thunder roared and lightning flashed, and in that blinding instant, he could see that the water streaming from those sprinkler heads wasn't white, it was red. Ronnie let out a fresh scream of horror and swerved to avoid those streams as he realized that Bill's blood was watering the seventh fairway.

Ronnie took off his glasses and wiped away the thin red drops of blood. He hurriedly put them back on, not wanting to take his eyes off the road for too long. The lenses were still smeared with red. As soon as his eyes focused, he saw that he was heading straight for a big rock at the edge of the grass near the drop-off circle.

"Shit!" he cried, and yanked the wheel hard to the right to avoid hitting it. The cup cutting tools rolled violently in the back and flipped out over the edge. They clattered to the concrete and rolled onto the grass near the big practice putting green. The cart's wheels missed the big rock by only a few inches. Ronnie remembered the day earlier this spring when Bill had put that rock there. It was meant to keep golfers from cutting across that little corner of sod in their golf carts and turning it into a muddy mess.

The memory of Bill brought it all crashing down on him. Bill was gone now, the killer got him.

That idea filled him with as much panic as it did sadness. Mark was dead too, and the others were probably dead. He was all alone. It was all up to him to survive now, to either call for help or to run home.

Me? Why me? I don't know what to do.

In the past, he'd always had Bill, Mark, or someone else to tell him what to do. He had always been Mark's "sidekick," as Butch and Pete were so fond of saying. Now he was thrust violently into figuring out this mess on his own. His brain felt too slow, too filled with terrible images of the dead for him to think clearly.

I just want to go home. That's all. I just want to go home and figure this out from behind the safety of my own locked front door. It was a childish thought, but it seemed like the only safe option at this point.

Then what though? What if he follows you home? He imagined that cracked wooden face peering in through the downstairs windows, searching for him, rearing back with that tomahawk to smash through the glass. His dad would know what to do though. It would be out of his hands again.

All of this flashed through Ronnie's mind as he tore across the parking lot, glancing back over his shoulder every few feet. He barely noticed as the first fat raindrops began to fall, and in his panic, he didn't notice Tanya's parked car at all. He was only dimly aware of the throbbing, bleeding coyote bites on his left arm. If asked later whether he could remember anything between the seventh fairway and the empty spot in the parking lot where his car had been, he would've drawn a total blank.

The cart began to sputter and stall out as he neared his parking spot, its headlights began to dim.

"Come on, come on," Ronnie urged.

As if in protest, it flat out died.

He hopped out and examined it. One of the

back tires was flat, he remembered the chief's arrow puncturing it. There was another arrow sticking out of the side of the cart, and he could smell the gasoline that was seeping out through the hole. This cart was done for, but at least he had the good luck to make it most of the way to the shop before it died.

Ronnie looked around, wondering why the parking lot was so dark. He tried to look up at the dark streetlights but raindrops just fell onto his glasses. He wiped them away with the bottom of his shirt.

He did something to the lights, it had to have been him. Whatever. Just get the hell out of here before he comes after you.

Ronnie scanned the dark parking lot for his old Mercury. There was Butch's old Ford truck, Pete's old Ford truck, Zeke's El Camino, and Joe and Jeff's clunkers (Brian and Bill usually parked closer to the shop). His Mercury was nowhere in sight, and Mark's Chevy van was gone too. He scanned all the cars again, then spun in a full circle to see the whole lot. For a brief second, he spotted Tanya's car at the far end of the lot near the restaurant, but didn't recognize who it belonged to.

"Wh--" he trailed off in confusion and frustration. "I coulda sworn--" He couldn't believe what he was seeing. "Where the fuck is my car?!"

This is not possible, he thought. *My keys--* He looked down at the power switch on the dead cart, saw the spare key, and remembered that someone else— probably Joe or Jeff—had driven off with his car keys earlier. They could be anywhere now.

"Oh no," he exhaled. He felt his shoulders sink in disappointment, then the fear and frustration surged again. "This is not happening. *This is not fucking happening!"*

He walked into his empty parking spot, looking forlornly in the windows of the locked parked trucks on either side. Of course there were no keys in either of them.

Could another golf cart make it all the way back to town? Will I even be safe in a golf cart? What about the rainstorm moving in? What if the cart runs out of gas and that guy comes after me on that farm land? What if--

Ronnie's ears picked up on something, a slow, steady beat, rhythmic and almost hypnotic, almost as if it were slow native drums played by a ghost tribe. The sound was coming from the maintenance shop. Ronnie backed away a step, thinking for a second that the killer was in the shop trying to beckon him in with those drums. That was impossible though, the killer was back at the pump house.

Boom. Boom boom. Boom. Boom boom.

"What the hell is that?"

Abandoning the dead cart, he slowly began making his way toward the shop, crossing over the parking lot median and the entrance driveway. As he came around the fence that shielded the maintenance dumpster from the parking lot, the drums became louder and clearer. They weren't native drums, they were a slow rock beat, and laid over them were a couple of twangy guitars and wailing harmonicas. He glanced back one more time before the dumpster fence shielded him from sight. The killer was nowhere to be seen.

Ronnie focused in on the music and started to feel a little hopeful. Maybe Brian had it playing loud and didn't hear Bill when he called over the radio, or maybe he'd had one of his tools running and hadn't been able to hear it. *Maybe he's still alive.*

"Brian!" he called out, and picked up his pace. "Brian! You there?"

The rain began to pour down as he ran toward the open garage bay door. When his eyes caught the puddle of blood running into the drain at the foot of the doorway, he slowed his steps.

Oh fuck, no. He's been here. "Brian?"

The smell of blood and exhaust became stronger as he approached the shop. He recognized the song as he came within earshot, it was "When the Levee Breaks," the last track on Led Zeppelin's fabled *IV* album. He knew that Brian was about twelve years older than he and Mark, and sometimes he liked to break away from the country music and listen to rock albums from his high school and college days, most commonly stuff from Led Zeppelin and Black Sabbath.

The lights in the shop were dim and slowly flickering. At first Ronnie thought they were somehow linked with the pounding drum beat of the song, but then they surged bright and flickered in a few of the offbeats. In that weird light and strange pounding music, this place felt less like a maintenance shop and more like some sort of modern day version of a medieval torture chamber.

Ronnie came to a stop just outside the garage bay door and caught only a glimpse of the tee mower that was up on the hydraulic lift. It had been raised up again, its tires level with Ronnie's head. All three of its blade reels were lethargically dripping with blood. Something big had been caught up in them, meaty lumps hung from the underside of the mower, dripping blood into the red river that flowed down to the drain in front of his feet.

He involuntarily gave a sharp gasp and turned away, his stomach rolling. *I don't want to look at that. Nope, I don't want to see it, whatever it is.* Another crack of thunder shook the sky. In a flash of lightning Ronnie saw that down near his feet, faint red footprints made by moccasins were washing away in the rain.

Gotta go into the office and call the police! Gotta get help, then find some place to hide until this is all over.

251

With a deep shuddering breath, Ronnie walked into the shop, keeping his eyes focused on the floor. He jumped over the wide river of blood and landed safely on the concrete on the other side. Now that he was facing the office door, he allowed himself to look up again.

The lights were fading in and out in here too. Ronnie rushed past the time clock and went straight to Bill's desk. He suspected that the old rotary phone in the corner of the desk might be smashed. For a second, he saw it in pieces, then he blinked and saw the truth. The phone still sat there, it hadn't been destroyed by the killer after all.

"Thank God." He picked it up and with shaking, nervous fingers dialed 911. Pressing the receiver against his ear, he listened for the ringing tone on the other end. It never came. Ronnie jiggled the cradle, expecting a dial tone, but the phone remained dead silent. "Come on, Goddammit!" he whispered impatiently, trying the cradle again. It was no use. He slammed the phone back down on the cradle. "Fuck!"

Cut off. I'm fucking cut off out here.

He looked around on the desk desperately trying to think. There were the keys of the picker cart on their plastic golf ball key chain. Bill had offered to let Ronnie take that caged cart less than an hour ago, and he had left the keys lying on the desk. Ronnie almost dismissed them as unimportant, then turned back.

Wait a minute, if I take the picker cart I'll be safe...I hope. And there's another phone up at the clubhouse, maybe that one will work. Now that he thought of the clubhouse, he remembered who owned that car sitting on the other end of the lot. *Wendy and Tanya. That's Tanya's car.* Mark had always pointed it out whenever they rode by, and gotten all excited to see her. *Those girls must be up there too, maybe they're still alive. What if he stops to get them first before he comes*

252

back down here looking for me?

Ronnie felt sick as he imagined Wendy vacuuming the floors, totally unaware of the masked murderer creeping up behind her. He left Mark out there, he left Bill, and he had left all the others. He couldn't just leave anyone else like that, especially not Wendy and Tanya.

Maybe I can save them. Maybe for once in my life I can be the hero instead of just the sidekick.

He snatched the key with the golf ball key chain off the desk and turned to make a run for the picker cart.

Two steps outside the office door, he stopped dead in his tracks. The killer was standing outside the garage door in the rain, holding his tomahawk reared back over his shoulder. Ronnie uttered a startled scream. The chief hurled the tomahawk and it spun through the air toward him.

Ronnie dropped the picker cart keys and ducked, raising his arms to shield his head. He tried to spin out of the way, but his shoes slid in the blood on the floor. The tomahawk missed him by inches, slamming into one of the speakers on Brian's portable tape player. The music cut off and the tape player fell back onto the concrete, sizzling and sparking around the stone blade.

Ronnie bumped into the tee mower's reels. The red mangled ruin of Brian's body dislodged and rolled out. His legs stayed caught in the back reels but everything from the waist down hung there swinging back and forth like a pendulum. Ronnie screamed again and jumped back out of the way, trying to avoid being touched by the bloody corpse. His feet slipped in the blood again and he fell backwards. With a sickening splatter, he landed hard on his butt.

The chief started forward. He reached back over his head, grabbed the bottom edge of the garage door, and yanked it downward. It rolled with a loud clatter and slammed down hard enough to shatter its narrow windows.

Ronnie felt rough hands sink into the wet ropes of his hair and yank him up off the floor. He screamed in equal amounts of pain and fear as the hands pulled his head back painfully to stare up into the wooden mask. It lowered its head toward him and he could smell the stink of rot and decay wafting out from behind the mask.

"Where is Hamilton?" it asked in a low gravelly whisper.

Ronnie couldn't believe what he was hearing. He was so stunned that he couldn't even comprehend what he was being asked.

"Hamilton! Where is Hamilton?" it repeated angrily.

The nightmarish truth suddenly came crashing down on Ronnie. This wasn't just some random psycho killer, this emaciated skeletal thing in the tattered buckskin clothes was Chief Tomahawk from Zeke's story. It was all true. All the rumors of the dead Chief coming back to life at night, the legends that said he was a...whatever the word was that Zeke used, all of it was real. Ronnie was looking up at an animated corpse.

"I-I--" Ronnie stammered. There was really only one place he could possibly imagine where Mr. Hamilton might be at this moment. It was almost four in the morning, he was most likely home in bed. "He-h-he's at home."

"Where?!"

"I-I...I don't know where he lives. He's just home, that's all I know. All I know, I swear."

The dead thing dragged Ronnie toward the tool bench. Ronnie screamed in protest. He reached out desperately to grab onto something, anything that he could use as a weapon. His fingers brushed past the grinder that was mounted on the corner of the tool bench and flicked the switch. The gritty disc started spinning, but with the sporadic power, it only ran in short little spurts. It was still spinning fast enough to cause serious damage. The chief stopped in his tracks and watched the spinning wheel for a moment, then began pushing Ronnie's face toward it.

"No! No!" Ronnie shrieked. His open mouth was pushed closer and closer to the spinning wheel. That thing would grind his teeth down into dust, then pull the skin of his lips into its narrow metal cover plate and shred what was left of his face.

Ronnie beat back at the chief madly with his fists. He tried to kick back at the chief's legs, but his tennis shoes only slid in the blood on the smooth concrete floor. None of his struggling kicks or punches did any good, his angle was too awkward.

His eyes rolled wildly, searching for any kind of weapon to use against the killer. The only thing within arm's reach was the propane torch that Joe and Jeff had used yesterday to melt that golf ball. Ronnie reached out with his right hand, groping for it. Brushing it with his fingertips, he made it roll a few inches closer to the end of the tool bench. He seized it.

The dead thing still held Ronnie's hair tight in its right hand. When it saw what Ronnie was doing, it reached over with its left hand to try and bat the torch away. Ronnie was too quick though. He re-positioned the torch and jammed his finger down on the ignition switch. A jet of blue flame hissed out against the dead thing's left hand, singing it. It yanked its hand back, apparently sensitive to the flame.

Ronnie brandished the torch over his head, waving the blue flame dangerously close to the black feathers of the chief's headdress. The chief rolled to the right to avoid the flame. It didn't fully let go of Ronnie's hair, but it gave his head enough slack that he could move away from the grinding wheel.

Now the chief's right forearm was in front of the spinning wheel. With a hard cry of effort, Ronnie shoved himself forward like a bull to escape the bony grip. The chief's arm caught against the gritty grinding wheel. It ground down part of the bone, causing him to let go of Ronnie's hair. The rough wheel bit into the bone and it sucked the chief's hand into the metal safety cover.

As the bones in the chief's hand began to grind into dust, it hissed and uttered a weird throaty, growling scream. It bucked, trying to yank the hand out.

Ronnie stumbled forward, sliding through the blood again. He absentmindedly ran his tongue over his teeth, thanking God that they were still intact. As he scrambled away from the chief, he dared to take only one look back. At the moment it seemed to be trapped in the grinding wheel, and panicking too much to simply flick off the switch. Ronnie didn't stop to watch. He snatched up the picker cart keys out of the blood puddle and ran out the door.

Bursting out into the rainy night, Ronnie sprinted for the parked picker cart across the yard. He practically slammed against the metal mesh sides when he reached it, and struggled with the temperamental door handle. Finally, it opened and Ronnie dove in, shoving the key into the power switch with shaking hands. He threw the gearshift into reverse, slammed on the gas pedal, and looked back to see if the chief was coming after him. For the moment, he was still alone in the yard.

The engine struggled. *"Go, go. Don't do this to me!"* He tapped the gas pedal, gripping the steering wheel with white knuckles. Finally the engine caught and Ronnie surged backwards. He yanked the wheel hard to the left, puddles of rainwater on the cart's roof slid off and splashed to the concrete. Then with a grinding of gears he shifted back to forward and sped off toward the clubhouse.

Dots of rainwater obscured the Plexiglass windshield and he could barely see. All Ronnie cared about was getting as far away as possible from the chief.

My God, he thought, his mind still reeling. *It was Chief Tomahawk, Zeke's stories were true. He must think we're all the white settlers from back in the old days, the ones that massacred all his people, or maybe their descendants. It's not possible, it's totally insane, but I saw it with my own eyes. I heard that cracked voice asking for Mr. Hamilton. I saw his rotting skeleton body up close.*

He desperately wished Zeke were here now. The old man was probably dead on his mower out there, the chief probably got him. Zeke would've known what to do, would've helped figure out a way to survive against the chief.

"God, what do I do? What do I do?" he asked out loud.

Had Ronnie still been outside the shop, he might have heard the sound of the grinder turn off, and then the low chant of an incantation in the old Kikawa language, the words of Chief Tomahawk's slaughtered people.

Wendy awoke with a jolt, she thought she'd heard someone scream her name from somewhere in another room. For a moment, she had no idea where she was. Blinking, she stared at the tight space around her, she was surrounded by shelves stocked with snacks and spare kitchen supplies. Adding to her disorientation, the light bulb above her was flickering in and out in random patterns. She could've sworn she felt something move underneath the floor where she sat, but that might only have been one last lingering piece of whatever dream she'd been having.

She slowly unfolded her memories from a few hours ago. She was at work cleaning up the shelves that had fallen down in the pantry. Tanya was here too and she was being a total bitch. A headache had been throbbing in her forehead, and when she reached a decent stopping point, she had taken a break to try to cure it. With her knees up and arms folded over them, she rested her forehead and closed her eyes, enjoying the calm, soothing darkness.

"Shit, what time is it?" she asked aloud. She rubbed her eyes and brushed her dark hair back behind her ears with her fingertips. Her butt felt numb from sitting on the flat kitchen tiles for so long, and her arms had fallen asleep and were now tingling. Her neck also felt sore from the awkward way she'd been sleeping sitting up.

Tanya's gonna be pissed at me, she thought. *I can just hear her now, 'What the fuck have you been doing in there? Taking a nap? I've had to clean this whole fuckin' pro shop all by myself.' Ugh, better get ready, prepare yourself for yet another bitch-fit.*

Wendy struggled to her feet, bending her head back to stretch her neck. Looking up, she caught sight of the flickering light bulb mounted high up on the wall and thought the bulb might not be tight in its socket. She reached up and tried to screw it back in with her fingertips, but to her surprise it was still tight. She pulled the long string that connected to the chain switch on the side of the fixture, and it went out. With another pull, it came back on still just as flickery as it had been before.

"Oh terrific, one more problem," she muttered. "This whole place is falling apart."

She opened the pantry door and was surprised to see and hear rain hammering against the windows. Thunder rumbled outside and she saw a brief flash of lightning.

"When did that start?"

Then she noticed that the dim lights hanging above the curved bar were flickering in the same way as the one in the pantry. Looking across the entire restaurant, she saw that all the lights were like that: the elk horn chandeliers above the dining room, the native-patterned wall sconces, the lights in the hallway outside

259

the restaurant, and even the little spotlights in the trophy case across the hall.

Under her feet she felt another slithering vibration, just like the one she had felt in the pantry. She took an awkward step back and heard a gritty scratching sound under the floor tiles. This was louder than before, there was no dismissing it as just a dream this time. She could even hear whatever was down under the floor scraping against the drain pipes that were under the sinks. A low subterranean echo floated its way through the pipes and up to her ears.

Her heartbeat began to pound in her ears, and her wide, staring eyes locked onto the floor tiles where she heard the noises. As much as she didn't want to believe it, there was something burrowing through the dirt under the clubhouse. She had a sudden irrational feeling that whatever it was knew that she and Tanya were here alone after hours, and it wanted them.

Thunder cracked loudly outside and broke her paralysis. She ran through the little aisle behind the bar and turned left past the coffee makers. She spun in a circle, cautiously watching the floor of the empty restaurant. All she wanted to do was grab Tanya and convince her that it was time to get the hell out of this creepy old clubhouse. To hell with cleaning. She bolted through the restaurant doorway toward the pro shop.

A sopping wet man spun around right in her path and they both screamed. Ronnie hadn't been expecting to see her. His black hair hung in wet ropes, clinging to his forehead, and his glasses were spotted with rainwater. He looked deathly pale and his eyes were wide. Luckily for him, the pouring rain had washed most of the blood off his clothes, shoes, and arms, otherwise the sight of him would've sent her running.

When he first came in through the back doors a

few moments ago, he had called both Wendy's and Tanya's names and got no answer. He had quickly locked the glass doors behind him and went straight to the pro shop to try the phone. Tanya's stiffening corpse had been there to greet him, and he figured that Wendy was dead too. The phone in the pro shop was dead just like the one down at the shop.

"Ronnie! You scared the shit out of me," she wheezed. She clutched her heart, relief flooding through her.

"Wendy," he gasped.

"Hey!" she cried, tensing her shoulders as he enveloped her in a hug with his cold, wet arms.

"Thank God! I thought you were dead. Thank God."

"Hey, what are you—Stop it. You're getting me all wet."

He let go. "Sorry. Where's your phone?"

"Back there next to the cash register, why?" Without another word, he grabbed her hand and pulled her back toward the kitchen. He stared out the windows, watching for any movement outside. "Ronnie, what are you doing? What's going on?"

The paranoid, frantic way he was acting brought the fear creeping back into her mind. Ronnie ignored her, going around the bar and straight to the phone. She stopped in front of the bar, not wanting to go back there again, and let her hand slip out of his. Her eyes flicked to that spot near the pantry and she wondered if Ronnie would hear whatever was crawling under the floor.

Ronnie dialed 911, and listened for a ring tone. Again, he jiggled the phone cradle and got nothing.

"Son of a bitch." He slammed the phone back down hard enough to make it ding once.

"Ronnie, stop it. You're scaring me. What the hell's going on? You look like you've seen a ghost."

261

Ronnie looked back at her with wide eyes. He couldn't find the words to tell her what happened, it would sound too crazy. All he could do was shake his head. The expression on his face confirmed that he had indeed seen a ghost.

Suddenly she remembered her sister. "Tanya," she cried. "Where's Tanya?" Ronnie swallowed a dry lump in his throat at the mention of Tanya's name, and he looked even more sick and afraid than before. A cold worm of dread drilled into her heart like an ice pick. "No." She turned to run toward the pro shop.

"Wendy, wait! Don't!"

Ronnie ran around the counter and grabbed her arms before she could reach the hallway. She struggled against him.

"Don't. Don't look at her. You don't want to see it. Trust me."

The color drained out of Wendy's face. "No, this...this is a joke, right? Just another one of Mark's sick jokes."

Ronnie shook his head gravely.

"Mark's gone. Bill's gone. Everyone's gone. It's just you and me. We're the only ones left."

"No, I don't believe you," Wendy moaned. Her face scrunched up as she looked in the direction of the pro shop. Ronnie spoke to her in a frantic whisper, trying to explain the dire situation they were in. She barely heard him, all her thoughts were focused on her sister.

"It's true. He got everyone else. I barely got away from him. I locked all the doors. Maybe we'll be safe if we just stay here and hide. Maybe we'll--"

Then Ronnie felt it, that weird slithering deep in the ground under the floor tiles. This time it was all around them, all over the kitchen, and under the carpet in the dining room. It sounded as if hundreds of living things were squirming around under the floor, struggling to claw their way to freedom.

Ronnie let go of Wendy and hopped up on a chair the same way he would have done if the floor had been covered with snakes. Wendy turned and sprinted for the pro shop, screaming her sister's name.

"Wendy! Wait!" Ronnie cried out. He jumped off the chair and chased her down the hall. Running with the shifting dirt under the floor and the lights flickering in and out made Ronnie feel like he was in some kind of haunted funhouse. Knowing that they were running toward Tanya's body sprawled across the pro shop counter made it even worse, it made him feel like he was going to throw up.

Just before Wendy rounded the corner, Chief Tomahawk came sprinting out of thick sheets of rain. He slammed against the glass doors and shook the handles violently. Ronnie thanked God he'd had the foresight to lock them when he stepped in here a few minutes ago.

Wendy shrieked and fell back onto the floor. The memory of the other day when she stood just outside these doors looking at the Chief standing across the lake came flooding back. She could feel the wormy vibrations under the tiles. Ronnie slid to a stop and helped pull her up by the shoulders.

"Oh fuck! Oh fuck!" Ronnie screamed at the sight of the chief. He could see the parked picker cart out there where he had left it. It was so close, yet impossible to reach. The chief glared in at Ronnie for a moment, then reared back and slammed his tomahawk against the glass. A spiderweb of cracks the size of a basketball spread outwards with a crunch.

"Come on! The other doors!" Ronnie dragged Wendy to her feet and they sprinted down the long hallway for the front doors.

The chief reared back and slammed the heavy

stone wedge into the glass again. The cracked area doubled in size, and one stone corner poked in. Ronnie heard a third and fourth crunch against the glass and a few shards tinkling and pattering as they fell to the floor mat.

Lightning flashed, revealing what was waiting for them at the front doors, and they skidded to a stop. Dozens of dead people stood shoulder to shoulder at the glass front doors and the long row of windows that looked out onto the patio. They mindlessly slapped their wet, muddy hands against the glass, clawing to get in. Behind them, more corpses were pulling themselves up out of the ground through the dirt in the flower beds that surrounded the clubhouse, the pouring rain washed chunks of mud off their gray skin. They wore frilled buckskin clothes and loin cloths. Most of their scalps were gone, leaving exposed yellowish-white skulls around sagging gray flaps of skin.

Ronnie remembered the most grisly part of Zeke's story. After the massacre up on Indian Hill, Hamilton and a few other white farmers had buried all the dead Kikawas in a mass grave somewhere down the hill. Now he knew that the mass grave was right where the clubhouse stood today. All the victims of the first Indian Hill massacre were closing in around the clubhouse for their revenge.

Ronnie and Wendy stood there clutching each other and helplessly shrieking. They both looked back and forth between the undead horde at the front doors, and the masked killer chopping his way through the back.

A large shard of glass punched out with the chief's next vicious chop. It hit the floor and shattered against the tiles. The chief punched and kicked out more chunks of broken glass, making himself a jagged opening. As he stepped into the clubhouse, his moccasins crunched on the shattered glass. Ronnie grabbed Wendy's arm and yanked her back into the restaurant.

"Come on!" Ronnie dragged her sobbing into the restaurant, frantically looking for a place to hide. Behind them they heard the thudding footsteps coming down the hallway toward the restaurant.

Wendy pulled Ronnie toward the kitchen. *"This way!"*

She led him through the narrow food prep aisle between the counters and the ovens. There was a side door exit at the opposite end of the kitchen that would lead back out into the hallway near the bathrooms and the broken back doors. They heard the chief wildly lash out with the tomahawk and smash the glass of the trophy case on the wall as he came toward the restaurant.

They glanced back briefly, but continued to the side door. Wendy pushed the door open, but Ronnie held her back, scanning the kitchen for something.

"What are you doing?" Wendy screamed.

"There they are," he said aloud. All the knife racks were on the side of the wall near the ovens. Ronnie dashed back and grabbed the meat cleaver off the rack, it slid out with a sharp metal rasp. He gripped the handle tight in his hands, hearing the chief thumping through the restaurant towards them, knocking over one of the chairs at the tall tables near the bar.

"He's coming! Hurry up!" Wendy screamed.

They pushed out into the hallway again right in front of the men's room door.

"This way. I parked the picker cart just outs--"

"What is the meaning of this?!" a stern voice boomed out.

Ronnie and Wendy spun around. Mr. Hamilton was standing at the front doors looking clean-cut as always. He held his keys in one hand, and a dripping umbrella in the other. All the dead bodies that had been clawing at the glass doors only a minute ago had vanished, the rain was already washing their muddy hand prints away. They couldn't feel those wriggling, squirming vibrations through the floor anymore either.

Ronnie and Wendy glanced at each other dumbfounded.

"Look at this mess!" Mr. Hamilton shouted. *"What in God's name do you two think you're doing?"* He was shaking with fury.

"Mr. Hamilton, get out of here!"

"Run!" Wendy screamed at him. He continued to shout over them.

"We're hosting the biggest tournament of the year in less than three hours! Do you have any idea how important that is? And just look at this place! Look!" Mr. Hamilton was practically screaming now. As he ranted, he stormed over to the trophy case with his hands out, gesturing at all the broken glass. He noticed that his great-grandfather's old musket with the bayonet was missing.

"Ronnie," Wendy called to him in a pleading voice. She was eyeing the kitchen door warily and backing toward the shattered back door.

"Go. I parked the picker cart right out there," Ronnie told her quietly but urgently. They began to crawl through the jagged opening in the broken glass door.

"Where do you-- *Hey! Get back here right now!"* Mr. Hamilton called out.

"Run, Mr. Hamilton! He'll kill you too!" Ronnie screamed. He slipped out through the hole in the broken glass door after Wendy without taking another look back.

"What are you talking about? *Wait!"* Mr. Hamilton called out, but Ronnie had already run out into the rain. He was so furious at seeing his clubhouse in such shambles that he couldn't see straight. He wasn't prepared to listen to a word the kids said, but something in Ronnie's last words had broken through the veil of rage. *He'll kill you too.* Who? Was someone else in here?

Before Hamilton could even turn and take a look around, he heard a low whisper coming from the restaurant. At first it sounded like a hiss of air, then it formed words, impossibly close to his ear.

"Hhhhhhhamilton."

He turned and faced the doorway into the restaurant. Out of the darkness the cracked wooden face of the old cigar store statue stepped forward, and something long and sharp stabbed through his clean sweater-vest and into his abdomen. Hamilton grunted and his hands flew up to pull the object out. It was the bayonet end of his great-grandfather's musket, the one that he had supposedly used to stab Chief Tomahawk and save Elias Hart's life so long ago.

The chief pushed him backward and lifted him up with the bayonet. Hamilton felt his body rising off the floor as the old metal tore through his insides. His expensive polished golf shoes barely brushed the tiles. He gripped the musket's barrel uselessly and uttered a painful scream.

He looked down into the grim mask of Chief Tomahawk and couldn't believe what he was seeing. All the stories he had been told as a boy came rushing back. He remembered one still night as a small boy before they moved out of the old farm house and into town. While he was trying to sleep, he had thought he heard a low, gravelly voice up on that hill calling his name. How that had terrified him. Now he knew this was the owner of that voice.

The chief slammed him backward into the

smashed trophy case, shards of glass ripping open his sleeves and the skin on his arms. The bayonet pinned him into the wooden back wall and several of the tall golf tournament trophies jammed into his back. Hamilton felt blood rising up into his throat like a flood of saliva. It began to drip out of his mouth. He leaned forward, automatically mindful not to get any on his clothes even in this desperate situation. Something in the twisting bayonet had hit a nerve in his spine and he jerked with pain.

The chief grabbed hold of Hamilton's tight curly Afro and pulled his head up to look him directly in the face. Hamilton tried to call out for his father to save him, but his father had been dead for thirteen years. Blood choked up in his throat as the chief brought the tomahawk down, chopping into his scalp.

Time was running short. Ronnie knew that if they didn't get away from this place as fast as they could, Chief Tomahawk would come running out of those broken back doors again. They could still hear Mr. Hamilton's screams echoing out of the clubhouse as they reached the picker cart.

Wendy got there first and yanked at the door handle, sobbing with frustration.

"It won't open!" she screamed.

Ronnie dropped the meat cleaver to the asphalt where it splashed in a puddle. He grabbed the handle and pulled on it with her. He knew that the trick was to lift up on the handle, at least that's what Mark had always told him. With a grunt of effort, they finally managed to make something snap inside and the metal mesh door flew open, banging against the side with a metallic rattle.

"Go! Get in!" Ronnie yelled. Wendy dove in while Ronnie bent to pick up the meat cleaver. He

hopped in after her, slammed the door closed, and handed her the cleaver. "Here hold this for me."

Now he struggled to pull the key out of his jeans pocket, his wet knuckles bunched up against the denim. He had taken the cart keys out of his pocket earlier before he went inside, just in case the chief tried to sabotage the cart. He got a hold of the key, fumbled to put it in the power switch, turned it on, and floored the accelerator.

The cart's engine began to crank lazily but it continued to sit still. Ronnie tapped the pedal with his foot and pulled the little choke lever near the gearshift.

"Comeoncomeoncomeon," he chanted.

Wendy looked back and watched the glass doors through the metal mesh.

Finally, the engine coughed and began to turn over reluctantly.

"MOVE!" Ronnie screamed, pounding on the steering wheel with the heels of his hands. Ronnie stomped down on the pedal and the cart sluggishly rolled forward, it was older and slower than the other maintenance carts.

Driving full speed around the side of the clubhouse, he wiped the rain droplets off his glasses with his bare hand. Even with his glasses somewhat clear, he could hardly see a thing past the sheets of rainwater rolling down over the windshield. Ronnie wished desperately that this thing had some windshield wipers.

"Where are we going?" Wendy asked.

"Anywhere but here," Ronnie answered without taking his eyes off the road in front of him. Suddenly, he had an idea. "You don't have Tanya's car keys, do you?"

"No, they're back inside with Tanya."

"Shit."

Just from the mention of her sister's name, Wendy thought about how she was abandoning her, and began to sniffle and cry in the passenger seat.

A beige round shape materialized ahead of them, it had to be the big circular flower bed in the center of the drop off circle. The parking lot was just beyond that, and just the sight of it gave him some relief. He took his eyes off the road to look at Wendy. He wanted to offer her some comfort, some words of condolence, but he just didn't know what to say. Just the sound of her crying made him want to cry as well, she wasn't the only one who lost someone tonight. There would be time for that later, now he had to focus on driving them as far away as possible. Still he had to say something.

"Look it's gonna be--" Through the window on her side, he saw the chief running straight at the cart. He had slipped out through the back door of the restaurant where they took out the trash. *"SHIT!"*

Ronnie instinctively yanked the wheel hard to the left. The cart veered over. Wendy looked up, immediately afraid again. She caught a fleeting glimpse of the wooden face running straight towards them on her side. Clinging to Ronnie, she dropped the cleaver to the floor and began to shriek again.

In his panic, Ronnie had forgotten about the triangular rock in the corner of the grass just outside the drop off circle. It was the second time he'd forgotten it tonight. Their right tires bounced up over the rock, jostling them around inside. The rock was sloped like a ramp, tipping the cart up on its two left wheels. Ronnie cranked the steering wheel back to the right hoping to get them back on four wheels, but the cart became unbalanced and tipped over onto Ronnie's side, smashing into the wet grass.

Ronnie felt his body being slammed against the metal sides of the cart, his glasses flew off his head. Wendy was flung into him as they landed. Their heads knocked together and bounced against the bent driver's

271

side door. Several long cracks splintered across the windshield. Pieces of metal mesh on Ronnie's side broke and bent up, cutting into their arms and legs, one even sliced open the skin on Ronnie's left cheekbone. The cart slid forward on the wet grassy hill and stopped on the edge of the big putting green.

Inside the cart, cold, dirty rainwater seeped in through the mesh on Ronnie's side. He grunted and winced, feeling the sting of all the fresh scrapes and cuts on his arms and legs. Lying on top of him in a heap, Wendy moved her head slowly back and forth. Ronnie groped for his glasses and luckily found them right next to his head. When he put them on, he saw that the right lens had cracked.

"Ugh, fuck. Wendy, you okay?" he asked. All she could do was give him her own wincing grunts in response.

The chief slammed his bony hands against the passenger door that was now above their heads. Ronnie and Wendy heard the rattling bangs, looked up, and began to scream. She tried to flatten herself against the floor to escape the chief's gaze.

The chief wrapped his fingers around the passenger door's handle and gave a hard yank. Right at the last second, Ronnie forced himself upwards with all his strength.

"No!"

Ronnie grabbed the handle with both hands and leaned back. The cart door opened a few inches, then slammed shut again. Ronnie let his body weight hold the door closed. The chief grabbed the outside handle with both of his impossibly strong hands and he and Ronnie began a tug-of-war. Wendy underneath him tried to kick out the shattered windshield with her thin tennis shoes, but they only bounced off the Plexiglass.

Ronnie felt himself being lifted against the

chief's strong tugs, and knew he was going to lose this battle. He was painfully aware that they were about to die trapped like rabbits in this overturned metal cage. He tried to think of some other way out of this, and then he remembered the cleaver.

"Wendy! The knife! Get the knife!" Ronnie screamed.

Wendy, also screaming, stopped trying to kick out the tough Plexiglass windshield and began searching for the knife. Ronnie couldn't see whether she was actually looking for it or not, and he kept screaming at her to find it.

After one big yank, the chief shot its skeleton hand—the one that hadn't gotten mangled by the grinder—inside the open gap of the doorway. It clawed at Ronnie's wrist. Ronnie tried to slap it away, but the bony fingers were too close. It latched onto his wrist, digging its thumb into the underside where all his veins and arteries connected with his hand. Ronnie cried out in pain and yanked his wrist back before the sharp thumb could pierce his skin.

The chief flung the door open and peered down at them. Rain fell onto their heads as that terrible wooden face leaned down. It lashed out with its long arm, grabbing for them. Both Ronnie and Wendy fell flat to the bottom again. Neither of them had ever felt more desperately claustrophobic and terrified.

Wendy finally pulled the cleaver up from in between the seat cushion and the crushed door underneath them. She began to swing the knife wildly at the chief's hand. The cleaver connected with a few glancing blows at the chief's arm, but it wasn't enough to stop him completely. He ducked back from a wild swing that almost chipped off a piece of his mask. He pulled his arm out, reached back for something, and held up the tomahawk. The rain washed Mr. Hamilton's blood off the blade and onto their faces as it reared back.

The backside of the chief's headdress suddenly lit up. All of the wet black feathers, and glittering raindrops became illuminated and were perfectly visible above their heads. The chief heard something coming but looked up a second too late.

Zeke slammed the huge fairway mower into the underside of the picker cart, pinning the chief between the two vehicles and shoving the picker cart back. The tomahawk flew out of the chief's hand and thumped into the thin grass. Ronnie and Wendy clung to each other as the impact shook them. The windshield cracked even more with the impact, but the Plexiglass still held. More broken edges of the metal mesh poked up at them. All they could do was brace themselves until it was over.

The fairway mower's momentum pushed them farther out onto the big putting green. They finally came to a sudden stop. Zeke was panting in fear as the fairway mower's engine died. The chief was still moving and struggling between the mower reels and the underside of the picker cart. It snarled and hissed, beating against the vehicles and trying to pull itself out. Only its top half was still exposed.

"Christ!" Zeke shouted as the dead thing leaned toward him over the mower deck, clawing at his legs. Zeke turned the fairway mower's ignition key and the engine turned over sluggishly as the chief continued to wriggle out. He had managed to get the tops of his pointy hips out now.

Finally, the engine fired, roaring to life. Zeke jammed the throttle forward and pulled up on the round red switch to start the blades. The chief's body began to shake violently as its legs were chopped up by the spinning mower blades. It let out a hissing scream of agony.

Inside the cart Ronnie and Wendy felt the

thrumming vibrations of the blades spinning and chopping. They scratched against the underside of the picker cart. The sound was deafening in their cramped little space. Both Ronnie and Wendy shut their eyes and waited for it to be over.

Finally the chief's animal screaming and shaking tapered off and it slumped sideways. One of its arms fell inside the picker cart, the other hung down on the outside. Its wooden mask turned to the side with the fairways mower's headlight glaring brightly against it.

Zeke hit the red stop button with his fist, and the blades wound down. He slowly throttled down and then killed the engine. He panted for a second, trying to catch his breath.

Everything fell silent inside the cart, and Ronnie dared to look up into the open doorway. The chief's limp skeletal arm dangled down inside the cart, inches above both of their heads.

"You kids okay in there?" Zeke called. Ronnie recognized his voice immediately.

"Zeke! You're alive!" he yelled. He heard Zeke's brief laughter outside and Wendy looked up. Ronnie smiled at her. "Come on. Let's get the fuck out of this thing."

Zeke slowly pulled himself up from his seat, wincing at the pain in his back and his broken leg. Hanging onto the steering wheel for support, and holding his broken leg up in the air, he leaned forward and held out his hand.

"I got ya, boy."

Ronnie and Wendy stood up, carefully keeping their distance from the chief's dead torso lying on the top edge of the picker cart. Wendy was grimacing with pain from the cuts and bruises covering her legs and arms. She had been wearing short shorts, and had sustained more injuries than Ronnie.

"Pull me out first, then I can help her down," Ronnie said. He stepped onto the cart's steering column and boosted himself up onto the metal mesh. Straining with effort, Zeke grabbed his hand and helped pull him up. Ronnie stepped onto the mower deck next to Zeke and looked him in the eyes.

"Thank you," he said solemnly.

"Don't thank me yet, least not 'til we've made it safely to mornin.'"

Ronnie jumped down off the mower deck and his foot landed on the handle of the cup cutter. He remembered avoiding the rock earlier tonight in the other cart, just after the pump house and the bloody sprinklers. He had felt his cup cutting tools fly out of the cart bed and roll onto the grass somewhere, but at the time he'd been in too much of a panic to care.

Zeke leaned over to help Wendy get out of the cart. She put the cleaver down on the metal mesh while she was being lifted. She was shorter than Ronnie, and was in too much pain to hoist herself up the way he had. Zeke had to ignore the pain in his leg and put more effort into pulling her up. Tears were streaming down her cheeks as she stepped up onto the side of the cart. She cautiously kept her eyes on the chief's still body.

Ronnie stepped up next to the underside of the cart, holding his arms out to help her down. She half jumped half fell off the cart, taking a wide step over the dead chief.

"I gotcha, I gotcha," Ronnie told her, grabbing her by the waist and helping her fall a little more gently than she would have otherwise. Zeke collapsed back in the mower seat grunting at his aching legs and back.

As soon as Ronnie let go of Wendy's waist, two dead arms wrapped around her neck and began to squeeze like boa constrictors. Ronnie and Zeke both jumped startled. The wooden mask turned and Wendy

276

could hear its hissing breath loudly in her ear. She tried to scream but he choked off the air from her windpipe. The chief unknowingly knocked the cleaver back down into the cart with his wriggling movements.

Wendy clawed at the arms and tried to sink to her knees. The chief let one arm go to hold onto the cart, but it wouldn't let her fall. It screamed out that whistling, haggard sound again.

Zeke acted on impulse, jumping forward and kneeling on the mower deck. His broken leg flared in pain but he ignored it and focused on grabbing the chief by the shoulders. He tried to pull the chief off of Wendy but only succeeded in pulling both of them closer to the mower blades. Its powerful arms were locked tight.

Zeke grabbed the chief's head and pulled, bending it back. He hoped that the chief still felt some pain and would let go of the girl. With its legs gone, it had less leverage and seemed to be robbed of some of its inhuman strength. Ronnie looked frantically for the cleaver, he hadn't seen when it fell back into the cart.

"Help us for God's sake!" Zeke growled at him. The chief whipped its head back and forth wildly, trying to free himself from Zeke's grip.

Ronnie stepped forward, meaning to help Zeke pry him off, then he remembered the cup cutter. He scooped it up off the ground and held it up like a javelin. Zeke gave the chief's head another hard pull backwards, exposing its chest. Ronnie ran forward roaring in rage and terror, and speared the chief directly through the sternum.

It finally let go of Wendy and went tumbling back off the cart. They heard it clatter and thump down onto the wet grass. Wendy collapsed to her knees coughing, and Ronnie knelt down beside her. Zeke took the weight off his broken leg and lay against the top edge of the cart panting.

"Wendy, are you okay? Can you breathe?" Ronnie asked. She didn't answer him but coughed and gasped, slowly regaining her breath.

Then they heard the chanting start up, a harsh whispering growl in the old Kikawa language.

"Nah way oh, hock chalahweh. Nee ho tawa'ay..."

Only Zeke knew why he was chanting. "Oh Christ, no!"

"What? What is it? What's he saying?" Ronnie demanded.

"He's callin' on them. Callin' down the dark spirits. We gotta stop him."

The wind began to pick up, rough gusts blowing their wet hair around. It sounded as if it were moaning in protest against the unnatural forces the chief was summoning. It blew so hard that they had to shield their eyes from the raindrops and hail that began pelting their faces. More lightning started to flicker close by, bright strobe light flashes in the darkness.

They had only one weapon left, the rubber mallet from the cup cutter. Ronnie ran to it, snatched it up by the handle, then sprinted around the side of the downed picker cart.

In the flashes of lightning, he saw that the chief's mask had fallen off. Chief Tomahawk's face was a skull with a few strips of dry leathery flesh clinging to the bone. He had black empty eye sockets that were filling up with rain, it almost looked like it was crying as they overflowed and water ran down the sides of the skull. Its arms were spread reverently to the sky, and its jaw worked as it chanted in that growl. The cup cutter stuck straight up out of its chest like a gravestone. The blades had pierced its rib cage and held tight even through the fall.

Clenching his jaw, Ronnie ran toward it as the

278

rain turned to thick pellets of hail. He reared back with the rubber mallet, realizing that this was to be the most important cup he had ever cut in his life.

He dropped to a kneeling position in front of Chief Tomahawk and slammed the rubber mallet down on top of the flat cup cutter blade. The dead thing's words were choked off into a scream. It began chanting again. Screaming, Ronnie pounded the cup cutter blade in deeper. The chief briefly turned its head and hissed at him like a vampire. He pounded it in a third, fourth, and fifth time as hard as he could. The chief's scrabbling fingers clawed at his legs. Ronnie ignored them and continued to pound the cup cutter's metal blade in deeper.

Zeke leaned up on top of the picker cart and watched. He looked up and noticed the clouds swirling around overhead, full of electricity. There was a charge building in the air, he could feel it. Even the hail began to lessen as if the weather was shrinking back for the coming strike. On the other side of the cart, Wendy saw the swirling clouds and covered her head with her hands.

"Ronnie! Get back!" Zeke screamed as he lifted himself up off the mower deck and collapsed into the mower seat. He tried to pull himself away from anything metal.

Ronnie didn't even hear Zeke, this was too important. He swung the mallet one final time as lightning ripped down from the sky.

Ronnie was blown backwards, the rubber mallet flying out of his hands and the glasses flying off his head. Zeke squinted and tried to shield his eyes against the blinding white-blue glare. It had been meant for Ronnie, but Zeke watched the electric bolt turn, attracted to the metal, and strike the cup cutter instead. Tendrils of electricity snaked out and hit the mower and picker cart too. A deafening crack exploded in their ears.

When Zeke looked up again, the hail had turned

279

back to rain, steady but not pouring like it had been earlier. Ronnie had landed in a heap on the flat green. Zeke slowly crawled off the mower deck and limped over to Ronnie. He sat down next to him and grabbed him by the shoulders.

"Talk to me, boy," Zeke said. "You all right?"

Ronnie coughed, the wind had been knocked out of him. Other than the cuts and scrapes from the picker cart, he was okay, the lightning had never touched him. He could barely make out Zeke's words over the loud ringing in his ears.

"Is he dead?" he yelled, overcompensating for the ringing.

"You mean again?" Zeke countered. Ronnie only heard a mumble.

They looked over at the remains of Chief Tomahawk. The blackened bones lay still and limp against a charred crater in the grass. The metal cup cutter was partially melted, molten metal had run down through the gaps between its ribs. Several of the feathers on its headdress were still smoldering, but the rain was quickly putting them out.

Ronnie got to his feet and cautiously walked over. He kicked the chief's arm and it didn't move. He stood there, preparing himself for yet another sudden movement. As the rain died down he just stood there, watching to make sure it didn't start moving. For the next hour they silently stood guard around the corpse, waiting for the sun to rise.

*   *   *

The man with the PGA who had scheduled all those meetings with Bill and Mr. Hamilton showed up just after sunrise. It was a dreary, overcast morning with thick humidity hanging in the air. Ronnie was wearing his glasses again, he'd found them and put them back on as soon as there was enough light to see. They heard the man's car coming and watched him get out, going straight for the pro shop. He saw Ronnie, Wendy and Zeke sitting there in their soaked clothes next to the crashed mower and picker cart and slowed down, the slight smile melting off his face.

"What the hell is going on here? Don't you people--"

Then he saw the haggard looks on their cut and bruised faces, their damp clothes, and the blackened skeletal thing lying in the grass near them. He instantly knew that no tournament would be happening today. They gave him only the briefest explanation and sent him off to get help.

Other golfers began trickling in over the next half hour. Either they had been scheduled to play in the tournament, or they didn't know about the tournament and were hoping to snag a tee time before the course got to be really busy. Ronnie heard a Journey song blasting out from one of their car radios, "Who's Crying Now?", and it instantly got stuck in his head. Ronnie, Zeke, and Wendy tried to give them only brief answers. A few of them tried to lead them off to their parked cars where they had first-aid kits. They reluctantly went with them, but kept glancing back at the golfers as they examined the wreckage.

"Don't worry. He won't move in the daylight," Zeke muttered to Ronnie. "At least I don't think he will." Ronnie didn't feel any comfort at that remark.

Two police cars arrived soon after that, their sirens roaring across the quiet parking lot. The police began to shoo away the curious golfers who were kneeling around mowers.

A stern young police officer with a mustache approached Ronnie, Zeke, and Wendy, and told them to wait where they were, they would have to answer some questions. The tone in his voice suggested that he thought they were all guilty and hiding something. After he walked away, Zeke spoke to Ronnie.

"You know, your little sidekick, Mark, would've had something snappy to say to that asshole."

Ronnie looked over at him astonished. It was the first time anyone had ever said that someone else was *his* sidekick, instead of the other way around. For a second, he felt that he had achieved some kind of new level of respect, graduated up to be one of the guys. Too bad the rest of the guys were all dead. Poor Mark, just the thought of him brought the image of his body lying dead on the bunker machine back into Ronnie's mind.

"Yeah, well, I'm not Mark," Ronnie said solemnly. It was all he could think of at the moment.

The paramedics arrived a minute later and ignored the police officer's commands to have them wait where they were. Zeke was hauled off into an ambulance on a stretcher. Ronnie and Wendy were told to sit down in the open back door of another ambulance, and were treated for their scrapes, cuts, bruises, and in Ronnie's case, coyote bites.

The police chief's voice suddenly boomed out of an electronic megaphone.

"Okay, if you're here to play golf, you need to clear this area right now. This course is closed. I need you to get in your cars and go on home."

From his spot in the back of the ambulance, Ronnie watched the other police officers ushering people away from the wreckage on the big putting green. As they slowly wandered back to their cars holding their golf bags, Ronnie recognized the two brothers that had laid the dead eagle to rest on Monday. One of them looked directly at him, then continued on toward their truck.

Once the golfers had cleared out, the police roped off the entrance and exit driveways with orange cones and yellow crime scene tape. The paramedics began pulling the bodies out of the clubhouse in black plastic body bags on stretchers. Wendy burst into tears at the sight of them, knowing that inside one of them was her sister. To Ronnie's surprise, she fell against him, needing his warmth and comfort. Ronnie looked down at her sobbing head, trying to think of something to say to comfort to her, something that would stop her tears and make her feel okay. He debated putting his arm around her.

I can't comfort her. I'm not even important to her. Maybe Mark would have had the guts do that but I can't.

Then he replayed his exchange with Zeke from a few minutes ago in his mind.

Your little sidekick would've had something snappy to say...

I'm not Mark.

Ronnie put his arm around her and held her close as she sobbed. They sat like that waiting for the police for a long time. In his mind, Ronnie remembered all of his coworkers, all his friends who were now gone. He wondered who would take care of the golf course now, and if Chief Tomahawk's curse would touch them too.

Epilogue:

Deep in the corner of the Kikawa reservation, twenty-five miles west of Indian Hill, sat a lone tepee in a grove of dead, knobby trees. An old man lived there, refusing to give up the old ways, and hardly anyone ever went to see him. On that dreary Saturday of Memorial Day weekend 1981, a truck approached the tepee. Through the windshield, the driver saw a thin line of smoke rising from the hole in the top and knew that they would find the old man in there.

They parked, and the two Kikawa brothers stepped out, still in their black shirts, acid-washed jeans, and cowboy boots. They hauled their golf bags out of the back of the truck, tossed their clubs back into the rusty bed, and lugged them into the tepee through the low circular opening.

An incredibly ancient old man sat cross-legged on the other side of the small fire in the middle of the tepee. Deep lines and wrinkles ran down his old dry skin. Wisps of thin white hair hung out from under the black feathers of the headdress he wore. Thin, frilled buckskin clothes covered his frail body. He had mashed up some kind of black concoction in a clay bowl, and was dipping a few stone arrowheads into the dark liquid

284

when the brothers came in.

"Chief Poison Arrow," the elder brother said, raising his hand in greeting. They spoke to him in English since they had been raised in the modern age. Neither of them had a very big Kikawa vocabulary. "We went back to Indian Hill like you asked." They held the golf bags out in front of them.

Chief Poison Arrow looked at the golf bags and tilted his head quizzically.

"What is this?" he asked in a soft croak.

"You asked us to go back there and bring him to you, remember?" the younger brother spoke up.

The lines in the old man's face deepened. To them it looked like he didn't understand what they were saying. Sometimes the older brother thought that he must be senile, but they still came to see him occasionally to hear stories of the old days and learn whatever they could about the dark spirits.

"We came to see you yesterday. Do you remember that?" The old man remained silent. "We told you that we had given the eagle at Indian Hill a proper burial. And you got all excited and told us to go back there and collect him. And when we asked who, all you said was, *'You'll know when you see him.'* Does any of that ring a bell?"

Chief Poison Arrow finally spoke up again. "My memory goes back two hundred years. I remember more than you'll ever forget, boy." There was a rough edge to his voice that caught both brothers off guard. It made both of them nervous. "You say you brought him, but I do not see him."

The brothers glanced at each other, then dumped out their golf bags. A pile of what looked like charred and broken sticks tumbled out next to the old man. A skull and a jaw bone thunked out on top of the pile, then a ragged pile of black feathers and a charred dead bat fell out behind them.

The younger brother delicately pulled two items out of a zippered pocket on the side of his golf bag and stepped forward. He held out a bloodstained tomahawk and a wooden mask. Chief Poison Arrow looked at them, then nodded. The younger brother set them down in front of the pile.

"Leave us," the old man ordered. Both brothers glanced at each other, then left the tepee without a word, dragging their golf bags with them.

The old man stared at the pile of Chief Tomahawk's black bones for a moment, waiting for the sound of the truck to start up and fade away in the distance.

Finally, he touched the tomahawk, and spoke up in Kikawa. "Brother, you should not have been so reckless. How many times did I tell you it would lead you to ruin? Now so many wasted years have passed. I am sorry I was not with you, but the great spirit set us on different paths. Rest now. The white men will think you have gone. I have learned that it is useful for those fools to think that. They thought that I died, yet I outlived them all. I lived on for many decades under their noses." He laughed. "I cannot die yet, not until this year of blood ends. That time is near, and when it comes, I will wake you."

Chief Poison Arrow closed his eyes and took a deep breath. He passed a wrinkled hand mystically over the pile of bones, and they began to click and rattle.

Cameron Roubique
Thornton, Colorado
January 13th 2018 – July 1st 2018

Afterword:

After my friend LJ Dougherty (who didn't work at the real life golf course Indian Tree with me) finished reading this book, he asked, "So how much of all these golf course shenanigans actually happened in real life?" My honest answer, "Umm...all of them." The best part about writing this book was getting to remember all of fun and hilarious times I had while working at Indian Tree during my college years. Back then, all I did was go to school, screw around at work with my best buddy Kyle Doran, and watch '80s slasher movies on youtube, primarily *Sleepaway Camp,* over and over. It was great times.

Outlining this book was like putting together a puzzle of all these stories and anecdotes that I wanted to include, and in some cases, turning them into scary scenes. I realize that some of the early chapters might be a little self-indulgent, but what can I say, I was having fun writing. Not everything I wanted to include made it in, like taking the boat out on seven lake to trim "Gator Island." One Indian Tree story was used as inspiration for a scene in another book I wrote called, *Kill River,* and it involved me crawling through a tight concrete pipe with a pitch fork to unclog some mud and tree limbs that were cutting off the water that fed the golf course lakes. Seriously, there is nothing better than working a summer job at a golf course, I highly recommend it.

Thirteen years ago, we started joking about the "Indian Tree Massacre," and I promised myself that one day I'd write it. Way back in 2013, after I finished writing *Kill River*, I tried outlining a version of "The Indian Tree Massacre," it seemed like a natural step for a second book. But back then I was stuck on Cyndi and Thrill River, so I set this one on the back-burner. In retrospect, I think that was the best move. The killer was originally going to be a regular living person and have a whodunit reveal at the end, and I never would have gotten to explore writing scary scenes for a supernatural killer. For some reason, I find supernatural stuff even scarier than real life and the idea of Chief Tomahawk and Chief Poison Arrow creep me out a lot more than some of my other characters.

I hope that if any of the members of my Indian Tree family read this, they don't find any of my character descriptions too close to real life and insulting. The characters' physical descriptions were all based on characters in horror movies or TV shows I've seen, as they usually are with all my books. I also hope my Indian Tree family knows that I think the world of them.

As always my dad, my wife Darla, and my best buddy Tim Taylor helped me edit this book. My friends LJ Dougherty and John Resetarits (also a member of the Indian Tree family) test read this for me and gave me a lot of great criticisms and feedback that helped make it a stronger story. And my Indian Tree friends Scott Gibson, Scott Bullock, and Danny Machuga helped me a lot with the golf course terminology and technical details. Thank you guys so much! If you spot any inaccuracies or typos, my bad, I often can't even write a damn tweet without some kind of typo.

Hopefully, you're enjoying my 1981 Year of Blood books. If you liked this book and haven't checked out *Disco Deathtrap* yet, I'd definitely check it out. It takes place almost five months earlier than *Golf Curse*, and the epilogue in that book kind of ties them both together. I'll be writing more slashery books in the future if you decide you want to know more about what happened back in that long, dark, bloody year. Or you can always watch the many amazing slasher films that came out back then too. Thanks for reading, and don't cut down any old trees if you can avoid it. You never know what might be hiding under the bark, scratching and waiting to get out.

Cameron Roubique
Thornton, Colorado
March 25th, 2019

Soundtrack:

The following is a list of songs that are either prominently featured in this book or inspired me as appropriate background music in some of the scenes. You really don't have to listen to these songs to enjoy *Golf Curse,* but all of them are excellent and if you're not already familiar with them, I highly recommend checking them out.

Cameron Roubique

1. "Take Me Home, Country Roads" - John Denver
2. "Stone in Love" - Journey
3. "I Love A Rainy Night" - Eddie Rabbitt
4. "Carefree Highway" - Gordon Lightfoot
5. "Wheel in the Sky" - Journey
6. "Anytime" - Journey
7. "Sundown" - Gordon Lightfoot
8. "Rhinestone Cowboy" - Glen Campbell
9. "Seven Year Ache" - Roseanne Cash
10. "When the Levee Breaks" - Led Zeppelin
11. "Who's Cryin' Now?" - Journey

About the Author:

Cameron Roubique lives in Thornton,
Colorado, with his wife, Darla, cat, Penny,
and pug Vader. He is an avid 80's slasher
movie, superhero, and water park fan.

You can follow him on his website
at www.yearofblood.com
on twitter at twitter.com/lil_cam_ron
and on instagram at instagram.com/cameronroubique.

He can also be reached through email at
cameron@killriver.com.

Made in the USA
Las Vegas, NV
03 June 2022

49759099R00173